A State of Grace

MYSTERY
and the
MINISTER'S
WIFE®

A State
of Grace

TRACI DEPREE

GUIDEPOSTS
NEW YORK, NEW YORK

A *State of Grace*

ISBN-13: 978-0-8249-4746-0

Published by Guideposts
16 East 34th Street
New York, New York 10016
www.guideposts.com

Copyright © 2008 by Guideposts. All rights reserved.

This book, or parts thereof, may not be reproduced, stored in a retrieval system, or transmitted in any form or by any means, electronic, mechanical, photocopying, recording or otherwise, without the written permission of the publisher.

Distributed by Ideals Publications
2636 Elm Hill Pike, Suite 120
Nashville, Tennessee 37214

Guideposts, *Ideals* and *Mystery and the Minister's Wife* are registered trademarks of Guideposts.

The characters and events in this book are fictional, and any resemblance to actual persons or events is coincidental.

All Scripture quotations are taken from *The Holy Bible, New International Version.* Copyright © 1973, 1978, 1984 International Bible Society. Used by permission of Zondervan Bible Publishers.

Library of Congress Cataloging-in-Publication Data

DePree, Traci

  A state of grace / Traci DePree.
      p. cm. — (Mystery and the minister's wife)
  ISBN 978-0-8249-4746-0
  1. Spouses of clergy—Fiction. 2. Church membership—Fiction.
  3. Tennessee—Fiction. I. Title.
  PS3604.E67S73 2008
  813'.6—dc22

                                          2008010574

Cover by Lookout Design Group
Interior design by Cris Kossow
Typeset by Nancy Tardi

Printed and bound in the United States of America

10 9 8 7 6 5 4 3 2 1

To Marjorie Lois Siedschlag Mielke.
I love you, Ma.

Chapter One

The aromas of fresh paint, new-sawn lumber, and varnish filled Kate Hanlon with a sense of wonder as she made her way into the quaint Tennessee church. So much had happened in the short time she and her pastor-husband, Paul, had been in Copper Mill, and yet it was as if this were their very first Sunday here—the Sunday that should have been.

Her mind flashed back to the scene. It had been a beautiful autumn day as they made their way into the valley, fresh from San Antonio. Leaves in shades of orange, red, and brown had obscured her vision of the town. Then she caught her first sight of Copper Mill from the road above, with its tree-lined streets and rows of houses. To the southeast she noticed a trail of dark smoke, and as they wended their way toward the town, it soon became evident that it wasn't from any campfire. The church they'd come halfway across the country to minister in was ablaze. The town was devastated. Suspicion floated in the air with the news that the fire had been intentionally set. So much grief and anger had poured out in those first days, along with sadness that trust had been broken in the small town. And yet, here they were today, starting anew. Kate crossed the threshold into the foyer and sanctuary as the organ began its prelude. It had a sweet sound, that organ, donated through the generosity of Eli Weston. The antiques dealer had purchased the piano-sized instrument at an auction the previous month just for this day.

Kate stopped to take in the sight. She'd been here daily, it seemed, while the workers were rebuilding, but she wanted to savor this moment. She thought of the Christmas service, held in the unfinished space, but aside from that night, the congregation had been meeting in her living room since the fire. Now construction was complete. White walls reached up toward thick wooden beams that girded the ceiling like the ribs of a giant whale. Plain windows along the sides of the sanctuary let in the bright sunlight. The Smoky Mountains were visible in the distance, as were Copper Mill Creek, shimmering with early morning mist, and the many hills surrounding the small town.

Walking into the sanctuary, Kate silently wished there were something more to brighten up the space, for while it looked habitable, it hardly looked homey.

She thought of the church they'd left behind in Texas. Paul had pastored Riverbend Community, a megachurch in San Antonio, for the past thirty years. Its stylish furnishings had been chosen by a decorating committee, and everything had been just so. But here in Copper Mill, Paul and Kate served the needs of a little more than 150 members; they hardly had the budget that the five-thousand-member church had had.

Kate passed rows of oak pews and greeted the members with a smile on her face and a wave here and there as she took her place next to Paul in the front row. The pew was sturdy, well built, though not particularly beautiful. She sighed and realized she wouldn't move back to San Antonio for all the decorating budgets in the world, for while funds might be tight at Faith Briar Church, they felt God wanted them here among these people, people who truly cared and would sacrifice no end of resources to help one another. She'd seen it firsthand in the rebuilding of the small church.

THE ORGAN THAT continued playing gloriously was on the left of the sanctuary. Sam Gorman sat on the bench, concentrating as his eyes scanned the hymnal before him. Kate enjoyed watching him—his head bobbed up and down with the melody as if he was doing more than playing notes, as if the song reached a place deep inside him.

Kate settled her purse on the floor and reached for her hymnal.

When she straightened up, she felt a tap on her back. She glanced behind her. Livvy Jenner leaned across the pew and whispered, "Good morning."

Over the past few months, Livvy had become Kate's closest friend. Although Livvy's teenage boys were still at home and Kate's were all grown and living on their own, the two seemed to understand each other. Perhaps it was their common love of books and their shared sense of curiosity, or that they naturally knew what the other was thinking. Whatever the case, Kate was glad to have made a dear friend so soon after moving to Tennessee.

"Don't you look nice today!" Kate said. The forty-something town librarian wore a smart-looking navy suit with a hint of floral in the blouse that peeked from underneath. Her auburn hair was up, as it often was, showing off her high cheekbones and hazel eyes.

Livvy blushed and whispered, "I had to dress up for such a day of celebration."

Kate nodded her agreement. She'd been looking forward to this day for months too. Now that it was here, it seemed time had evaporated with their labor.

As the prelude ended, Paul rose and made his way to the platform, where he took his place behind the podium. He flashed Kate a lopsided smile, which she returned with a wink. He looked so handsome in his dark suit with his salt-and-pepper hair and stunning blue eyes.

The organ paused, then Sam began to play the first hymn. Paul motioned for everyone to stand, and she turned her attention to the hymnal. She could hear Paul's rich tenor above the rest, lilting to the tune of "O the Deep, Deep Love of Jesus."

Kate let the words seep into her being, filling her with a sense of contentment. "Vast, unmeasured, boundless, free! Rolling as a mighty ocean in its fullness over me . . ."

It was one of her favorite hymns, and she was glad Sam had chosen it for this special morning.

When the song had ended and people had taken their seats, Paul paused, gazing at his congregation and taking in a deep breath. Kate could see the shimmer of moisture in his eyes and the satisfaction in his expression.

"What a glorious morning," he said. His gaze traveled around the simple sanctuary as he gestured with a broad sweep of his hand. "Look at this place, at what God has done in restoring what we all thought was lost. What was a horrible tragedy, God has turned into a blessing." His grin broadened. "Isn't that just like him? I look at each of you, who were once strangers to Kate and me, and today I see friends. A family forged by adversity. No welcome party could have done what this hardship has done, for it has created a bond between all of us unlike any other. I'm grateful to all of you who worked so hard to get us to this point." He paused as his eyes met those in the congregation, then he continued. "Your perseverance has shown me what an awesome church we're serving. Your willingness to sacrifice—" Paul's voice broke as he said the word.

Tenderness swept over Kate at seeing her husband so overcome. It wasn't often that he cried, and when he did, she knew it came from a deep place within his heart. She watched in rapt attention as tears formed in her own eyes.

Paul regained his composure and said, "This is God at work. Right here in Copper Mill, Tennessee. He can take the worst situation and make something beautiful out of it. That's what he does."

A tear escaped Kate's lashes and coursed down her cheek. She dabbed at it with a tissue she pulled from her purse.

For Kate and Paul, driving all the way from Texas and arriving in Copper Mill to find a burned-down church and a devastated congregation had been a rough start, to be sure, but Paul was right; it had birthed a deeper connection with the people than there ever could have been without it. There had been obstacles and struggles, but together they'd worked through them, and now they were stronger, more unified.

Kate thought of others in the congregation, especially Eli Weston, who had accidentally started the church fire. He'd been devastated by the fire and, before that, by the death of his fiancée, Diedre. The church hadn't pressed charges, and Eli had come through the ordeal stronger in faith and character, a more integral member of their community than he'd ever been.

Her gaze lifted upward as Paul continued his sermon. So much was right about this moment. The people had made it that way, and yet Kate sensed there was still something more to do to make it complete. To show in some tangible, outward way what had happened in the inner life of Faith Briar as a church body.

Her thoughts turned back to the austerity of the sanctuary. While it held a certain beauty, the freshly painted walls were devoid of the touches that made a place a home. Even a simple cross at the front would do much to give it the boost it so badly needed.

Paul's words resounded in her ears: *What was a horrible tragedy, God has turned into a blessing*. It was so like God to do that—to bring life from death, to bring beauty out of ashes, to turn the dark of winter into the brightness of spring.

As she pondered, she realized there was something she could do. She had the ability, after all. And it could be a gift for the members of Faith Briar who had done so much to make them feel welcome.

She'd have to work and plan to make it just right. And she'd need to get the approval of the board of elders, though it might be fun to make it a surprise . . . even for Paul.

She smiled. What would he say if he knew she was keeping such a secret from him? The idea grew.

It would be a huge undertaking; she'd never done anything of this scale before. But maybe, just maybe, she could pull it off.

THE COUNTRY DINER was abuzz with the chatter of after-church patrons. Paul and Kate waited by the front door to be seated. The smell of biscuits and gravy, cooked sausage and hash browns, and the smoky scent of barbecue permeated the air. There was a reason this place was popular —and it wasn't the atmosphere, though with its gingham curtains and blue Formica tabletops, the diner did have a certain quaintness that grew on a person.

The counter was filled with regulars—Sheriff Roberts and Deputy Spencer, both in uniform, sipped coffee as their plates of barbecued ribs arrived. Betty Anderson and her husband were sitting next to them. Betty's bleached hair made the beauty-shop owner hard to miss. Her husband was a smallish man whom Kate only seemed to recognize when he was accompanied by his wife. Kate gave them a wave.

"Be right back, y'all," LuAnne Matthews called over her shoulder as she flew past. The heavyset redhead delivered water to a nearby table, then stood pencil and pad in hand as she took the diners' orders.

Paul reached for Kate's hand. "You okay?"

"I'm fine." Kate smiled up at him. "I was so proud of you today."

Paul arched a teasing brow. "Really?"

She shrugged. "You've accomplished so much with this church in such a short amount of time."

Paul reached an arm around her waist. "I don't know that I did all that much."

"You're too modest," Kate said.

"All I know is I'll be glad to get back to the business of regular life and being a pastor instead of a construction supervisor."

"Is there such a thing?" Kate asked, wrinkling her nose. "*Regular life*, I mean?"

"Maybe not, but a little less stress would be nice. I'm picturing that quiet, simple pastoral life we came here for." The lines around his eyes crinkled as he smiled.

Kate smiled too. "Are you sure you're not living in a fantasy world?"

"Never."

While her husband yearned for a quiet life, Kate wasn't sure how she would fare in such a state. All the busyness of the past months—remodeling the run-down parsonage and raising funds to rebuild the church, not to mention finding out about Eli's unwitting role in setting the fire—had been energizing for her. She loved the hub-bub and activity. It vitalized her.

Kate sighed as LuAnne returned to seat them. "Hey, Pastor . . . Kate. How are y'all? It's hoppin' today!" she said, wiping her brow with the hem of her apron and setting her horn-rimmed glasses firmly back on the end of her nose. "Where were you wantin' to sit?"

"A booth?" Paul nodded toward the front of the Country Diner that looked out onto Hamilton Road, one of Copper Mill's main streets. Cars and pickups ambled up and down the road. To the east, Copper Mill Creek was visible beyond the Town Green that was now frosted in white. Rolling, sugar-coated hills rose in the distance.

"Alrighty," LuAnne said and led them to the only open booth.

Kate and Paul took their seats as LuAnne slid the menus onto the table in front of them.

"The special today is barbecued ribs for $3.99." She gave Paul a look that said she knew he'd like that. "Loretta made the best stack cakes this morning . . . *lots* of apples." Then she was off to greet another group at the front door.

Kate leaned toward her husband. "I can make ribs for you at home," she offered.

Paul's clear-blue eyes sparkled. "You'd add wheat germ or bran flakes to the sauce! No thank you. I'll get them here where they're untouched by your health-conscious hands."

Kate smirked and looked down at her menu. They'd been here so often already that she had practically memorized the sheet.

"So . . . ?" Paul said.

"So, what?" she asked, still reading, trying to choose between a blackened chicken salad and a roast-beef sandwich.

"You sighed before. You never sigh unless something's bothering you. So out with it."

LuAnne arrived with their water and then dashed off to the next table before Kate could ask what kind of dressing came with the salad.

"It's nothing," Kate said, shaking her head.

"We've been married thirty years, Kate Hanlon. I know when it's nothing and when it's something."

She shrugged, then relented. "I guess I'd gotten used to all the activity after we first got here. Unpacking, fixing up our new home, getting acquainted with the ladies at Faith Briar, discovering who started the fire . . . I don't know. I'm wondering what I'll do to keep busy now that I don't have a hatful of to-dos on my list. It's silly."

"Figuring out how to use that new cell phone of yours is sure to keep you busy," Paul teased. He had insisted she get a cell phone after her investigation into the church fire had nearly gotten her killed. At his request, she carried it with her so she could call for help.

Kate laughed.

Then Paul's tone grew serious. "But it's totally under-standable that you'd wonder, although I assumed you'd help me at the church. At least counseling couples, and the women . . ." He reached across the table and gave her hand a squeeze.

Kate paused for a moment in thought. "I want to be available for whatever the church needs. You know that. But it's not the same as working full-time like I did in San Antonio . . . having a reason to get up every morning."

"You could look for a job." Paul raised his eyes from the menu that was spread before him and took a sip of his water.

Kate met his gaze. "You've never complained but I know it's hard on you when I'm working so much, and it doesn't exactly leave me available to help when things come up."

Paul smiled, then paused in thought. "You could set up a stained-glass studio, really do something with that hobby of yours."

"You're kidding, right?"

"I'm completely serious," Paul said, his eyes reflecting his sincerity. "You're a gifted artist. Why not take this time to explore that gift? The kids are grown. We have an extra bedroom . . ." He sat back while Kate considered the idea.

Kate couldn't believe that Paul suggested exactly what she'd been thinking. It had long been her dream to have her own glass studio, where she could create beautiful works of art, but in San Antonio, the time had never been right. There were always kids to raise or church activities to plan, not to mention the demands of her job as an executive assistant in an accounting firm. Yet there was nothing as exhilarating as seeing an idea fully crafted into a stained-glass masterpiece that caught the light in a kaleidoscope of color. Her excitement began to bubble as the possibilities dawned.

"I could make some lampshades for the kids, and maybe a window for our bathroom, and of course . . ." her words trailed away when she realized she was about to spill the secret she'd thought of at church that morning.

"'Of course' what?" Paul asked.

Kate waved a dismissive hand. "You know me . . . My mind starts spinning with ideas."

Paul laughed, then went on, "You'd be busy doing something you love to do. That's a good thing. It would make you happy."

Kate reached across the table and squeezed his hand again.

"Pastor . . . Kate," a voice broke in. "I tried to catch you at church but you slipped out so quickly!"

Paul and Kate looked up to find Renee Lambert standing there. The elderly woman appeared to be in her early seventies, though with all the makeup she had on her face, it was often hard to tell. Her hair was a pale blonde with an inch of black and gray along the roots. In one manicured hand, with ruby red artificial nails, she clutched a small shivering dog, whose rear end disappeared into her large designer bag. It licked her palm with its tiny pink tongue and gazed at her with soulful eyes.

"There, there, Kisses," Renee said to the pooch. She pursed her too-red lips for emphasis as she turned her attention to the dog.

"Renee," Paul said. "How are you this fine January day?"

The woman coughed into her manicured yet wrinkled hand. "I'm doing well..." Renee had been a thorn in Kate's side from the moment they arrived in Copper Mill, but underneath her controlling ways, Kate sensed that she really had a heart for the church.

She placed a hand on her chest and let out a heavy sigh.

"Is something wrong?" Kate asked.

Renee shook her head. "I've just gotten some very bad news, I'm afraid. It's just so sad..."

Paul sat up straighter and said, "I'm so sorry, Renee. Please, won't you join us?"

"Is your mother okay?" Kate asked, sliding over in the booth to make room. Renee's mother, Caroline, had come to stay with her daughter in November while she recovered from a broken hip and had recently decided to live with Renee. Kate knew it was hard for Renee, who was no spring chicken herself, to care for her ailing mother.

Renee dabbed at her eyes with a tissue and sat down, careful to adjust her purse—and Kisses—just so in her lap.

"She's fine." Renee fluttered her fingers at Kate's question. "As ornery as ever. But it's not about Mother. I heard from a dear friend in Chattanooga"—she leaned in closer—"that little Marissa Harris has cancer." She whispered the last word, as if by saying it too loud, she might spread the horrid disease.

"Marissa who?" Paul asked.

"Harris," she repeated. Then she waved a hand. "I forgot. You're still new here. You don't know the Harrises." Kisses whined from his perch in the bag, and Renee patted his quivering head. "They're members of Faith Briar, though they haven't attended in months."

"I don't believe we've met anyone by that name," Paul said. He looked at Kate, who had no idea who the Harrises were either.

"Patricia Harris is in her early forties," Renee went on. "Nice enough looking. She's a widow. She lost her husband just five months ago in a horrific accident. It was right before you came. Ray was an electrician."

At this she raised a thinly plucked eyebrow. "He had been working down on Ashland Street, on one of those tall poles, when he was electrocuted. It was just horrible. That poor woman. Pastor Jacobs delivered a lovely eulogy at his funeral," she went on. "Anyway, according to a nurse friend of mine in Chattanooga—she's the one who told me about Marissa—the poor girl has been going to chemotherapy for a while, was in the hospital for an extended stay, and didn't have a *single* visitor . . ."

Paul ignored the barb. "How old is Marissa?" Kate asked, imagining a five-year-old.

"She's just out of college, I believe. Went to the university in Chattanooga."

Kate sat forward in the booth, her elbows resting on

the Formica tabletop. LuAnne arrived just then and took their orders.

"Did you want something too, Renee?" the waitress asked with a raised brow.

"I'll have a lemon water, please, and one of those chef's salads—no dressing."

LuAnne left to call back their orders. Once she was out of earshot, Renee leaned in and said in a loud whisper, "There isn't much in terms of *health* food in this place, but we don't have much choice, do we?" She smiled as if pleased with herself.

"What were you saying about the Harrises?" Paul asked.

"Oh yes. The way I hear it, Marissa's been having chemotherapy treatments for leukemia down in Chattanooga. My friend is a registered nurse there. Marissa was admitted for a full month with only her mother at her side. I just think that's a crime when the church should be stepping in and helping out. Don't you?"

"Has Patricia called anyone at the church or on the prayer chain?" Paul asked. Concern filled his eyes.

"No. And she won't, either." Renee raised an eyebrow and readjusted her designer bag with its resident dog before continuing. "Patricia hasn't come to Faith Briar since shortly after Ray died. I don't know what this will do to her. I just don't know. If it were me, I don't think I'd be able to carry on at all. After all she's been through . . ."

Chapter Two

K ate fidgeted with the scarf around her neck, wanting to get the knot just right, yet knowing it was fine to begin with. She glanced in the visor mirror of her jet-black Honda Accord and reapplied her lipstick. She'd been rehearsing what she would say to this stranger all morning, yet nothing sounded quite right.

Hello. I don't know you, but I heard you lost your husband ... and now your daughter's sick. With each practiced sentence, Kate envisioned the front door slamming in her face.

People didn't take kindly to strangers showing up unannounced, especially wanting to talk about personal things. Not in this day and age, anyway. Sure, she was the pastor's wife, but that gave her no more right than it did anyone else. And Patricia had obviously stopped coming to Faith Briar Church for a reason.

Kate's heart went out to the woman. What must it be like to lose your husband and then face the death of your only child? She couldn't get it out of her mind. She'd revisited Renee Lambert's words all the previous day. When she called each of her three children for her weekly update, the thought had stayed with her. She'd even dreamed about being widowed and then finding out that her daughter Rebecca was on her deathbed. She awoke in tears, afraid that something had happened to Paul. But he snored on next to her.

Yet that deep sense of concern had pushed her all the way to Patricia's house, and she knew it would keep pushing until she at least tried to comfort the poor woman.

Paul had wanted to come along too, but a previously scheduled meeting had kept him at the church.

I don't know what I'm doing here, God, Kate prayed. *But I know you care about Marissa and Patricia, so do what you will. Help me to be sensitive to their needs.*

She climbed out of the car and took in the red Colonial house on Mountain Laurel Road at the western edge of town. It was a lovely two-story home with a green door at its center and four white-trimmed windows in perfect symmetry on each level. Flower boxes rested under the windows, though their contents were now snow covered. A light flutter of snowflakes wafted through the barren aspen trees that created a parklike atmosphere in the yard. Birdhouses in all different styles and colors were spread in clusters around the property. Northern cardinals and Carolina chickadees flew between them like fickle girls at a dance. A blue jay dove in to steal seeds and spread them across the ground.

Kate made her way up the cobblestone walk to the

front door and rang the doorbell. Suddenly the words she'd rehearsed left her completely. She scrambled to think of something to say, but nothing would come. She heard the sound of footsteps before the door opened tentatively. The woman inside was trim and petite, with short, pale blonde hair and vivid blue eyes. She appeared to be in her forties, though Kate had never been a good judge of people's ages.

"Can I help you?" the woman asked.

"Are you Patricia Harris?" Kate ventured.

"Yes . . ."

Kate cleared her throat. "I'm Kate Hanlon." She held out her hand, but the woman simply looked at it. "My husband is the new pastor at Faith Briar Church."

The woman's eyes glazed over at the announcement. "Listen, I'm not interested in any sales pitch to get me to—" Patricia began.

"I'm not here to try to get you to come back to church."

Patricia gave her a curious look. "Then why are you here?"

"I'm sorry," Kate said. "I'm not trying to intrude, truly." She inhaled and smiled kindly at the woman. "I just heard that your husband died, and I wanted to offer my condolences." That sounded lame even to her ears. She held out a plate of freshly baked oatmeal cookies, all the while praying that Patricia wouldn't turn her away.

Patricia eyed the cookies for a long moment, then her shoulders relaxed. "Well, I suppose it wouldn't hurt to say hello. Would you like to come in?"

Kate let out a breath of relief.

Patricia held the door open, and Kate followed her inside.

The front entry was flanked by an open staircase leading to the second floor, and the hallway opened to a dining room on one side and a den on the other.

The wall beneath the staircase was lined with photographs —mostly black and whites, all in assorted black-painted frames. Some of the photos featured a pale girl with dimpled cheeks, dark hair, and luminous dark eyes, through all ages of childhood and adolescence. Others bore the image of a man—good looking in a rugged way, with a sheen of stubble on his dimpled chin and penetrating pale eyes—and a pretty woman, whom Kate assumed was Patricia in her younger days.

In one photo, the man was holding the girl on his lap as they swung high on a city park swing. The joy the two shared was tangible, him holding her tight with one arm as the swing flew, while her expression carried the child-like rapture of the moment. Kate wondered if Patricia had been the photographer of the beautiful collection, since most of them were of father and daughter, with only a few of her.

At the center of the wall was a cross-stitched picture with "Marissa Lauren Harris" in tall letters across the top, and her birth date, weight, and length intermingled with teddy bears and blocks. It was a sort of birth announcement in thread. Kate had similar ones for each of her three children, given to her by an elderly aunt.

"August 16th . . . I have one of these for each of my kids too," Kate said, realizing that Patricia was watching her. "These photos are amazing. Did you take them?"

Patricia waved her hand. "An old hobby of mine. I don't do much of it anymore."

"Well, your place is lovely. Have you lived here long?"

"Twenty years. My husband built the house shortly after we were married." She nodded to a framed, poster-sized black-and-white photo of the same man on a cata-maran. The boat was tilting precariously toward the water as the man leaned back in counterbalance. His hair was tousled in the wind, but by the wet grin on his face, it was obvious that he was having a great time.

"Looks like he was quite the sailor."

"He was." Patricia's expression was wistful, then her face twisted in grief, and she turned away, heading down the hallway toward the back of the house. "Like I said before, I've had about all I can handle of the church. You're not going to recruit me to come back."

"That's okay," Kate said simply as she followed.

The hallway opened up into one large room with a nicely decorated kitchen to the left and the living room to the right, where a wall of windows let in the bright day. Wide pine boards in a warm hue lined the floor. Red Wing jugs and yellowware bowls lined the open kitchen shelves, giving the room a homey feel, as did the many antiques in the space.

"What was your name again?" Patricia asked as she set the plate of cookies on the counter and turned to get some cups from the cupboard.

"Kate, Kate Hanlon. I don't usually knock on strangers' doors like this."

Kate laughed nervously, and Patricia gave her a sympathetic look before saying, "That accent . . . You're from where?"

"Texas." Kate blushed. "Paul was pastor of a church in San Antonio. I was born and raised there . . . and have lived there most of my life."

Patricia nodded. "It was that megachurch, right? I heard about it. How many members did you have?"

"A little over five thousand," Kate said.

"Wow. I hope you're not thinking you'll be able to do that here in Copper Mill. People around here . . ." She paused as if to search for the right word. "Let's just say they're a bit set in their ways. You'll soon discover that folks want things to stay the way they've been for the last hundred years."

Feeling no need to challenge her, Kate let her go on.

"Folks like me, well, we're . . ."

"Folks like you?" Kate asked.

"Never mind," Patricia said. She bit her lower lip, then asked, "Would you like some coffee?"

"I'm always good for a cup of coffee."

Patricia turned to ready a pot, then got down two small plates and napkins for the cookies.

"Tell me about your husband," Kate urged, hoping the request wouldn't seem too intrusive.

"You don't want to know my life's story," Patricia said. But by the faint smile that tilted the corners of her lips, Kate knew her interest had pleased the woman.

"You must miss him a lot," Kate said.

Patricia's eyes turned cloudy, and she reached for a tissue from the far end of the counter. She wiped her eyes before any tears could escape, then responded, "Yes, I miss him . . . For our twenty-fifth anniversary, we were going to take a sailing trip around the world. We were going to rent an oceangoing sailboat like we did when we went to Alaska. But he died five years too soon." She nodded her head toward the picture again. "That was the boat he used to race on lakes around the area and in the Midwest, but he loved taking bigger boats out East or to the Pacific Coast . . . It was his favorite activity. Especially cruising around Alaska. Our trip there was so . . . Then he . . ." Her words trailed away, and she raised one hand, lightly covering her lips. Then she sighed and turned to busy herself with the coffee.

Kate waited, watching the petite woman.

"I'm sorry," Kate finally ventured.

When Patricia turned back to Kate and met her gaze, it was obvious that she'd been shaken. "I sold the boat right after the accident," she said. "It held too many memories."

Kate reached out a hand and touched Patricia's arm in sympathy.

"So, who told you?" Patricia asked.

"About Ray?" Kate clarified.

Patricia nodded and slowly drew her arm away.

"Renee Lambert."

"Oh, that old biddy." As soon as the words slipped out,

Patricia blushed. "What other rumors did she spread about me?"

"She wasn't unkind . . ." Kate began, but then she heard the sound of a timid-sounding voice at the entrance to the hall, just off the kitchen.

"Mom?" said a girl who looked to be in her early twenties. She was a petite thing, like her mother, and wore an African-print head scarf that accentuated her dark eyes in a pale face. Her features were delicate, reminding Kate of Snow White. A blanket was wrapped around her thin shoulders and trailed down almost to the floor, leaving only leopard-print slippers showing from under its length.

Patricia must not have realized that her daughter was there either, because as soon as she heard Marissa's voice, she rushed to her side and helped her walk to the couch in the living room. Marissa lay down as her mother straightened blankets and fussed with pillows.

"You need your mask," Patricia said, quickly returning to the kitchen to retrieve a blue surgical mask for her daughter.

Marissa smiled over at Kate, revealing deep dimples in both cheeks before she slipped the rubber band over her head that held the mask in place.

"Hi," the young woman said through the mask. "I'm Marissa." Then she turned to her mother. "Why didn't you tell me we had company? I would have at least put a robe on."

"She wasn't exactly expecting me," Kate said apologetically as she prepared to go, but Marissa motioned for her to sit. Her weary eyes, darkly circled though they were, looked grateful for the company.

"Mrs. Hanlon brought us some cookies." Patricia offered the plate to her daughter.

"I love cookies," Marissa said, taking a large one from the plate. "So you're . . . ?"

"Kate Hanlon. My husband is the new pastor at Faith Briar."

"Oh." Marissa's eyes lit with recognition. "I read about the fire in the paper, and everything that's been going on there. That was rough."

Patricia returned to the kitchen to check on the coffee on the other side of the long room.

"We're doing better now," Kate said. "The church has been rebuilt, and we're back to regular services."

"I miss going to church there," the girl confessed. "I've been sick, so it's been hard to get out." She lifted the bottom of the mask and took a bite of the cookie before letting the mask drop back over her mouth.

"I'm sorry to hear you're sick," Kate said.

"Well, not as sorry as I am." Marissa laughed, then she lowered her gaze as her laughter faded. "I have leukemia," she said simply. "I've been doing chemotherapy for what feels like an eternity." She looked at Kate and shrugged.

"And how is that going?" Kate asked as she moved to the wingback chair across from Marissa, setting her purse on the floor next to it.

"Hard to know. If I measure effectiveness by how sick the treatments make me feel, I'll be just fine."

Kate liked this girl. The twinkle in her eyes showed good humor, and while Kate couldn't see her smile with the mask covering her mouth, she could see the laugh lines at the corners of her eyes that turned up in sincerity. Kate felt a motherly protectiveness for her almost instantly.

"So, how long does that course of treatment last?" Kate prompted.

"I just finished four weeks, so I guess it depends on my next test results. It could go on for quite a while. If they could find a bone-marrow donor, I could be done soon . . ."

Kate glanced at Patricia, who'd gone silent. She set the tray of coffee and the accoutrements on the table between Kate and Marissa.

"Sweet or unsweet?" she asked Kate, pointing to the coffee.

"Sweet," Kate said. "But I can fix my own. You don't have to."

Patricia handed Kate a steaming cup, then added sugar and cream to another, stirred it, and handed it to her daughter.

"Thanks," Marissa said before going on.

Kate readied her own cup while the girl continued.

"There's no telling how long it will take to find a match, though. People don't know how easy it is to be tested—just a swab from the inside of the cheek. But even if there was a match right in Copper Mill, I might never find them if they aren't tested. Of course, family is my best bet for finding a match anyway. Mom was tested, but she isn't a match. Parents rarely are, since they represent only half the gene pool."

"Do you have any siblings?" Kate asked.

Marissa glanced at her mother, and Kate sensed nervousness in the look. "No," she said.

Patricia was staring hard at her cup. The way she seemed to be avoiding eye contact, even with Marissa, gave Kate pause. Then sadness flickered in Patricia's eyes, and something else Kate couldn't put her finger on. But whatever it was, it disappeared behind that resolute shield almost as quickly as it had appeared. Kate wondered what the woman was hiding. Then she shook off the thought. The last thing this woman needed was Kate criticizing her.

Each of us has our own way of coping, Kate scolded herself. *And why shouldn't she, especially after losing her husband a few short months ago and facing a hardship like this alone.*

"I could talk to people at the church about being tested," Kate offered. "You never know. Someone could—"

Patricia rose suddenly and cleared her throat. "Marissa really needs her rest," she began, her tone markedly sharp, impatient.

"Mom, I'm fine," Marissa protested.

Patricia let out a breath. "No, I think you need to go, Mrs. Hanlon." Her eyes met Kate's. "You'll excuse us, won't you?"

"Mom!" Marissa protested.

"Your mom's right," Kate said. "I need to go." She stood and picked up her purse.

Patricia lifted the tray and returned to the kitchen, the sound of clattering dishes spreading across the rooms.

"Will you come back to visit?" Marissa asked. "Mom gets so discouraged. She seemed to be enjoying your company before I came in." Her voice was low as if she was trying to keep her mother from hearing.

Kate smiled as she looked into the girl's eyes. "I'll come back," she said. "I promise."

Then Patricia led Kate to the front door. Her thin shoulders were stiff, and Kate noticed that she was shaking. Patricia stood facing the closed door while Kate waited behind her, then a moment later, she broke down in sobs and turned to face Kate, her blue eyes made bluer with the tears.

Kate lightly touched her arm. "I know this is hard," Kate said. "I just want to help. You have to believe that. If there's any way I can . . ." Her words trailed off, then she said, "I didn't mean anything by offering to look for donors."

Patricia nodded, letting out a shuddering breath. "You are the first person to darken my door," she squeaked. "I've been doing this all alone for so long, without Ray . . . I can't lose her too." Her gaze flittered toward the other room, then back to Kate. "And it's all my fault. I could stop it, if I chose, but I'm so selfish—" Her words stopped short, and her eyes darted from Kate's gaze.

"What do you mean you could stop it?" Kate asked.

"Nothing," the woman said quickly. "Forget I said anything."

"I don't understand." Kate knew she was pushing, but

she couldn't help herself. What guilt could Patricia possibly be carrying that would lead her to think that she was the cause of her daughter's leukemia? "You can't blame yourself."

"I said forget it." Patricia's tone was firm, so Kate decided to let it go.

"I don't mean to pry. I'm sorry." Kate met her eyes. "I want to understand and to help you and Marissa. That's all. No strings attached."

When Patricia finally raised her eyes, Kate could see the agony that seemed poised to drown her.

KATE CLIMBED into her Honda Accord and turned the key, her thoughts still with Marissa and Patricia as she began the short drive home. The dusting of snow that had been falling earlier had turned into a full-fledged snowfall that gave the quaint town a Currier and Ives look. Kate turned on her wipers to push the fat flakes off the windshield.

She didn't hold Patricia's curt attitude against her. Instead, she thought once more about what it would be like to lose Paul so tragically and then to be alone as her only child faced leukemia. She couldn't even fathom it. She sent up a quick prayer for Patricia as she turned onto Smoky Mountain Road and made her way home.

A tangle of questions nagged at her mind. Why had Patricia said she could end her daughter's suffering? And if she could, why hadn't she already done it? And why had she been so resistant at the mention of testing others to see if they were a match for Marissa? Wouldn't most mothers want that? Any chance to save her daughter's life? It was obvious from the tender way she cared for Marissa that she loved her—so what was it?

Kate pictured the stiff way Patricia had moved about the kitchen after her daughter had come into the room, the sideways glances when Marissa had talked about her leukemia and treatments, and the way she had abruptly ended the visit when her daughter so obviously wanted to talk. Something else was there. Kate could feel it. An undercurrent, but of what? Fear? Certainly that was understandable. And a protectiveness of her only daughter —that too seemed completely reasonable. But why the guilt?

No doubt she was just imagining things.

Chapter Three

Energized by the idea of creating a stained-glass studio, Kate rose early the next day and spent some time reading her Bible and praying, then she began preparations for converting the third bedroom into a studio. Ever since Paul had mentioned turning the spare bedroom into a stained-glass studio, the idea had grown within her. She'd had a small workspace in San Antonio, but with a full-time job and all her responsibilities at the church, she'd never had the time to really enjoy her hobby the way she'd wanted.

For years she'd kept files of project ideas—sketches of windows, sun catchers, and lampshades she wanted to create someday. Now, she realized, she could really invest in the hobby, turn it into something more substantial. Who knew what could come of it?

The previous evening, she'd jotted down a list of supplies she'd need and ideas for the surprise project for the church. She'd also sketched out some design ideas that had been floating around in the recesses of her mind.

The coffeemaker beeped from the kitchen as she pulled a thick folder of project ideas from a small file box in her bedroom closet.

She padded back down the hallway and across the large living room to the cute but tired-looking kitchen. She lifted the coffeepot off its warming plate, then pulled out a delicate china cup and saucer from the cupboard. Lifting the blue stylized pot, she poured the hot brew, releasing its aromatic scent. Then she settled down at the kitchen table, opened the folder, and peered through its contents.

She'd been collecting design ideas ever since she'd taken her first class in stained-glass art. She'd had many art classes in high school and college, and she'd always been good at drawing, but there was something about stained glass that held a particular attraction for her. It allowed her to use her love of drawing, but it took that ability one step further, turning the one-dimensional concepts into a living, breathing creation. The interplay of shadow and light meant that her creations were ever changing, fresh, with a life of their own. That, to Kate, was the best part of being a stained-glass artist, watching her pieces grow into something more than even she had imagined. Letting the light have its way. She supposed God was that way too, as his light took over and transformed a person into someone they never could have ever been on their own.

She'd made a small sun catcher during that first art class and then moved up to larger and larger pieces until she began making more intricate Tiffany-style lamps, complete with the requisite dragonflies and butterflies. Her house was filled with them, as were the homes of her children and friends. Everyone she gave them to said she was an exceptional artist. Whether or not she was the most talented artist, she couldn't say, but she felt happiest when she was creating, and that was motivation enough to keep at it.

She paged through a stained-glass supply catalog and wrote down a list of the items she needed: additional glass cutters, glass in a variety of colors, caulk, foil, jewels, lead came, soldering supplies, some zinc framing materials, and a new grinder. She did have several boxes of sheet glass in the basement storage room, but she knew she'd need a bigger variety. She added "large table for layout" to her list, and a light table she could use to see how the light would play through any given piece. And she would definitely need more storage for her soldering supplies, tools, and any special trims the pieces might need. It seemed there were always a multitude of small pieces she needed, and she liked to hang on to scrap glass for mosaic-type works. That, of course, would mean bins for sorting scraps by color.

Next she took a sheet of clean paper and drew the layout of the extra bedroom. It was a basic square with one end occupied by a closet with bifold doors. If she bought an organizing system for the closet, it would allow her to maximize the room itself as a workspace. She positioned the light table in front of the room's only window, which looked out on the backyard. She liked feeling connected to the outside world while she worked, even if she was alone in her studio. Then she drew a square to indicate the large divided storage unit for the glass sheets that she'd brought with her from San Antonio and a smaller square representing a file cabinet for any paperwork that might need filing.

She liked to keep track of her costs so she could feel good about how much she'd saved whenever she saw similar lampshades or windows in stores. And who knew, if she did decide to sell a few pieces, it was always good to know where her price points were. After all, it paid to be optimistic about one's ventures, she told herself.

The worktable would take up the majority of the space behind her. She needed something durable, with a top that wasn't fussy, since cutting glass and soldering seams didn't lend themselves to keeping the furniture pristine. She wondered where she could find such a table and decided to give Sam Gorman's Mercantile a look-see. If he didn't carry anything along those lines, she could always see what was available in Chattanooga or search online. She was amazed at what she could find if she simply let Google do the work for her.

She glanced at the clock and realized it was seven. Paul must have already left for his morning run. She'd been so engrossed in her plans, she hadn't even heard him go.

Making her way to the spare bedroom, she stood in the doorway and pictured how it would look without the boxes and clutter that currently occupied the space. The room had become a sort of catchall while she decorated and remodeled the rest of the house. If she didn't know what to do with something, she'd put it in here.

Having to downsize was part of the price of moving into a smaller space. Yet, to her surprise, she discovered she enjoyed the process of clearing out the clutter. It felt cleansing, more than simply a reduction of possessions but an inner release as well. As if getting rid of the physical encumbrances that surrounded her freed her mind and spirit.

Things she'd held on to for years, she was now able to let go of. In their place was the satisfaction of simplicity. Who'd have thought it of her? She used to love going shopping, hitting the antique stores, looking for those perfect trinkets to fill her life with.

Perhaps people could change. She smiled at the thought. Already, Copper Mill was changing her.

Entering the room, she began sorting through the piles. Soon she had four large garbage bags filled with items to put on the curb with Monday's trash and another three boxes of usable items to take to Goodwill on her next trip to Pine Ridge. She took the boxes out to her Honda and placed them in the trunk, then came back in and hung her coat back in the front hall closet.

She returned to the room that was already taking on a semblance of order. The remaining miscellaneous items she placed in two boxes to be distributed in their rightful spots around the house. All that remained was a pile of boxes containing the stained-glass supplies she already owned. She went down to the basement and brought up the colored glass, still in its shipping box with her San Antonio address on the label.

As she stood assessing her next task, her mind drifted to her visit with the Harrises the day before. She sent up a prayer for Patricia and her daughter, that they would find comfort and healing during this hard time, that God would draw them close. God had a way of doing that in difficulties, drawing people to himself, giving them the tools of faith and perseverance just when they needed them, and not a moment before. She wondered how God would get ahold of Patricia. The woman certainly had a hard shell when it came to matters of faith. Surely, losing her husband was a devastating blow, and now Marissa's ill health ... Kate shook her head. What must it be like to face such hardships without hope?

Whenever God had allowed Kate to suffer, she had leaned more heavily on his comfort during that time. She couldn't imagine life without that assurance. How bleak the future must have looked to Patricia, especially since she seemed to be blaming herself for Marissa's condition. What had she meant when she said she could stop her daughter's suffering if she chose to? That comment continued to nag at Kate. Her heart ached at the thought.

She remembered her promise to Marissa that she would return. She wondered if Patricia would slam the door in her face this time. She sighed, allowing her prayers for mother and daughter to float upward. She'd just have to pray that Marissa would answer the door.

When she heard the front screen door slam, she raised her head. A moment later, Paul appeared in the bedroom doorway. His face was red from exertion. He was wearing red wind pants over his sweats, and the hood of his East Tennessee State Buccaneers sweatshirt was sticking out of the top of a navy bubble vest.

"I was wondering if you went running," she said.

"I ran a little ways, but it's cold out there! So I stopped at the Country Diner for a bite to eat with the other pastors."

Kate glanced at her watch. "Which explains why it's nine o'clock." She lifted a brow.

"Spending time with the locals is part of the job, honey, part of the job." He grinned, then said, "Oh, and remind me to pay Pete MacKenzie back for breakfast."

"You borrowed money from the Presbyterian pastor for breakfast?" Kate teased.

"You don't expect me to carry my wallet in my running pants, do you?" He was grinning as he said it, then he lifted his gaze to the room and cleared his throat. "So, what are you doing in here? I haven't seen this room so clean since we moved in."

"I'm setting up my stained-glass studio, remember?"

"I'm glad to see you're moving forward with that."

"This is fun, actually." She held out the studio layout sketch for him to see.

He took it from her and studied it. "Looks like you have everything covered." He handed the sheet back and asked, "You think you'll make mostly lampshades or windows?"

"I'll let time and my whims dictate that, I guess. I was thinking about talking to Steve over at Smith Street Gifts to see if he'd be interested in carrying some of my work. What do you think?"

"I can't think of a good reason not to." Paul gave her a lopsided grin.

"Maybe I could even teach a class on glasswork. I'd need to prepare a curriculum of sorts . . . decide what I'd have the students make first. Perhaps I could offer several levels of classes—beginner, etcetera . . ."

"That's what I love about you, Katie. When you're onto something, you're like a pit bull!"

"Hey!"

"I mean that as a compliment, honey. Entirely complimentary."

Kate blushed, then shrugged. "I guess I'm a little excited. I'll start small, just do a few projects that I enjoy, stretch my abilities as an artist."

"I have no doubt you'll be branching out, building a large facility, and starting a full-out business in a few short months. Maybe you could hire me to be your errand boy."

"Don't tease me, Paul Hanlon. Besides, you're already my errand boy."

Paul sidled next to her and bent over to kiss the top of her head. "Well, I suppose I should get crack-a-lackin'." He pointed to his watch. "Say," he paused to add, "I was thinking maybe I should stop in on Patricia Harris, pay her and her daughter a visit, since I was too busy with my meeting to go with you yesterday."

Kate shook her head. "I think she's going to need gentle nudging. If the pastor shows up on her doorstep . . ." Kate shrugged. "Well, I think she'll bolt."

"I just thought—" he began.

"You have good intentions, hon, but God had a reason for keeping you busy yesterday. Patricia is skittish. She's been hurt. I don't know the details, but I can see it in her eyes. We can't push her. Besides, just because you're the pastor, it doesn't mean you have to personally meet every need. Let the church be the body of Christ, not a one-man show."

"Fair enough," Paul said, his hands in surrender pose. "You know I trust your judgment."

"I'll tell you when she's ready for the big guns."

"That's not a very nice way to put it," he protested.

"I actually thought you'd like the he-man image."

Paul flexed his arm muscles and lifted an eyebrow. Then he turned and said, "Have fun, honey. I need to get down to the church."

Soon Kate was back to dreaming and planning. And praying for Patricia and Marissa Harris.

AFTER A QUICK SHOWER and shave, Paul headed to the church. By the time he'd walked to the otherwise vacant lot, it was 9:47. The church secretary's ancient red Datsun was in the spot closest to the door.

When he came in the side door that led directly to the church offices, stomping the snow from his shoes, Millie Lovelace raised her gray head and eyed him suspiciously. She had tight curls from a perm gone awry, and her face seemed more wrinkled than her sixty years seemed to justify. Whenever she came near, Paul was always certain he could smell the faint scent of cigarettes, though he'd never seen her partaking. He wondered if her husband or sons were smokers.

She pointed to the clock on the wall and said, after clearing her throat, "I was here at nine o'clock." The implication was unmistakable.

"I'm glad to know the church secretary is on the ball," Paul said with a wink. Millie blushed and sputtered.

"You know I'm only here till noon. I have to get to my job at the SuperMart in Pine Ridge this afternoon. I can't be sticking around to tie up your loose ends because you meander into the office whenever it suits your fancy."

"Understood," Paul said.

He walked past her desk and into his office, which was directly behind hers, pulling off his winter coat as he went. He'd had the walls painted a warm cocoa color to give the room an intimate feel, and a bookcase filled with all manner of study books covered the wall behind a large oak desk. Though he had a study at home, where he often worked on his sermons, he used this office to conduct most of the church business.

Paul clicked on a green banker's lamp, then another brass table lamp at the end of the desk. He opened the miniblinds for the window overlooking the parking lot, then he turned on the computer, and it hummed to life. It seemed particularly cold in his office this morning, so after placing his coat in the closet, he put on the cardigan he kept on the hook behind his door. Then he returned to the outer office, where Millie was on the phone.

"If you ask me, he needs to learn what his priorities are," she was saying when her eyes met Paul's. She cleared her throat again and blushed. Paul walked to the coffeepot and reached for his ceramic mug with "East Tennessee State" in big letters on its side. "Renee," she went on. "I need to go."

Paul heard the phone click and Millie straighten in her vinyl office chair. He turned to face her.

"Renee Lambert?" he asked.

She nodded, and he let the topic go. He'd learned long ago that it was often better not to know what people were saying, though he had a pretty good idea anyway.

Then he took a long sip of his hot coffee. "So, what's on our docket for this week?" He leaned against the low filing cabinet that sat opposite her desk. The copier hummed next to him. He set his mug on top of it and rubbed his palms together to warm them.

Millie paged through the paper calendar she kept for him. She'd refused to put the information on the computer despite Paul's argument that he could access the information from home and help keep it updated. She'd merely replied, "You never know who will get into your information if you put it out there for everyone to see."

"It would be private."

She shook her head. "The only way to be sure such things are private is if you don't put them there in the first place." Then she'd held up the calendar and said, "Sometimes the old ways *are* the best, Pastor Hanlon."

He'd smiled and let her have her way. Hers was a small world, and if he could help her feel secure in it by writing his daily appointments into a calendar and doling them out like candy at a dentist's office, then he could accommodate that. Though who she thought was so desperate to know his comings and goings, he couldn't guess.

"You have a board meeting tonight . . . and your nursing-home visit is tomorrow in Pine Ridge. Joe Tucker called to say he has firewood for anyone in the church who might need some."

Paul picked up his coffee and took another sip. "Oh, that's nice of him."

"Fifty dollars a cord," she added.

Just then the phone rang. Millie picked it up and said, "Faith Briar Church." She paused while the person on the other end talked. "Yes, he's here." She nodded for Paul to step into his office, which he did, closing the door behind him. The phone buzzed, and Paul picked up the handset as he settled in his chair.

"Good morning," he said.

"Pastor Hanlon? This is Eli Weston." Eli ran the local antiques store. He was a good guy. Quiet. And though they'd discovered that he was the one who'd accidentally set the church on fire, he'd been forgiven. He'd confessed and done all he could to make restitution. Eli had done so much to help rebuild the church, and Paul had watched that very process bring healing to the young man's broken heart.

"Eli. How are you?" Paul asked.

"Fine, fine," Eli said.

"Say, I wanted to thank you again for the beautiful trunk you gave us. Kate just loves it. She put her mother's handmade quilts in it. It has a permanent spot at the foot of our bed. You know women . . ." Paul let his words drop away.

"I'm glad to hear she likes it," Eli said, then cleared his throat. "Um. I'm calling . . . well. I have a question to ask . . ." He sounded tentative, and Paul wondered why.

"Go on," Paul coaxed.

"I have some neighbors, they're brothers, actually—the Wilsons. They're really going at it."

"You mean they're fighting?" Paul sat up straighter in his chair.

"Arguing very loudly is more like it. I thought about calling Deputy Spencer, but that's not always so good for keeping peace in the neighborhood, if you know what I mean."

"Sure, I understand," Paul said.

"I was wondering . . . hoping you could come over and . . ."

"And break up their fight?"

"I remember how diplomatic you were with my situation with the fire and everything. How you helped me smooth things over with the church. Well . . . I hoped maybe you could help Jack and Carl resolve their issues. But if you don't want to—"

"No, no. That's okay, Eli," Paul assured him. "I hear what you're saying. It's totally understandable."

"I tried to talk to them, but they slammed the door in my face. And since then, the shouting has just gotten louder."

"Are you afraid they'll get violent?"

"No. I know these boys. They've been my neighbors for a long time. They're both good guys. But you know brothers."

"Oh, I do," Paul laughed. "My brother and I used to fight like cats and dogs when we were small." He paused, thinking of his brother Charlie, who'd lost his life in Vietnam. He still missed the times they used to share, even the fights. Then he said, "I'll be over in a few minutes, okay?"

"Thanks, Paul."

Paul hung up the phone and rose to take off the cardigan and put on his winter coat. For some reason, the image of Mister Rogers came to mind, and he smiled. He bet Mister Rogers never went to break up fights in the middle of his day in the neighborhood.

PAUL DROVE his blue Chevy pickup to Eli's house and parked in front. The downstairs was the storefront for Weston's Antiques, a business Eli had inherited from his grandfather, and upstairs was Eli's living quarters. The two-story building was set back from the street. Rocking chairs in various sizes and colors lined the porch, and a white picket fence surrounded the yard. A large wooden Weston's Antiques sign brought in the tourists year-round.

Paul tugged the gearshift into park. As soon as he

opened the door, he could hear loud voices coming from the house in back of the store, intermingled with the high-pitched yipping of a dog. He wondered how long the brothers had been arguing and why someone else hadn't called the police. But other than Eli's place and a few businesses, there weren't any other homes nearby, and Paul expected that most people would be at work in the middle of a Tuesday morning anyway. He decided to pow-wow with Eli before attempting to talk to the brothers, so he made his way up the snowy brick walkway and entered Weston's Antiques.

The interior was dark, and it had that smell of age—not quite moth balls, but a bit musty. Antique collectibles filled every square foot of the place, with narrow rabbit trails here and there for walking. The walls were covered in pastoral scenes of sheep and meandering brooks all in shades of blue and green, as well as turn-of-the-century lithographs of stern-looking ancestors in stiff, unsmiling poses.

Paul walked to the back of the store as Eli emerged from the hallway where his office was. He was drying his hands on a dishtowel and set it down on a 1950s baby buggy when he realized the pastor was there.

"I thought I heard someone come in," he said. "You got here quick." Eli Weston was a large man with a husky build and a shock of blond hair that contrasted with his dark brown eyes. He had a gentle, almost shy smile that was partly hidden behind tortoise-shell glasses. "Thanks for coming, Paul." He held out a hand, which Paul shook.

"Don't mention it," Paul said.

Eli crossed his arms over his barrel chest, while Paul

scratched his head and asked, "So, do you know what the argument's all about?"

Eli shook his head. "I think it's something about their dog. They've been fighting off and on all day. And that poor dog is beside herself."

Just then the sound of shouting grew louder, and a door slammed outside. The brothers had moved their fight into full view. Paul glanced out the side window at the two. They both looked to be in their early twenties, trim and good looking if it wasn't for the torrent of loud accusations streaming from their mouths. The noise was muffled as it filtered through the store windows, but Paul and Eli could hear every word as clear as day. The blond boy was considerably taller than the other. He held a golden cocker spaniel in his clutches, while his smaller, dark-haired brother pointed and reached for the dog, whose teeth were bared in a snarl.

Paul and Eli took that as their cue to head outside.

They crunched across the snow, and when they reached the neighboring backyard, the brothers paused in mid-rant. The dog also turned to look and sent several yipping barks their way.

"What's going on here?" Paul said.

"He's stealing my dog!" the smaller brother said. His brown eyes flashed in anger.

"Scout is not his dog," the blond one said, turning back toward his brother. "He decided he wanted her when he opened my mail. Didn't Ma ever tell you it was rude to open other people's mail? He's so annoying!"

Eli cleared his throat, gaining the attention of both

brothers. "Would you two like to go back inside and talk reasonably? What you're doing obviously isn't getting you anywhere."

"Eli, you know how stubborn Jack is!" The blond brother said to the antiques dealer.

"Yeah, right," the dark-haired one added. "Like Carl isn't just as stubborn! *Stubborn* is his trademark."

"I think Pastor Hanlon can help, guys, really." Eli held up his hands in an attempt to calm the brothers.

"Who?" they said in unison.

"Pastor Hanlon." Eli nodded to Paul, who gave the brothers a little wave.

Just then an elderly woman passed on the sidewalk. She stared at the boys as if to say, "Can't you kids control yourselves?" and then continued on her way.

Paul took the hint and said in a lower voice, "Perhaps Eli's right. We should move this conversation back indoors."

The younger and smaller of the two, whom Paul had deduced was Jack, led them toward the ramshackle house they shared on the opposite side of the block from Eli's store. Carl followed close behind. A lean-to of sorts served as the back entry. It was in such a state of disrepair that it looked as if it would crumble away from the house at any moment. Piles of old newspapers were stacked in the entryway, and coats in all shades of camouflage bulged from the hooks that lined its walls. The space smelled of old shoes and man-scented dankness. The rest of the house wasn't much better. Ceiling tiles were missing overhead, and there wasn't a spot on the kitchen counters that wasn't filled with dirty dishes and moldy food. A gray Formica table in the center of the room harbored four chairs in the sea of mess.

Carl set the dog on the floor. Scout immediately turned to inspect Paul and Eli, jumping up and yipping between sniffs. Jack filled a stainless-steel bowl with dog food from the fifty-pound bag of kibble that leaned against the small, old Frigidaire. Then he filled a similar bowl with water and placed both on the floor next to the table. The dog ran to her breakfast and chewed noisily, leaving particles of kibble trailing down her orange-colored beard.

Carl cleared away bowls of day-old cereal and several boxes of Lucky Charms and Frosted Flakes from the table so they could sit down. The brothers sat on opposite sides, eyeing each other like playground bullies who wanted the same swing.

"So," Paul began. "What seems to be the problem?"

"I already told you," Jack said, tossing his dark hair out of his eyes with a flick of his head. "He's stealing my dog."

"I am not! Argh! You're so infuriating."

"Since you live together," Eli broke in, "can't you just share the dog?"

Both brothers looked at him with an expression that said he was insane.

"I'm not understanding either," Paul said with a shake of his head.

"Whoever gets the dog gets the money," Carl explained, then pointed at Jack. "He's the thief." He leaned down and scratched the dog on the head as she ate. Scout bared her teeth, though this time without a growl.

"I thought he was trying to steal *your* dog," Paul said to Jack.

"It's *my* dog and *my* money," Carl corrected. "I entered Scout in one of those mail-in contests and won. I even wrote an essay on why she's a great dog. But my brother here thinks he can claim anything he wants and just walk away with it." He leaned toward Jack and spat the words, "Didn't Mom teach you better than that?"

"How much did you win?" Eli asked.

"Five grand," both brothers answered.

Paul whistled. "That's a lot of money."

"You ain't just whistlin' Dixie. That's why I'm not going to roll over and let *him*"—Carl nodded toward his brother —"take what's rightfully mine! He always gets everything he wants. Spoiled brat. Well, not this time!" he insisted, his voice rising in intensity. Then he got up, stomped over to the kitchen counter, and shuffled through a pile of paperwork before returning with the official-looking letter from the How Now Dog Chow Company of Pine Ridge, just a few miles up the road from Copper Mill.

He handed the letter to Paul and sat back down. Paul read it through. The document looked legitimate, and it contained details for prize acceptance, including a requirement that the winner pose with his or her dog in an ad campaign for the obscure dog-food company.

"I don't even know what planet you're from!" Jack

countered, "You know Scout's mine. I can't even fathom that you'd lie to a pastor about it!"

"*You're* the liar!"

Paul and Eli exchanged frustrated looks.

"Let's take the volume down, boys," Paul said. "You don't want the neighbors calling the police, do you?"

Both brothers crossed their arms over their chests and turned their chairs slightly away from each other.

"Jack, Carl," Eli said. Their gazes shifted to him. "I called Pastor Hanlon here in hopes that he could help you resolve your differences. Could you at least listen to him?"

Jack uncrossed his arms and sat back in his chair. Carl picked up the dog, who settled in his lap to sleep. He stroked Scout's auburn coat.

"I'll take that as consent," Paul said with a smile. He scooted his chair back a bit and began. "This seems pretty straightforward if you ask me. Just answer a few questions, okay?"

Jack lifted a dark eyebrow as Paul turned to him.

"How did you get the dog?" Paul asked.

"He was a gift from my dad," Jack said.

"Yeah," Carl added, "to *me!*"

"Okay." Paul raised his hands to signal a time-out. "Carl, you said you entered Scout in the contest. Do you have a copy of the essay you wrote?"

Carl shook his head. "I sent the only copy in. I didn't know he"—he pointed at Jack—"would try to steal the prize money."

"Just because he entered *my* dog in a contest doesn't make the money his!"

"Oh, come on, Jack!" Carl stood, still grasping the dog. His chair toppled to the ground with the motion. Scout raised her head and started barking again.

"You know what?" Jack continued, pulling the dog from his brother's grasp. "I'm out of here! I'm taking Scout, and we're going to Aunt Susan's."

"Not with my dog, you're not!" Carl grabbed for the dog, but by now Scout was howling at the top of her lungs.

Jack set Scout down, and she started running in circles, snarling at everyone.

Paul reached down to try to calm the pooch but nearly got bitten as she lunged at him.

"I think our job here is done," Paul said, glancing at Eli, who was looking utterly confused. "Let's go."

They rose from the table to leave. Scout was still howling and running around in circles, and the brothers were glaring at each other.

Once outside, Eli said, "We didn't solve a thing."

"No, we didn't, did we?" Paul agreed.

"So, what now?"

Paul shrugged. "It looks like my quiet pastoral life is slipping into the Smoky Mountain mist."

Chapter Four

The January day had turned warm, with temperatures rising into the upper fifties. Rivulets of snowmelt meandered along Smoky Mountain Road where Livvy Jenner—the town librarian—and Kate were taking a noontime walk. It had become a ritual for the two, walking during Livvy's lunch hour a couple of times a week. Kate would arrive at the library on days when the temperature was pleasant, and the two would make their way up Smith Street, past the Town Green, take a right onto Hamilton Street, then head north out of town along Smoky Mountain Road to Kate's house, where they'd make banana-and-yogurt smoothies before heading back the mile or so to the library. They had it timed to perfection, always arriving back just when Livvy needed to return to work.

Kate lifted her face to the warming sunshine, the sound of their sneakers on the pavement filtering toward the towering pines on either side of the country road as they made their way back to town.

"You seem in a good mood today," Livvy observed. Her auburn hair was tucked behind her ears and her white sneakers peeked from underneath her black-nylon walking pants.

"I *am* in a good mood," Kate said. "I got started on setting up my stained-glass studio early this morning. I feel as if it's a new adventure for me. I don't know...I'm excited about it."

"I thought you'd been making stained glass for years." Livvy slipped her hands into the pockets of her jacket.

"Yes, but this is different. I really feel ready to do something with it, you know? Really create something special."

"Like starting a business?" Livvy raised an eyebrow and smiled at her friend.

"If I had customers, who knows what it could grow into? I'll just be glad to be working at it again. It's energizing to feel like a creative, imaginative person."

They came around a bend in the road, and a car slowed down to pass them. They walked single file as it did, then Kate moved back up next to her friend as Mountain Laurel Road came into view straight ahead. To the east was the Hamilton Springs Hotel, in its final phase of construction. It was said to be lovely, though Kate had yet to see it. It was supposed to be open for operation any day now. Kate couldn't wait to try out their spa and Bristol's, the new restaurant.

Kate glanced to the west, in the direction of Patricia and Marissa Harrises' home, just off the hilly stretch near Quarry Road.

She sighed as the image of that frail girl appeared in her mind's eye. She was barely older than Kate's youngest daughter, Rebecca. Dark circles had ringed those luminous eyes. She'd seemed hungry for someone to talk to, someone who wasn't already overwhelmed by the heavy burdens of life. Kate thought again of her promise to come visit.

"What's wrong?" Livvy asked. She was gazing at Kate with an expression of concern.

"It seems you know my cues as well as my husband does." Kate chuckled. "Nothing's wrong. I was just thinking of the Harrises. Poor Patricia—she's lost so much already. I can't imagine what she must be going through to lose a husband and now to have a child stricken with leukemia . . ." Kate shook her head.

"It is a shame," Livvy said. "And so young. If my James were to be diagnosed with leukemia . . ." she paused. "It's just too unimaginable to even consider. And since Patricia lost Ray, she hasn't been the same."

"You know her?" Kate asked.

"Kate, Copper Mill isn't that big, and I'm the town librarian. I know pretty much everyone, especially if they like to pick up a book every once in a while. Patricia and Ray used to come into the library every Wednesday evening for date night while Marissa was at youth group. They'd usually read periodicals, though Patricia might bring whatever book she'd been reading from home if it was one she just couldn't put down. She always was quite a reader. Even after Marissa was older, she and Ray kept

coming. I can still picture them sitting in that maroon
love seat by the front window, reading side by side. He
usually picked up *Outside* magazine or anything that
related to sailing and the outdoors, and Patricia would get
out the *Country Living* or *Parenting* magazines. It's
funny..." she paused.

"What's funny?" Kate prompted.

"There's so much you can learn about people by what
they read. I'd be interested in doing a character study of
people based on their reading choices." She shrugged,
then went on, "Anyway, Patricia barely ever comes in at
all anymore, not since Ray died."

"What else did she like to read?" Kate couldn't help but
feel curious. It was who she was. She supposed if Livvy
looked at her reading habits, she'd discover a decided bent
toward Sue Grafton and Mary Higgins Clark.

"Oh, Patricia probably could've taught parenting
classes, she read so much on the subject. From Dobson to
Spock, she read it all. Books on miscarriage and even
adoption." Livvy paused in thought. "She and Ray had so
much trouble having any more children after Marissa was
born. I always wondered why they didn't adopt. But she
sure doted on Marissa, and Ray... he adored that girl."

Before making their way across Mountain Laurel
Road, they stopped to let a semitruck and a lumbering
motor home pass in front of them.

"So when did she become such a...loner?" Kate
asked.

"Patricia?" Livvy clarified.

Kate nodded.

"That was a recent thing. After Ray's passing. She was actually one of the popular girls in high school. Very pretty. A cheerleader. She went for years with . . . What was his name? He moved away right after graduation. What was his name?" Livvy shook her head as she struggled to recall the name. "Anyway, Patricia was a few years older than I was. She was a senior when I was a freshman. I remember she was in youth group back then, and quite active. She participated in a lot of the discipleship training."

"Really?" Kate said. "I'm surprised. She seems so . . . against faith somehow. I don't know her, but she seemed very closed when I talked with her. She didn't want me trying to convince her to come back to church."

"That happens to a lot of people when life tests them." Livvy smiled, then shrugged. "I just knew her from church, really, at youth group. I looked up to her as a leader. She went to college in Chattanooga, I think. Then a couple years later, she came back married to Ray and with a baby."

"She must've been pretty young when she had Marissa, then."

Livvy nodded. "Nineteen, maybe? Twenty? Her folks moved away shortly after she left for school. They'd lived here all their lives, then as soon as Patricia was gone, they moved. That seemed odd to me. People in small towns tend to stick around, especially when they're older like those two were. Matt! That was his name. Matt Reilly. That was her boyfriend."

Kate nodded absentmindedly and continued walking.

Something still didn't seem right. "Why would Patricia tell me that she could stop Marissa's leukemia?"

Livvy stopped too. "She said that?"

Kate nodded.

"That's an odd thing to say."

"I thought so too," Kate said. "It was almost like a confession. Then she pulled inside herself—like a tortoise retreating into its shell." She shook her head. "I keep thinking about it. It just doesn't make sense to me."

"Maybe she feels guilty," Livvy offered. "Isn't that what mothers do? Feel responsible for everything that happens in their children's lives?"

"Well, that's true," Kate admitted. "I'm probably just imagining things. You know." She smiled shyly. "After the fire investigation, I'm starting to see mysteries everywhere!"

Kate paused for a moment in thought, then said, "So, her parents moved away while she was in college?"

"Somewhere out of state."

"And she moved back here . . . not near them after she got married?" Kate was thinking out loud, not really asking a question. She couldn't put her finger on what exactly was niggling at her. They came to a stop at the corner of Smith and Main, at the entrance to the parking lot for the library. An old pickup with a rusted front quarter panel rumbled up the street and past them, toward the Town Green. Two young mothers with babies pushed their strollers along the sidewalk.

"Was she ever in any kind of trouble?" Kate asked.

"Not that I recall." Livvy shrugged. "Like I said, she

was a leader in school, and even after she and Ray moved back, they were members of the Rotary. Ray volunteered with Habitat. Patricia was always helping out at the school. As for her folks, near as I could figure, they had a normal parent-child relationship. Of course, she was young, eager to get out on her own when she was eighteen ... And Copper Mill was home for her, even without her parents here."

Livvy folded her arms across her chest as another vehicle passed. "What are you thinking?"

"I don't know. Life is hard enough, but without her parents nearby ..."

"But Ray, he was an exceptional man—devoted, kind. Always willing to lend a hand. They loved each other. Anyone could see that. When she came home married to him, she was the happiest I'd ever seen her. Just really good people. He thought the world of her, right until the day he died."

"So, where are Patricia's folks now?"

"I heard that her parents died a few years back. Some sort of accident, and she was an only child."

"*Hmm.*"

"What?"

"It seems our mission is clear," Kate said as they made their way across the parking lot and up the stairs to the front doors.

Livvy paused to give Kate her full attention.

Looking at her friend with conviction, Kate said, "Those two lost souls need us."

WITH A POT ROAST in the oven and the table set for supper, Kate meandered back to her studio. Paul was at the
nursing home in Pine Ridge for his regular Wednesday
visit with the church members in residence there.

Much was still in disarray in the small studio, but defi-
nite areas had been set aside for each phase of the
stained-glass process. Kate had been looking up the cost
of light tables online and found a nice one for a reasonable
price on a stained-glass-supply Web site, so she placed
an order. The shipment was due to arrive in a week.

She already had that large divided organizer she'd
brought from San Antonio for the colored glass sheets
she kept on hand. This she moved alongside the spot
where her light table would eventually be. She began
placing the large sheets in the vertical bins. The smaller
pieces she placed in drawers that ran horizontally at one
end of the organizer. Then, following the Roy G. Biv rain-
bow pattern, she sorted the colors left to right beginning
with red, orange, yellow, green, and so on. Soon she had
all the glass distributed into its correct spot.

Then she got out her glass-cutting saw, small miter
saw for zinc framework, her ancient grinder, many soldering irons and scrub brushes for cleaning off her tabletop,
and a myriad of small tools and laid them in a line on the
floor. Once she installed the closet organizer, she'd have a
spot for each of these items.

She decided that a Peg-Board on the wall over her layout table could hold items like squares, pliers and what-
not. She wondered if the hardware store in town would
carry such a board.

Tired from all her work, she sat in the room's only chair, a padded office chair on wheels, and gazed out the window at the winter evening. The waning light of day illumined the yard. It had been so warm that bald patches showed where the snow had melted. Headlights shone from the country road, and Kate listened as her husband's Chevy pickup pulled into the drive. She heard the door slam and the screen-door spring stretch and complain before slamming shut behind Paul.

"I'm in here," Kate called.

A moment later he was at the door to her studio. "Hey, sorry I'm late." He leaned against the doorjamb. His graying hair fell across his eyes, and he pushed it back with a hand. "Wow. You've gotten a lot done in here." His gaze drifted across the room.

"Not too bad for two days' work," Kate said. "How about you?"

"*Mmm.* I had quite a visit at the nursing home today."

"Good or bad?"

"Good. Very good," Paul said. "The residents are always so glad to see a new face. It doesn't matter if they're from our church or not, I end up visiting with a whole slew of folks. Mrs. Roberts wheeled herself right up to me and said, 'I expect you'll come to call in my room today, Pastor Hanlon. Right?' Well, what could I say to that?"

"I don't think I know her," Kate said.

Paul shook his head. "You wouldn't. She's been in the home for several years. She has Parkinson's quite bad, but she's sharp as a tack. That's always hard to see—those trapped in uncooperative bodies despite being fully aware mentally . . ." His words broke off, and Kate gazed into his kind eyes. Paul took a deep breath. "It always gets to me," he said. "And yet it's such a blessing."

"I'm sure they appreciate your visits."

"No, I mean it's such a blessing to me."

Kate stood and walked to her husband, kissing him on the cheek. "That's why I love you, you know. That heart for people." She patted his chest.

Paul blushed slightly, then gave her hand a squeeze. "I know I'm a big softy. I can't help but think about James 1:27—'Religion that God our Father accepts as pure and faultless is this: to look after orphans and widows in their distress.' I always think I'm doing my good deed when I set off, yet I end up receiving so much more than I ever give."

THE COLD RETURNED on Thursday with a steady snowfall and gusting winds. After Paul left for work in the morning, Kate decided to mix up a batch of Nestlé's Toll House cookies. They were Paul's favorite, so she doubled the batch to make sure he'd get his share, unhealthy though they were. The only alteration she made to the famous recipe was substituting butter-flavored Crisco for the butter. The cookies always turned out just right with that switch, moist without being a gooey mess as the butter ones always seemed to be, at least whenever she made them. Leaving the mixer to run, she slowly added the chocolate chips until they were mixed into the batter. As usual, she let her thoughts wander to the current mystery she was puzzling over and tried to settle on why Patricia might be able to help her daughter, but nothing seemed to make sense. She switched off the machine and lifted the beater.

These cookies were intended for a mission—to soften the heart of one Patricia Harris. Kate smiled at the thought, as if the human psyche were so simple that a basic concoction of sugar, flour, and chocolate chips could change the heart. If only that were possible, she would've saved the world ages ago with a big Texas-style cookie bakeoff.

Retrieving the large cookie sheets from one of the lower cupboards, she began scooping the dough onto them, making sure to leave enough space between so the cookies wouldn't run together once they started baking. Soon the enticing aroma of chocolate-chip cookies filled the quaint kitchen. Kate put on her oven mitts and pulled out the first sheet, then the second. She waited a few minutes, then carefully placed the cookies on the cooling racks she'd set up on the counter. When she had placed the next batch in the oven, she leaned against the counter to sample the goods. They were just right, melting in her mouth as the taste of semisweet chocolate filled her senses.

Once the cookies had cooled, she neatly placed a dozen and a half on an inexpensive yet decorative plastic serving plate, gathered the clear blue cellophane wrap just so around the plate, and tied a pretty bow on the top using a white satin ribbon. Then she slipped the other gift from her studio into a flowered envelope and attached it to the bow like a greeting card.

When she set off for the Harrises', the snowfall had ceased, leaving a shimmering glitter across the landscape. The sun was shining brightly, almost blindingly, as Kate made her way along Mountain Laurel Road. She pulled up in front of the spacious home and saw that there was no car in the driveway. She walked up to the garage to peek through the side-door window—no car there, either. She had turned to climb back into her Honda and return home when Patricia and Marissa pulled up in an off-white Mercedes.

"What are you doing here?" Marissa asked as she got out of the car, a wide smile on her face when her eyes landed on the cookies in Kate's hand.

Kate lifted them slightly and said, "I had a little something for you."

Patricia closed the driver's door and gave Kate a questioning look. Then she moved to the front door and unlocked it, motioning for Marissa to go inside.

Once her daughter was out of earshot, she turned to Kate, "I appreciate you trying to reach out to us and all, but I thought I made myself clear the last time—"

"I know you're hesitant to let anyone into your life right now," Kate began, "but you shouldn't go through this alone. It's hard enough with a support system, but alone . . . You need a friend."

Patricia's shoulders slumped, and tears welled in her pale eyes. Finally she sighed. "I wasn't very kind to you—"

"Don't you worry about that," Kate said, gently touching her hand. "That's in the past."

"After the day Marissa had, I know she'll be glad for the company. At least for a little while." Then she led Kate into the back of the house, where Marissa was already lying on the couch.

Once Patricia had peeled off her coat and scarf, she took the plate of cookies from Kate's hands and said, "These look delicious."

She took them over to her daughter, who asked, "Can I?"

"By all means," Kate said. "I brought them for you."

Marissa carefully slipped the envelope off the ribbon and tore it open. "Oh, look, Mom, it's a sun catcher. How pretty!" She held it up for her mother to see. The stained-glass miniature caught the light in shades of green and blue.

"It's a *coquí*," Kate said, "a Puerto Rican frog. Actually, I made it myself."

"You *made* this?" Marissa's face held amazement. "What a gift you have!"

Kate waved a hand through the air. "Oh, anyone could learn to do it. It just takes practice and patience."

"Thank you." Marissa smiled up at her. "I really, really like it. It was so thoughtful of you." She turned toward her mother. "Mom? Can we put it up in the window now?"

Kate glanced at Marissa, wondering at the request. It wasn't as if sticking a suction cup to a window was a difficult task. But when Kate studied her more closely, she could see how very weak the girl was. What little color she had had drained from her face in the short time they'd been in the house.

Marissa raised herself to stand, but then her legs seemed to give out from under her. Kate caught her and was amazed at how light she was. Under her bulky sweats, she was skin and bones.

Patricia had come alongside her as well. Her eyes met Kate's, and she could see that they were filled with worry.

"Do you want to put it up in here?" Patricia asked her daughter.

Marissa shook her head. "No. Let's go in my room. I'll be okay."

"Are you feeling nauseated?" Patricia asked.

Kate realized then that they must have just come from a chemotherapy treatment, and she remembered Patricia's words about the rough day Marissa had had. Her heart ached at the thought, yet Marissa was undaunted.

"I'm okay, really," the girl insisted. She smiled as if to reassure her mother, then said, "Come on, let's put the *coquí* up on my bedroom window. I'll be able to see it from my bed when I wake up."

Gingerly they helped Marissa walk, though it seemed the fainting spell had passed. She quickened her pace, so Kate let go of her, though Patricia still kept a grip on her arm.

Marissa's room, off the short kitchen hallway, was a cheery place. High shelves that ran the length of the room

held Elvis Presley memorabilia in all shapes and sizes—
Elvis paper dolls, greeting cards bearing the singer's
image, dolls, buttons, you name it. And on the walls, aged
posters from many of Elvis's movies shone with
Technicolor brightness, including the singer's famed *Blue
Hawaii* pose in red shirt with white flowers and a yellow
lei around his neck.

"It looks like you're an Elvis Presley fan," Kate said.

"Can you tell?" Marissa let out a chuckle, then lowered herself onto the bed, which was covered with a
pretty aqua blue silk comforter, matching pillows, and
embroidered white-on-white accent pillows.

Her mother helped her move up further onto the full-
size bed, then covered her legs with a crocheted coverlet
that had been draped over a nearby rocking chair.

"Yes, I've always been a big Elvis fan," Marissa went
on, "though not as big as Mom used to be. Being born on
the anniversary of Elvis's death—that pretty much sealed
that I was destined to be an Elvis fan for life. But Mom
used to date Elvis." She pointed her chin toward her
mother in a teasing gesture.

"I did not!" Patricia protested. "The man was way too
old for me."

"But you had a crush on him in grade school," Marissa
persisted, which made her mother blush.

"You don't have to confess anything you don't want to
confess," Kate said, smiling. She took a seat in a padded
chair near the window. Bright sunlight diffused by sheer
white curtains warmed the spot.

"I don't mind saying, I did have a crush on Elvis," Patricia finally admitted, "and I did own every one of his singles. I still have them on the Jukebox downstairs. And"—she lowered her head—"I actually had my picture taken with him once."

Marissa clapped her hands in glee. "See? She still has that picture too if you'd like to see it."

Patricia shook her finger at her daughter. "I doubt I could find it if I wanted to."

"So, are you going to put my sun catcher up?" Marissa asked. She sat back on her bed as she held the glass ornament out to her mother. Patricia took it from her outstretched hand and pulled the curtain back.

"A little to the left," Marissa said, sounding slightly out of breath. "It'll catch the morning sun there." She closed her eyes slightly, and a moan escaped her thin lips.

Kate glanced at her, her heart aching at the sight of the girl in obvious discomfort, while Patricia adjusted the sun catcher and pressed the suction cup against the window to hold the ornament in place. Then she stepped back and moved to her daughter's side.

"I'm okay," Marissa insisted, her eyes on the sun catcher. "I like that, don't you?"

Kate felt humbled as she watched Patricia stare lovingly at her ill daughter, who was trying to be so brave despite her circumstances. And yet she felt powerless too.

Chapter Five

The next day, Kate returned to the Harris home at noon, this time with a batch of her homemade chicken-noodle soup. She knew that with the previous day's chemotherapy treatment, Patricia and Marissa would need support and a little comfort food.

When Patricia came to the door, she looked exhausted. Her hair, which was usually neatly styled, was a rumpled mess, with tufts standing out at odd angles from her head, and her eyes were clouded from lack of sleep.

"Did she have a rough night?" Kate asked.

Patricia nodded, and tears filled her eyes. "She was up all night throwing up." She began to cry. "She has to get better. She just has to."

Kate reached out to give her a hug, but realizing the pot of soup was in her way, she set it on the entry-hall table and then held the distraught woman until the sobbing lessened.

"I'm so tired of crying," Patricia said as she took a step back, wiping her cheeks.

"I know," Kate said. She waited for Patricia to calm herself, then retrieved the soup and lifted it to eye level. "Can I set this on the stove? It's hot if you're hungry now. Or you can eat it later."

Patricia shook her head. "I'm not hungry, and I doubt Marissa could keep anything down anyway. She's sleeping right now."

"Then we'll let it simmer until you're ready. Why don't you go lay down too?" Kate suggested.

"I have laundry that needs folding, and if Marissa needs anything . . ." She shrugged.

"I can do those things for you," Kate assured.

"No," Patricia said. "Really. I'm the one who should be—"

"That's silly," Kate said. "You're no good to her exhausted. I'll sit with her if she wakes up, and I'm as good as the next girl at folding laundry."

That brought out a weak smile.

"I don't understand why you're doing this for us."

"Because it's the right thing to do," Kate said. "Come on." Kate led the way into the kitchen and placed the pot of delicious-smelling soup on a burner, turning it on a low simmer. "You go on," she insisted. "I'll listen for Marissa."

"You'll get me up if she needs me?"

"Absolutely."

Patricia smiled gratefully at her and obeyed, padding up the stairs to her bedroom.

Kate made her way into the tidy laundry room, which was just off the garage. Kate thought of her own washer and dryer in the garage, which were usually piled high with unwashed loads of clothes. Looking around, she saw that there was a basket of what looked like clean sheets on the folding table opposite the washer and dryer, and another load of darks in the dryer. She made quick work of folding both loads and leaving them in neat piles on the table for Patricia to put away later.

Then she made her way down the hall to Marissa's room. She opened the door a crack to check on the girl and saw that Marissa was sitting in her rocking chair. "Hey," Marissa said, lifting her head. "I didn't know you were here."

Kate opened the door wider. "I thought I'd give your mom a break . . . and I brought some homemade soup for lunch."

"That's so kind of you." She motioned Kate into her room.

Kate took a seat on the edge of the unmade bed. "How are you feeling today?"

"A little better." Marissa smiled, and the dimples in her cheeks deepened. "I was just enjoying my *coquí*." She motioned toward the window. She was wearing a blue chenille bathrobe and leopard-print slippers. When she shifted in her seat, Kate caught sight of the catheter in her chest that peeked from underneath her pj's.

"Are you hungry?" Kate asked.

Marissa shook her head. "I will be in a bit, maybe, but right now I'm just glad to be sitting up and welcoming the day. When did you find time to make soup?"

"Ever since the kids left home, I've been amazed at the free time I suddenly have." Kate smiled into the young woman's eyes.

"How many kids do you have?" Marissa asked.

"Three—a son and two daughters. They all live too far away."

"That must be hard." She tugged the blanket on her legs up higher.

"I miss them," Kate said, "but we talk on the phone often and try to get together once or twice a year."

"I can't imagine living far from my mom. She needs me too much." Her eyes lit up. "And I need her."

As they talked, Kate wondered what Marissa's life had been like before the loss of her father. Their family seemed close-knit and loving, held tight by the trials of life.

AN HOUR LATER, Marissa sat back in the dining-room chair after she had finished the last of her chicken-noodle soup. The color had returned to her cheeks, along with the vibrancy Kate had noticed the first time she'd visited.

"That was delicious," Marissa said.

"Old family recipe," Kate said as she gathered the bowl and spoon, took them to the kitchen, and placed them in the sink.

"So is it top secret?" Marissa asked when Kate returned, teapot and cups in hand.

"I'll let you in on the secret cheap, Vinnie," Kate said in her best mafioso accent.

Marissa laughed. It was a rich sound to Kate's ears.

"So, tell me about yourself," Kate said as she poured

herself and Marissa cups of steaming black tea then took the seat adjacent to Marissa's.

"*Hmm*," Marissa said. She wrapped her narrow fingers around the cup as if to warm them and gazed up toward the ceiling in thought. "Well, I'm an only child, as you know. Twenty-two years old. I got my BS from college last May. I want to be a physical therapist. Oh, I was engaged for a little while too."

"You were?" Kate said. "I didn't know. What happened?"

"Oh," Marissa said. "It just didn't work out. He was . . . immature." She scrunched up her nose, then continued. "When he found out I was sick, he came to see me less and less. It was shortly after Dad died. Then he finally broke it off last month." She shrugged her shoulders. "It's for the best."

Kate studied her, wondering if she really believed it was for the best.

"Who wants a husband who can't handle the 'in sickness' part of their vows?" Marissa added.

Kate reached across the table and squeezed her hand.

Marissa took a long sip of her tea. "Besides," she said. "Once I'm feeling better, I'll meet the right guy. Hey, maybe I'll meet him because of my illness. You never know, right?"

"That's true," Kate agreed. How she wished she could will wellness into that thin frame and make Marissa whole without all the heartache and struggle she had ahead of her.

"Makes me miss my dad, though. He knew what commitment was all about."

"He was a sailor, right?" Kate asked.

Marissa nodded.

"Are there a lot of places to sail nearby?" Kate continued.

"Not really, but he'd trailer his boat and head up to Lake Michigan or rent a larger boat at the coast. He loved it so much, he didn't care that Tennessee wasn't the sailing capital of the country. He was good too—won several races. I'll have to show you his trophies sometime. He was very proud of them. He grew up outside Philadelphia, so it was something he took up as a kid."

"You and your mom have a lot of good memories," Kate said.

Marissa's eyes clouded. "She hasn't been the same lately . . ." Her words trailed off. "At first I thought she was just missing him, you know? He was her backbone in many ways. Not that she didn't have her own opinions and manage everything around here perfectly, but he knew how to encourage her. I'm not so good at it. Maybe it's because I'm too much like her." She chuckled. "But she's withdrawn into herself. It scares me. And sometimes I catch her looking at me . . . I don't know. I think she's really scared."

"Any mother would be," Kate assured.

"I worry about her. She needs someone to encourage her . . . like Dad did."

"So who encourages you?" Kate asked.

Marissa thought for a moment before answering. "People like you, I guess. Sometimes I really wish I'd had a sibling, you know? It's not always comfortable talking to your mom about some subjects, and a sibling, especially a sister I could confide in . . ." Her sentence trailed away, and she took another drink.

"My daughters talk to each other about things they'd never share with me," Kate admitted. "And I'm pretty sure most of their conversations are *about* me!"

Marissa grinned at her. "You can't assume that's all bad, though."

"I suppose not. Why didn't your parents have more kids?"

"They tried for a long time. Finally Mom was so heartbroken that we stopped talking about it. I could tell Dad felt awful. He really wanted a son."

"So that's why you seemed so hesitant when I asked you if you had any siblings before?"

Marissa nodded. "I know how hard that all was for her."

"Did they look into adoption?"

Marissa finished the last of her tea and set the cup on the table. "The topic of adoption was always so . . . I don't know . . . taboo. I never knew why. I remember a couple of Mom's friends bringing the topic up, one even brought her a brochure from some agency out of Chattanooga. Mom got totally freaked out by it. She got really mad and told her friend that she was being meddlesome. She was moody for days afterward. I'd never seen her like that. Dad never brought it up, and I sure didn't either. I thought adoption sounded like a great idea. At least I'd have my baby sister or brother, right?" She shook her head. "So that was that. I was destined to be an only child." A smile touched her face, and she said, "Do we still have some of those chocolate-chip cookies from yesterday?"

"I was wondering when you'd ask," Kate said. She rose and retrieved the plate, still wrapped in its cellophane, and set it on the table. Once she'd untied and peeled back the noisy wrapping, she handed a cookie to Marissa and kept one for herself. They each took a bite. Marissa closed her eyes in enjoyment.

"It's so good to be able to keep food down," she said. "Especially this kind of food. Chocolate is my all-time favorite. Last night I thought I'd never eat again, the way I was feeling."

"So, what's your next course of treatment?" Kate took a bite of her cookie.

"I have a couple more weeks of chemo, and I'm on several drugs. If there was a marrow donor that matched, I'd need to go through a couple days of heavy-duty chemo that basically kills not only the cancer but the marrow as well. Then I'd get the transplant. But the doctor said the odds of finding a match are fifty-fifty. If I go into remission after this round of chemo, I could have them set aside marrow for myself for later, providing there aren't any cancer cells left . . ."

"And the prognosis?"

"There's a sixty to seventy percent chance of remission. That's without the marrow transplant. With it, my odds would be much higher." She'd said it so matter-of-factly that Kate found it hard to believe that Marissa was talking about herself.

"This may seem forward," Marissa interrupted Kate's thoughts. "But I know you're a pastor's wife. We used to go to church before Dad died, and I still believe . . . even though Mom's become so . . . well . . ." She raised her eyes. "Would you pray for me?"

Kate placed a hand on Marissa's and said, "I'd be honored."

Then she offered up a simple prayer of gratitude for this girl and her life. "Lord," she went on, "Marissa has so much yet to do on this earth. She has a mother who's already suffered more than her share. She has friends who care about her. Please bring healing to her body through the treatments she's getting now. And if that is not to be, bring a donor. And most of all, bring your comfort to her troubled heart, and your presence to this home."

When she opened her eyes and gazed into Marissa's, the hope she saw there revealed her utter trust. *God*, Kate added silently, *don't let that trust be broken*.

AFTER THEY RETURNED to her bedroom and Marissa had finally dozed off again, Kate tiptoed to the bedroom door and closed it silently behind her. Marissa had looked peaceful, sleeping in the sunlight as its rays kissed her pale face.

So much about their talk made Kate wonder, most notably why Patricia couldn't talk to her own daughter about her devastation at not being able to have more kids. True, there were many who kept such hurts bridled, yet to not talk with those closest to her, Kate couldn't imagine that. She knew she had only to pick up the phone to talk to Rebecca or Andrew or Melissa about anything that was on her mind, even the most intimate of details. What else was family for if not to be a support in difficult times? She'd been at the Harrises' for well over three and a half hours. Wondering if Patricia was still asleep, she decided to check on her. Making her way up the stairs, she noticed that Patricia's door was ajar, and through the opening she could see Patricia sitting in a rocking chair, her back to Kate and her head tilted down.

Kate quietly knocked on the jamb. "I hope I'm not interrupting—" she began.

Patricia jumped to her feet, and a photo album tumbled to the floor. She quickly swooped down to gather it up, clutching it to her breast. Her vivid blue eyes were wide, darting.

"I—I didn't hear you . . . You startled me," Patricia said.

"I'm sorry," Kate soothed. "I didn't mean to . . ." She could see that Patricia's cheeks were wet with tears.

The woman moved to the open closet and shoved the album into its depths before turning back to Kate. She swiped at her tears and tugged her shirt down, but the guilty expression on her face was unmistakable. "I didn't know you were there," Patricia said. "Does Marissa need me?" She began to move toward the door.

"No. She's fine," Kate assured. "She just fell asleep. She ate a good lunch and even had tea and cookies."

Patricia stopped and wiped her cheeks again. "Oh, good."

"Are you okay?" Kate asked.

Patricia nodded.

"I'm sorry you're going through all this," Kate said. "Especially alone."

"We're going to be okay," Patricia said. She sounded almost defensive, and Kate wondered why. "Once the chemotherapy is done, she'll have a clean slate. Really." She lifted her chin and turned away slightly.

"I was hoping I could come tomorrow if—"

"No," Patricia said curtly. "We have plans."

"Well, then the next day—?"

Again Patricia shook her head. "Marissa will be busy all week, I'm afraid."

Kate thought of the hope, the utter belief, she'd seen in Marissa's eyes just a few minutes before. If only Patricia would open her heart to that comfort beyond anything that human contact could offer. Yet Kate knew Patricia was struggling. Kate would simply have to take what she was given and let God do the rest. When the right time came, she would be ready. That was all she could do.

IT WAS LATE AFTERNOON when Kate climbed into her Honda Accord to head back home. The sun hung low in the western sky, creating brilliant designs in hot pink and tangerine across the mountain ridges.

It had been a hard day, yet a good one. A sense of weariness overtook her. This hurting family needed so much, yet she was only one woman. And how could she help them unless she could find a way to soften the hard shell Patricia had encased herself in? But only God could do that, she reminded herself.

Then her admonition to Paul came back: "Let the church be the body of Christ, not a one-man show." She smiled to herself.

It was good advice. There were many others in the church who would be blessed in the helping, though she wanted to be sensitive to Patricia's desire for privacy. The least she could do was to call the prayer chain, without mentioning names, of course. Perhaps she could encourage those she knew to join the National Bone Marrow Registry. Even if there wasn't a match for Marissa, perhaps another leukemia patient in their midst would find life. She would call the hospital when she got home and go get tested—Paul too. At least that was something she could do instead of sitting around feeling helpless. And if there was one thing Kate hated, it was doing nothing.

The image of Patricia bolting upright when Kate had knocked on her door returned again. Kate couldn't seem to get it out of her mind—and the change in Patricia's attitude too. What had happened? Had she offended Patricia in some way? She couldn't think of anything she'd done, intentionally or otherwise. Yet Patricia had been so jumpy, so defensive.

What was it she was holding in her lap? A photo album? That was hardly something worth hiding. Yet it seemed that was exactly what she had been doing, judging by the way she had shoved it into the back of the closet.

Kate sighed as she turned left onto Smoky Mountain Road. What sense did it all make?

It seemed that instead of gaining a clearer knowledge of Patricia Harris, Kate was finding the woman more elusive than ever.

Chapter Six

The weekend passed in its usual manner. Paul added the finishing touches to his sermon on Saturday while Kate tidied the house and did some baking. On Sunday Paul mentioned a member of the church needing prayer "for health concerns." Kate felt better knowing there were others carrying the burden of prayer for Marissa. Paul even went so far as to mention the need for people to add their names to the National Bone Marrow Registry.

"There are many people," he said, "not just here in Tennessee, but across the nation, who need marrow donation, whose lives could be saved if we did our part." His eyes searched the congregation. Kate felt pride and love welling within her for this man.

"Kate and I are going to be tested this week. It's a simple swab of the cheek—that's it. But if you're a match, it could save someone's life. Isn't that a worthwhile thing to do this week?" He smiled, then glanced down at Kate.

She hoped people would take his words to heart and get tested—if not for Marissa, then for someone else.

SINCE PATRICIA HAD MADE it clear that she didn't want Kate's help anytime soon, Kate decided to spend the next week continuing the work on her stained-glass studio. So after she and Paul stopped at the hospital on Monday to have their cheeks swabbed, she drove to Pine Ridge and purchased a closet organizer with plenty of drawers and solid-surface shelves for the assorted supplies and tools her craft demanded. Then she labeled each drawer for easy identification. She had everything from foil to lead to jewels and nuggets, which were particularly pretty in lampshades, to caulk and the assorted chemicals she would need, as well as soldering supplies and leading tools, a stack of framing materials for window work, a small miter saw, a glass saw, her old grinder, soldering irons, and on it went.

When everything was in its allotted place and correctly labeled, she stood back in satisfaction. All she needed now was her light table, which was scheduled to arrive that week, and a large worktable that was essential in her craft. She wondered if Sam Gorman carried anything like that at the Mercantile, or at least if he had a catalog of such furniture. She liked the idea of supporting local businesses if at all possible, and she had discovered that if she ordered such a large item on the Internet, the cost of freight would be prohibitive.

So, on Tuesday afternoon she headed to the Mercantile. She parked on Main Street and entered the store's cluttered interior. Sam Gorman's warm smile met Kate as the bell above the door tinkled when she entered.

Aisles in the store were narrow, and the shelving was tall, giving the place a claustrophobic yet cozy feel. Sam carried every item imaginable—from milk and food products to knitting supplies, camping items, jewelry, clothing for every member of the family . . . you name it. A few shoppers perused the shelves near the back of the store.

"How are you this fine day?" Sam asked. The church's organist, he had become one of Paul's best friends in the months since their arrival. He was in his late fifties, loved fishing, and was one of the nicest people Kate had ever met.

"Oh, not too bad," Kate said as she set her purse on the counter.

"Anything in particular I can help you find?"

"Actually," Kate began, "I'm looking for a large table."

"Like a kitchen table?" He scratched his stubbled chin.

"No. More like a large craft table. Something square that I can lay my stained-glass projects out on, with a surface I don't need to worry about scratching. Something I can drive a nail into without worrying."

"So, a real craft table . . ." he said. "*Hmm.*" He chewed on his bottom lip as he thought, then said, "I think I have just the thing."

He reached down beneath the cluttered counter and pulled out a voluminous binder that he laid open between them. "There's some furniture like that in here, I think." He paged to the back. "Ah, here we are."

He turned the book so Kate could see it right side up.

"Says here it's thirty-one inches high, and the top is forty by eighty. That about right for you?"

"Do you have a tape measure?"

Sam nodded and retrieved the item, also beneath the counter. He held one end while Kate pulled the tape out to the correct length. "That's a good-sized table," she said. "What's it going to run me?"

Sam reached for his calculator with the large buttons and punched in some numbers before looking up to give her the total.

"Let's get it ordered," Kate said.

Sam began copying down the details on the special-order pad alongside the cash register as Kate watched.

"Heard through the prayer chain that Marissa Harris has been sick," Sam said as he wrote.

"Paul didn't mention her name—"

Sam shook his head. "News like that is pretty hard to keep hushed in a town like Copper Mill," he said. "Besides, Renee Lambert has been in."

Kate nodded her understanding. "That poor child," Kate said. "I wish there was more we could do to help."

"I've heard several people say they're going to be tested for the marrow-donation program." He glanced back and forth between the catalog and his notes, as if to be certain he'd copied everything correctly.

"Really?" Kate said, amazed at the quick response to the plea for help. Sam raised his head.

"No one likes to see a young person suffer," he added. "Especially that one."

"You know Marissa?" Kate asked.

"I knew her dad. Nice guy. Good friend, and a great sailor. He used to take me on his boat on occasion. Played a mean cello, so we shared a love of music. Even played duets together in church a couple of times."

"Patricia didn't mention that Ray was a musician," Kate said.

Sam closed the binder and placed it back in its spot beneath the counter, then straightened up again. "That woman keeps a lot to herself," he said. "Ray was kind of her opposite when it came to that."

"What do you mean?" Kate asked.

Sam shrugged, and his ocean blue eyes twinkled. "Ray was just a very open guy. Wasn't afraid to talk about things, like how much he adored that daughter of his. He wore his affection for her on his sleeve." He shook his head. "It's a crying shame he died so young. A crying shame."

A moment of silence stretched and yawned.

"He always wanted a son. When he found out he couldn't . . . well, that was a hard blow."

"*He* couldn't?" Kate said.

"Oh, they went through that whole barrage of tests the doctors have out there. It was a miracle he and Patricia had Marissa in the first place, I say. But he was heartbroken. I think that's why he worked extra hard to make Patricia and Marissa feel loved. He felt to blame."

"From everything I've heard, he sounded like a pretty extraordinary person," Kate said.

"Oh, that he was," Sam agreed. "He really cared. And it wasn't just an act with him—he really did care. Went the extra mile, you know? He had these vivid blue eyes. I can still see them. They drew you in with their caring." He took in a deep breath, then he cleared his throat and said, "Well, enough about that."

Kate picked up her purse from the counter and said, "I appreciate your ordering that table for me. It sure will be a help."

"It should be here in about a week. I'll bring it out to the house."

Chapter Seven

The next day, winter made itself known. Snow had fallen in a thick coat during the night, covering the landscape as well as the streets of Copper Mill. Paul was outside snow-blowing the driveway and sidewalk as Kate watched from the window of their bedroom. A cup of hot coffee steamed between her hands as she sipped. The loud snow-blowing machine sent an arc of white onto the front yard as Paul walked along behind.

He had been out there for a while and was just about done with the job when the county snowplow came by, leaving a ridge along the edge of the driveway. Paul stood upright, then his shoulders slumped as he looked at the long mound that now blocked the driveway.

Kate chuckled to herself before returning to her studio and the task at hand. She set the cup of coffee back on its saucer and picked up her pencil.

When she'd returned home from the Mercantile the day before, she'd been delighted to discover that UPS had left a large box on the front stoop. Her light table had arrived a day early. Considerably smaller than the table she'd ordered from Sam, this table had a glass top with a light underneath that made it possible to see how the colored glass would look in bright sunlight. She'd had it out of the box and assembled by suppertime.

She sat at it now with a large sheet of paper before her and her laptop computer alongside it. She'd been looking up pictures of different objects for her surprise for the church and had finally settled on one in particular. She didn't want Paul to suspect what she was doing, so when she'd seen all the snow, she'd been glad to know he would be outside giving her a little time to begin her design before Paul left for work.

She was immersed in her drawing, enjoying the moment, sipping her coffee and then sitting back to decide whether she liked the placement of this or that item, and erasing and redrawing as needed. She didn't want to make it too intricate, since that would eat up more time than she wanted, but she also wanted a sense of realism for the piece. It was a delicate balance, but one that she enjoyed finding.

Her thoughts turned to her talk with Sam Gorman the day before. He'd added a couple of pieces to the puzzle that was Patricia Harris—most notably that the reason she'd never had another child was because of Ray's infertility. Kate wondered if Marissa knew that detail. The young woman certainly hadn't mentioned it, but, Kate supposed, most men wouldn't share such intimacies with their daughters. What was it Sam had said about Ray's blue eyes? They drew you in with their caring. Kate hoped people could say the same of her when it was her time to go.

"What are you working on?" Paul stood at the door, his cheeks red from the cold.

Kate hadn't even heard him come in much less open the entry closet to put his winterwear away. Quickly she shut the laptop and turned her sheet of paper face down. When she faced him, she saw that his eyebrows were raised in question. She cleared her throat.

"It's nothing . . . Just a new project."

He took a step into the room, grinning. "Can I see?"

"Oh no!" she said a bit too loudly.

He stopped walking and looked at her. "Why not? Are you hiding something?" he asked in jest.

"Don't be silly. It's just . . . You know us artists. We want to wait for the big unveiling." She raised her hands in an awkward "Are you buying this?" gesture.

He crossed his arms over his chest. "Is that so? I can let it go . . . I guess."

"Thanks, honey," Kate said. "It's something special that I want you to see when the time is right."

"Well, I can't argue with that." He walked over to her and kissed her forehead, then pretended that he was going to sneak a peek. She smacked his hand.

"Just kidding!" he said as he reached for her cup instead and took a sip of the steaming brew. "It's so cold out there! Did you see what that plow did to all my good work? Talk about frustrating!"

"I did. Poor baby."

"So much for my ideal life."

"You keep learning this lesson, don't you?" Kate said.

"I guess some of us never learn!"

"Speaking of never learning," Kate said, "did you ever figure anything out with the Wilson brothers and their dog, Toto?"

"The dog's name is Scout," Paul said. "And no . . . Actually, Eli and I were going to head over there later this week. The younger brother is digging in. I don't get it."

"You're not alone on that front. I'm still trying to figure out Patricia Harris too. She has no parents or husband or extended family to speak of, yet she's completely shut me out so I can't help her. It's as if she's afraid of something." She reached out for her coffee cup, taking it from her husband's hands and setting it on the light table.

"Don't take it personally," Paul said.

"And how about you, Pastor—are you taking your own advice?"

"I think the Wilson brothers enjoy the attention they get by keeping this feud going," he admitted. "Jack actually moved out of the house with the dog, to their aunt's house. Carl is threatening to sneak in and kidnap the animal. I thought it was all talk, but these two are serious."

"All for some prize money?" Kate said. "You've got to be kidding me."

Paul shook his head. "I wish I were. Eli and I are going to take another shot at reasoning with them. If that doesn't work, I don't know what we'll do. Brothers shouldn't treat each other this way. In all my years of counseling, I've never had this much trouble getting through to two people."

"Why don't you go talk to Nehemiah about it?" Kate suggested. "We live nearby now. You should take advantage of that. Besides, you know he'd love a visitor."

Nehemiah Jacobs, the previous pastor at Faith Briar, had been Paul's mentor growing up and into his adult life. There was no one's opinion, other than his own father's, that Paul valued more.

"You know," Paul said, the light of an idea dawning as he looked into her eyes, "I should get Nehemiah's advice on it."

"Oh really," Kate deadpanned.

Paul gave her a wry grin. "I love it when I get good ideas like that." Like a mountain climber on a frosty morning, he took a deep breath of air. "I'll go see him just as soon as I check in with Millie. You know how she gets if I'm tardy!"

He bent for another kiss, which Kate happily returned, and then he headed to the church.

IN TENNESSEE, winters oscillated on a yo-yo string of highs and lows. By the time Paul got to Chattanooga to see Nehemiah Jacobs, the temperatures had risen to the midfifties. The snow that had covered everything was melting, and the runoff was flowing through the city streets in a shimmering sheen. Paul made his way up Dodson Avenue and pulled into the lot for Orchard Hill, the assisted-living facility where the seventy-nine-year-old former pastor now made his home.

Tucked beneath the hills of the Smoky Mountains, Orchard Hill looked more like a grand home than a medical facility. Divided windows lined the front near the entrance, and white pillars gave the place an almost regal feel.

Paul could see several of the residents inside, gathered around the grand piano that was the focal point of the front sunroom. The television in the corner sat silent. Paul made his way inside the door and to the piano room to the left. Men and women with varying degrees of graying hair sat mesmerized by the ragtime sounds that the pianist brought forth. She was a dark-haired woman with bright red cheeks, and she reminded Paul of a gypsy.

Nehemiah Jacobs listened from the couch nearest the window. His eyes were closed, yet a smile touched his wrinkled face, and he was swaying ever so slightly with the rhythm of the music. Paul took the seat beside him, and Nehemiah opened his eyes.

"Look who's here!" he said, sitting upright and clapping Paul on the knee. "What brings you to Chattanooga, Paul?" Several heads turned to see who was talking.

"You do, actually," Paul whispered. "I could use a visit with my old friend, but it looks like you're enjoying a nice concert."

Nehemiah's gray eyes turned toward the piano, and he nodded. "She comes every Wednesday. She's more punctual than the trains in France. This week it's ragtime. Last week it was classical. She has a large repertoire."

The woman who was sitting in a wheelchair closest to the front gave Nehemiah a scorching look, then she added the universal "shushing" signal with index finger to lips.

"Do you want to stay and hear the rest of this, or shall we take our talk elsewhere?" Paul asked.

"Oh, don't mind her," Nehemiah said. "She gets bent out of shape by most anything. But maybe we should go talk in the dining room."

Paul and Nehemiah stood to leave, then weaved their way through the wheelchairs and walkers that dotted the room. Despite his age, Nehemiah still got around without the aid of either. He said it was simply his stubborn nature not to submit to such contraptions, but Paul was sure it was that same stubborn nature that made him as fit as he was. He still walked two miles every day, either outside when the weather permitted or on the treadmills the facility had in its physical-therapy section. He also faithfully followed the vitamin regimen his wife, Rose, put him on years before when she was alive. And every morning he did the calisthenics routine he'd first learned in the navy during World War II.

In part, his example was the reason Paul had taken up running. It wasn't that he wanted to live as long as Nehemiah. The old man was always sure to remind him that "to die is gain." The thing that inspired Paul was the quality of life the man still enjoyed.

The two men made their way to the dining room, which was directly behind the piano room. It had several tables with white cloths; each table had already been set for the next meal. The room extended off the back of the building so that there were banks of windows on three sides, and it overlooked a pond where swans and geese made their home in the warm months. Paul could see children on the opposite bank playing in the melting snow.

Paul chose a table nearest the back window and sat facing the view. "Is this good?" Paul asked.

"Perfect." Nehemiah settled into his seat. Then he pointed toward the door to the kitchen, where a coffee station was set up. "Would you mind?"

"Not at all," Paul said. "Still take it the same way?"

Nehemiah nodded.

Paul got up to make two cups of coffee. He returned with the steaming cups and took his chair.

"Those kids play there all the time," Nehemiah said, his eyes still fixed on the children outside the window. "Makes me wish I had some snow pants." His smile belied his words. "Still, it's good to watch them having fun. Sometimes I wonder if they don't play there just to give us old folks a show."

His statement reminded Paul of the Wilson brothers. He cleared his throat and said, "That brings me to one of the reasons I came to see you today, Nehemiah."

"Oh?" The old man took a sip of his coffee.

"I was hoping you could give me a bit of advice. I always value your wisdom."

"I don't know that that's the best idea." Nehemiah laughed. "There's a reason the cliché 'old fool' exists, you know."

Paul leaned back in his chair and chuckled.

"Go ahead." Nehemiah's tone turned serious, his eyes meeting Paul's. "Whatever it is, it's obviously troubling you."

Paul thought for a moment before speaking, then he said, "There are two brothers—Jack and Carl Wilson. Do you know them?"

"I know Zeb Wilson. I think he was their dad. I vaguely remember the boys. They don't go to Faith Briar, do they?"

"No," Paul said. "Getting them to church is a bit beyond my reach. Right now I'd be happy if they could get along and not kill each other. Eli Weston called one day about some neighbors who were arguing loudly. Wanted me to come mediate."

"The Wilsons?"

Paul nodded. "Seems they're both laying claim to ownership of the same dog."

"So, buy another dog," Nehemiah said with a shrug of his shoulders.

"The problem is, whoever gets the dog gets a five-thousand-dollar prize. I haven't been able to get anywhere with them; they go round and round to the point of exhaustion. The youngest has even taken the dog and moved out of the house. Have you ever come across anything like it?"

"Oh, I've seen much worse," Nehemiah said with a laugh. "It's amazing what greed will do to a person. It'll twist you inside out if you let it."

"I've tried reasoning with them, but that gets me nowhere. I've thought about talking separately with each of them, but I don't know what good it would do. Each just accuses the other of lying . . ." Paul sighed. "You see my dilemma?"

Nehemiah sat in thought for a long time, his eyes trained on the children. Paul thought he'd forgotten the subject, when he finally turned back to him. "Seems to me," the old man began, "you need to heed the words of James 1:5 that goes something like 'Pray for wisdom and God will give it to you.' It's as simple as that, Paul."

But it didn't sound simple.

Chapter Eight

By the following Tuesday, Sam had delivered the work-table Kate had ordered from the Mercantile and set it up in the center of her studio. She was pleased with her purchase. It was a good-sized table, though not so huge as to completely dwarf the small studio, and the top was a durable plywood that would stand up to the abuse of soldering and glass cutting. She couldn't wait to use it.

She had completed the template for her surprise project for the church. Circular in design, it would have a diameter of thirty-six inches, making it one of the largest stained-glass windows she'd ever attempted. It would be a big undertaking, especially since it was so detailed. But Kate loved a challenge, and she couldn't wait to see people's faces when they saw it brightening the plain-Jane sanctuary.

The next step in the process was selecting the colored glass for the piece. She chose several shades of green and brown, with blue and white and touches of red and purple, deciding which she wanted where. Then she taped her template to the table and began the meticulous task of cutting the glass; first in measured strips to make the small cuts easier to accomplish. Then from those strips she cut the smaller pieces, setting each one on its designated spot on the template, careful to make sure it would fit exactly when the time came to put all the pieces together.

As with drawing, the glass-cutting phase of the process seemed to pull her into another world, a calm world where only she and her creation existed. There were few things like it. Cooking had the same effect, as did baking, and she relished those tasks almost as much as this.

She wondered if God felt the same way about creating the world. Did he get a sense of purpose and fulfillment in watching something new come from his own hands as she did? She couldn't imagine that he wouldn't, especially since people were created in his image.

She pushed the small glass-cutting tool into the green glass as she followed the lines of the template. The cutter made a zipping sound and left a tiny line on the glass's surface. Kate lifted the glass and tapped along the line's edge, then with a quick flick of her wrist, she snapped off the perfectly shaped piece. It was a job that took a little getting used to. At first she'd been timid about snapping the glass, afraid the whole piece would shatter with the motion. But in a short time, she'd come to trust her ability to press hard enough with the cutter so that the glass would break off easily after she tapped it. Any pieces that weren't exact after the first cut were either recut and snapped off using the pliers or taken to the grinder for more precise finishing. The rounded pieces she took to the glass-cutting saw, which was made just for curves.

She'd been working for hours before she raised her head and realized it was eleven o'clock. Rising from her stool, Kate stretched the muscles in her back that had gone rigid from being bent over in the same position for so long. Sometimes getting older wasn't all it was cracked up to be. She extended her arms and shook them out as well.

She walked into the living room when the sound of the mail truck pulling up to the box drew her attention outside. She waved to the long-bearded mail carrier whose nickname was Fish. She'd never heard what his real name was, but he seemed happy enough with Fish, though why any grown man would want to be known by such a smelly pseudonym was beyond Kate. Slipping on her shoes, she went out to the mailbox, which contained the usual smattering of bills and junk mail. She padded back into the house, tossed the items on the kitchen counter, and poured herself another cup of coffee.

It had been more than a week since Patricia had told her that Marissa would be too busy to see her. Kate wondered how she'd be received if she came by today. She'd been thinking of the pair nonstop since their last visit. Marissa had been so in need of a friend. Kate's heart ached at the thought of the ill girl all alone in her room, and poor Patricia doing her best to care for her, yet bedraggled and worn down by the task.

The savory aroma of the barbecued beef she'd put in the Crock-Pot earlier that morning tempted her senses and drew her to look through the glass lid. It was a simple recipe, just a pound or two of beef with pickle relish and her homemade barbecue sauce. She'd set it to cook when she'd first gotten up, so now it was bubbling in juicy tenderness. Then a thought occurred to her, and she pulled down a package of buns and scooped some of the barbecue into a glass bowl, which she covered with its plastic lid. She retrieved a container of coleslaw from the fridge, then found her purse and car keys and headed to the Harrises'. Food had worked before, she decided. Maybe it would work again.

When she arrived at the red Colonial, it was dark inside. The blinds were drawn tight against the day. Kate rang the bell, half expecting no one to answer, so when Patricia opened the door, she was surprised.

"Good morning," Kate said tentatively. Then she lifted the paper bag that held the barbecued beef, buns, and coleslaw. "I brought lunch."

Patricia's expression softened, and the vulnerability in her eyes nearly tore out Kate's heart.

"Let me feed you," Kate urged. "It's the least I can do . . . Okay? See, barbecued-beef sandwiches and coleslaw."

A trace of a smile tugged at Patricia's lips.

"Ah, a weakness!" Kate said.

Patricia blushed, and the women shared a chuckle as they made their way to the kitchen. Patricia pulled down three white ironstone plates. Then she retrieved a scoop, flatware, and three glasses. Kate took up the scoop and prepared the hot sandwiches, with a heap of coleslaw on the side. Steam rose from the delicious-smelling meal.

"Marissa will like this, and having you back," Patricia admitted. "I'm sorry . . . again. You've been so persistent, and so kind . . ."

Kate smiled kindly. "Don't you worry about it—you've been under tremendous stress."

She handed a plate to Patricia, then took the other two herself. She followed Patricia to Marissa's room, which was quiet except for the faint sounds of "Blue Suede Shoes" coming from the CD player next to her bed. Marissa's eyes were closed, and her head scarf had slipped, revealing her bald head beneath. Her face was gray and had a waxy appearance. Kate waited as Patricia bent over to talk to her daughter, setting her plate on the bedside table.

"Hey, honey," Patricia said. She lightly touched Marissa's shoulder. "You want to wake up? We have some lunch for you. Kate's here. She brought barbecued-beef sandwiches. Doesn't that sound good?"

Marissa nodded in response.

"She had another round of chemo yesterday," Patricia explained. "She's still feeling pretty weak from it. They said her red count might be down a little." She turned back to her daughter. "Come on, honey. Time to wake up. You need some food to help you gain your strength."

Marissa opened bleary eyes that were longing to droop shut. Then when her gaze turned to Kate, she released a glimmer of a smile. "You're here."

"You didn't expect me to stay away, did you?" Kate said. She raised the plate for Marissa to see. "I brought you lunch. Are you up for it?"

Marissa nodded and struggled to push herself to a sitting position, but she fell back exhausted.

"Come on," her mother said. She reached her arms

around her daughter's back and helped her to sit. Then she propped pillows behind her and set the tray across her legs.

Marissa gave her a grateful look.

Kate handed her the plate of food along with a spoon. The three sat and enjoyed the meal together, though Marissa ate very little.

Patricia was sitting on the edge of the bed, alongside her daughter. She placed a hand on the bedspread where Marissa's legs were. "The treatment has seemed far worse than the leukemia at times," she said.

Kate nodded her understanding.

"Next week is the last one," she went on. "Then we'll find out if she's in remission."

"Maybe I'll grow some hair again," Marissa said, and weak though she was, that touch of humor in her voice warmed Kate's heart. "Maybe you'll get to meet the old Marissa after that."

"Let's hope that happens," Patricia said.

THAT AFTERNOON Paul, Eli Weston, and Jack Wilson met at the home of Jack's aunt. As they sat in the small living room, sounds of Aunt Susan bustling about the kitchen in the back of the house filtered down the hall. Scout ran frantically around the threesome, eager for anyone to give her a pat on the head.

No one had said a word since they'd all taken their seats. Jack traced circles on the country-blue fabric of the couch with his finger while Paul waited. Eli folded his hands together and let out a heavy sigh.

Aunt Susan's home was a pleasant enough place on the northeast corner of Ashland Street and Quarry Road. A Cape Cod, the house had a classic feel with a country touch. Handmade quilts and coverlets were draped across the backs of padded chairs and the couch. A fire in the Ben Franklin wood-burning stove at the center of the living room glowed with midwinter charm. Paintings of old farmhouses and horses with buggies spoke of a home that was well loved, as did the many antiques throughout the room. Hardwood floors were covered by a thick area rug in a deep shade of blue that complemented the couch where Jack now sat.

"This isn't getting us anywhere," Paul said. "Come on, Jack, surely you know that moving to your aunt's house won't resolve anything. It will only escalate matters."

Scout came alongside Paul and nudged her nose into his knees, the jingle bell on her blue collar tinkling. He patted the animal on the head, which only served to further excite the dog. She tried to climb onto Paul's chair with him, but he pushed her back.

"Down," Paul said. The dog tilted her head at him and sat.

"Carl can end the fight whenever he's ready to admit the truth." Jack pushed his dark bangs out of his eyes and glanced down the hallway.

"How likely is that to happen?" Eli asked.

Now Scout was beside Eli, begging for attention. She jumped up and made a *whoof* sound. Eli ignored her.

Jack merely shrugged his shoulders. "Scout's my dog. What else can I say? Carl wrote that essay to try to steal the prize that belonged to Scout's rightful owner—me." He punched his forefinger into his chest.

Paul wanted to believe him. He wanted to believe Carl too, but they couldn't both be telling the truth. What bothered him most was that they were so willing to tear apart their relationship over it. That he couldn't understand. He thought of his own brother, Charlie. He'd give anything to have him back for a day, and he wouldn't waste it with silly bickering.

Just then Aunt Susan came into the room bearing a tray of desserts. "How are you boys handling yourselves in here?" she asked. Paul noted a faint Scandinavian accent in the way she said *you* with a long *o*, as if it were spelled *yoo*. When Scout saw her, she was instantly at the woman's side, nudging into her legs as she walked and circling her.

"Oh, you silly pooch," Aunt Susan said.

Eli offered her a smile. "We're doing fine, Miss Wilson."

"Call me Susan," the plump blonde woman said. In her late sixties or early seventies, Jack and Carl's aunt was about five feet tall, if that. She had a double chin and a jovial smile. Her pale hair was caught up in a sort of beehive, though Paul was sure that couldn't be the right name for the style. Hadn't beehives gone out of vogue in the sixties? She wore a pearl necklace and matching earrings, and a blue-and-white-checkered apron covered her pink housedress.

"Would you like some cheesecake and hot cocoa?" she asked Paul.

The thought of Kate's reaction to the sugar-filled

dessert gave him pause, then deciding he'd exercise later, he took a plate and a mug.

"Thank you," he said. "You didn't have to go to all this trouble."

She offered the same to Eli, who also reached for a helping.

"It's no bother," Susan said. "I keep treats like this on hand since Jack came to live with me. Got to keep up his strength, ya know."

Paul looked dubiously at Jack, who simply smiled in return. The fog was beginning to clear.

"It's just a crying shame these boys can't get along," she added. She set the tray on an end table, then took a seat in the gliding rocker that flanked the glowing fireplace. Scout was right beside her, trying to nose into the cheesecake on her tray. Susan patted the dog's head and said in a milquetoast tone, "No no." Surprisingly the dog obeyed. Scout took a step back and sat facing Susan.

She reached for the poker and gave the fire a nudge. Once the flames were back on course, she retrieved her own snack. "My brother, Zeb, would be so upset if he knew what his boys were doing to each other. Thank the Lord he's fairly oblivious to such things these days. Jack," she said, turning her attention to her nephew, "surely you and Carl can come to an agreement."

Jack ignored her.

"Susan, do you know who owns the dog?" Paul asked her.

She shook her head no. "When I moved from St. Paul, Scout was already at the house."

At hearing her name, Scout turned her head and opened her mouth in a sort of smile.

"I have no idea how they got her, and of course the boys aren't exactly helpful in telling us that story, are they?" She leaned forward as if she'd just spoken a big secret. "She's a good doggie, though, aren't you, girl?" Susan's voice dissolved into baby talk.

Jack rolled his eyes and cleared his throat. "Don't you have something to do, Aunt Susan? In the kitchen?"

"Oh, I'm sorry," she said. The hurt expression on Susan's face was unmistakable. "I'm interrupting. You're absolutely right, Jack. You boys need to have your talk." She stood, cheesecake and cocoa in hand, and Scout stood with her. "I'll make myself scarce."

She left. The sound of Scout's nails on the hardwood floor followed her to the back of the house.

"You didn't need to send her away," Paul said.

Jack made a *hmmph* sound and took another bite of his cheesecake. "You should be talking to Carl. That's who you should be talking to. He's the one who's lying, not me."

Paul thought of his conversation with Nehemiah the day before and offered up another prayer for wisdom, but no great burst of inspiration came to him. *Thanks a lot*, he thought.

Instead, a scratching sound near the front door sounded in his ears.

"Oh, that dumb dog," Jack muttered. "Aunt Susan, can you take Scout out?" he hollered.

There was no reply.

A STATE OF GRACE   105

"Why don't we take her out?" Eli suggested. "It'll give us a chance to get some fresh air."

"Fresh air?" Jack repeated sarcastically.

The three men rose and walked to the entry closet to put on their coats. "Aunt Susan, we're taking Scout for a walk," Jack called.

She came out of the kitchen, wiping her hands on a dishtowel. Her eyes were ringed in red, and splotches on her cheeks told them she'd been crying. "That's fine, dear," she said, sniffling before returning to the kitchen.

When they opened the door, Scout ran out ahead of them. A blast of cold air bit at their cheeks. Paul tugged his Columbia jacket closer around himself, then he tucked his mittened hands into his pockets. Scout was nosing the ground in a frantic pace, sniffing here and there as if something exciting was under the snow.

"Get back here," Jack called to her. The dog raised her head to look back at him, then returned to her sniffing. "I said get back here, you dumb mutt!"

Scout ignored him this time.

"You and Carl could share the earnings, you know," Eli offered.

"Are you kidding? After all the work I do to take care of that dog? Why should I give Carl anything?"

"He *is* your brother," Paul said.

"Brothers don't steal from each other," Jack said.

Scout had found something interesting across the street; she trotted toward the railroad tracks.

"Get back here!" Jack shouted. Scout only quickened her gait.

The men picked up their pace to try to catch up, but Scout must have thought they were playing tag, because she took off in a full-out run.

"Scout!" Jack shouted again. But within moments she had disappeared up the railroad tracks, headed north toward the Depot Inn, one of the fanciest restaurants in Copper Mill. They all called for her, to no avail.

"Let's get the truck," Paul suggested.

With Eli in the lead, they ran to Paul's pickup, which was parked on Quarry Road next to Susan's house. Jack squeezed into the middle, and Eli slammed the passenger door just as Paul squealed the tires and pulled out, headed toward Main Street. He sped north, careful to watch for traffic as his eyes searched for the small cocker spaniel. "Do you see her?" he asked.

"No," Eli said. "Wait a minute . . . There she is." He pointed ahead.

The dog darted across Quarry Road, causing a black Ford Focus to screech its brakes. The car just barely missed hitting her. But she was still on a tear. She flew across snow-covered lawns, making it difficult to track her from the truck's street-side view. Paul took a quick right onto Main, only to have to stop at the intersection while a mother and three toddlers crossed the street in agonizing slowness. She looked at the men curiously, as if wondering why they were in such a hurry. Or perhaps she'd never seen three grown men crammed in the front seat of a pickup truck.

Once she was across, Paul hit the gas.

"Where did she go?" he asked.

"Try left," Jack said as his eyes scanned the neighborhood. "I saw a movement over there." He pointed toward the Baptist church on Hamilton Road. Paul turned that direction, but when they neared the church and slowed down for a closer look, it was obvious that what Jack had seen was a poodle wearing a thick orange-wool doggie sweater. His owner glanced at them and gave a wave.

Paul pulled a U-turn and stopped the truck across from Carl and Jack's home, which was right next to the *Chronicle* building. "What now?" he asked.

"Let's just drive the streets," Eli said. "She's got to turn up."

Jack merely crossed his arms over his chest and grunted. "Dumb dog," he muttered under his breath.

They drove for well over an hour, combing the streets of Copper Mill. They even went so far as to head north on Smith Street toward Joe Tucker's backwoods cabin, but there was no sign of Scout. She had simply disappeared.

Heading back toward town, Paul made a left onto Mountain Laurel Road and drove east toward the high school. Still no Scout.

"We'll have to call the vet, see if anyone turns her in to the Humane Society," Eli finally said.

The Humane Society in Copper Mill was actually a part of the local veterinary clinic. A few cages for stray cats and dogs were kept in the back of the clinic, where the animals were well taken care of until either their owners showed up or kindhearted citizens came to adopt them.

Eli pulled out his cell phone and searched for the number, then relayed the information on the lost dog. "We last saw her on Hamilton—" he began.

"No," Jack interrupted. "That was the poodle. We last saw Scout headed east toward the Town Green."

"Oh, the Town Green," Eli corrected himself. "Yes, she's a cocker spaniel, orangish in color, female." He placed a hand over the mouthpiece. "Did she have a collar?"

Jack nodded. "A prissy blue one that Aunt Susan bought her, and a jingle bell."

"Did you get all that?" Eli asked the person on the other end. The person on the other end of the line must have heard because Eli didn't need to repeat the information. He pressed the End button and said, "They said they'll call if she turns up."

"Great," Jack said. "Now I'll never get my prize money."

"I don't get it," Paul said. "Why do you need to have the dog to collect the prize?"

"Part of the prize is a photo shoot of me with the dog. You know, one of those ads for dog food or whatever."

The thought crossed Paul's mind that Jack could simply find another cocker spaniel for the shoot, but then he decided not to mention it. The last thing he needed to do was encourage more deceit on the part of the two Wilson brothers.

In the few minutes it took for them to get back to Susan's house, Eli's phone rang with news.

"She's been spotted," Eli relayed the news. "Over on Sweetwater Street down by the old quarry. We'll meet you there," he said to the person on the line. "She can be hard to catch, that's for sure."

Paul hit the gas, heading south out of town toward the strip mall, where the old quarry was located. Before they even reached the spot, however, they saw Jim Hepburn's rusty white pickup truck parked along a wooded section of the road just before the entrance to the parking lot. Paul pulled his pickup to a stop behind it, and the three men got out. Sounds of barking and shouting emanated from the woods, so Paul, Eli, and Jack took off, following the noise. They darted around tall pines and into a stand of deciduous trees, where the undergrowth was quite thick. The snow grew deeper, slowing their movement and filling their shoes.

"Where are you?" Paul called out to the volunteer dog-catcher he'd met only once before.

"I'm up here," a voice returned.

They followed the sound up the ridge. It was steep going, and the dog's barking was incessant as they approached the spot. Paul wondered what was causing her such stress, but when they came into a clearing, the answer to that question was all too evident.

Scout had cornered a skunk.

Chapter Nine

The hair on the ridge of Scout's back was standing up as she snarled at the terrified skunk, who was backed against a thick log. Scout crouched low with teeth bared. Jim Hepburn stood at the edge of the small clearing with Eli, Paul, and Jack. He was a grizzled-looking man with ruddy features and a creased, wrinkled face. He held a muzzle and chain leash in one hand and what looked like a cattle prod in the other. He turned to the group, "Whose dog is she?"

Jack raised his hand and said, "Mine."

"We don't want to provoke that skunk any more than the dog already has," the man said, "or we're going to have a much worse situation on our hands. Let's just sit tight for a bit."

They watched as dog and skunk faced each other. Neither seemed ready to relent, and the dog's barking only seemed to increase. Finally Scout snarled and took a step forward. That must have been the end of the line as far as the skunk was concerned, because it suddenly bit the dog on the snout, then turned and unleashed its nasty smell straight in the dog's face.

"No!" Jack yelled as Scout yelped in pain and the skunk waddled off.

Paul had never heard a more pitiful cry of agony, either from the dog or its supposed owner. When Scout turned toward them, he could see that her eyes were closed and tearing badly. The smell of skunk was over-whelming. Paul had to fight to keep his stomach from turning on him. He clutched a hand over his face. Eli held a handkerchief over his nose and mouth, while Jack muttered something unintelligible under his breath.

"I'll get her," the dogcatcher said.

She was rolling on the ground now, pressing her face into the snow as if to wipe out the agitation and swiping her paws across her eyes. The old man moved forward cautiously, the hand with the muzzle held out to the side. "Good doggie," he crooned.

When Jim was a few feet from her, Scout raised her head and growled loudly. "No no. You don't want to do that."

Finally Scout's rescuer squatted down. "It's okay," he said.

Scout kept growling, her teeth a menacing warning as she pawed at her eyes, trying to remove the irritant. Letting the stick fall to the ground, the dogcatcher reached toward the dog. He leaned forward, his attention on the dog's col-lar. He was within inches of his prize.

Then Scout turned on him.

She attacked full force, biting the old man first on his outstretched hand and then on his leg. She held the limb in her teeth and shook her head back and forth. Finally Jim grabbed her in his hands, practically hanging her by the collar, and pulled her off his bleeding leg.

Quickly he pulled the muzzle over her mouth and tightened it under her jaw and around her neck. Paul and Eli rushed forward to help hold the dog.

The man sat back in the snow in obvious pain. "I hate this job," he said through gritted teeth. Then he looked over at Jack. "You need to keep your dog under control!" He lifted the hand that covered the wound on his leg. "Man, that hurts!"

Knowing Eli had Scout in hand, Paul moved forward to have a look. The cut was visible through the hole in the dogcatcher's pants. The laceration was jagged, a good three inches long, dark purple in color, and deep.

"You're going to need stitches, Jim," Paul said. He reached into his coat pocket for a handkerchief and pressed it over the open wound. "This will help the blood clot. Hold it tight."

The old man obliged.

"She wouldn't have bit you if it hadn't been for the skunk," Jack said.

Paul was amazed at Jack's lack of concern for the injured man.

Jim raised his hands. "Hey, I don't care how we got here. All I know is I have a bleeding leg from your mutt! She better be up on her rabies shots."

"She's *up* on her rabies shots." Jack rolled his eyes.

Paul sent Jack a look that told him to be quiet. Then Paul turned to the volunteer dogcatcher. "Are you up to walking down to your truck?"

Jim nodded and said, "I'm not going to sit up here all day smelling this way."

Paul reached around the man's thin shoulders and helped him stand. Jim gingerly placed some of his weight on the leg and winced with the pain, but then he straightened and released his grip on Paul. "I'll be fine." He waved Paul away.

Eli led the way down the steep embankment with a now-docile Scout in his arms. The dog whimpered and nuzzled into the crook of one arm. Paul and the old man slowly worked their way down the hillside together behind him. Paul wanted to be near the man in case his bleeding leg gave way, but the dogcatcher toughed it out despite the pain that arced across his eyes.

Brooding and sullen, Jack was last to return to the truck. Paul felt like spanking him, if he could have done such a thing to a boy who was no relation to him.

When they reached their vehicles, the dogcatcher said to Jack, "You'll need to get that dog to the vet right away. The skunk bit her good on the nose."

"I can take care of my own dog," Jack snapped.

The man raised his hands, then clapped them in an "I've said my piece, the rest is on you" sort of gesture. He climbed into his rusty pickup, turned the key, and drove toward town. Eli and Jack were already in Paul's pickup by the time he got there. Scout was on Eli's lap, near the passenger-side door, the smell of skunk in her fur unbearable. A low growl lingered in her throat as she looked toward Jack.

"Knock it off," Jack whispered, though not loud enough that the dog seemed threatened. She stared at him for a long moment, then stopped growling.

Paul took his seat behind the wheel and started the pickup. As they made their way back into town, Paul realized he was getting a headache. He never got headaches.

He pulled up to the vet clinic on the corner of Smoky Mountain Road and Ashland and glanced over at his partners in crime. Both men looked exhausted—their eyes were red, and neither of them could drag a smile out of a pocket.

They climbed out and made their way into the squat brick building. The receptionist raised her dark curly head. She was younger than Paul had first thought, probably in her early twenties, though she still had braces on her teeth. And her nametag bore the name Ashley.

"Can I help you?" A look crossed her face as the scent of the men followed them in. "Ewww!" she said, waving her hand in front of her nose. "What in the world?"

"Skunk," the three said in unison.

"I can tell that!" She plugged her nose. "That is so nasty!"

"Imagine how we feel," Eli added.

The vet came around the corner from a long hall of examination rooms. He was a short bald man with sharp black eyes. "What in the—? Oh!" he said, pinching his nose. "Which one of you got sprayed?"

All three pointed to the dog.

Paul said, "Dr. Milt, she got it right in the eyes, and the skunk bit her nose. See." He pointed to the small tear on the dog's nose. The vet reached for the stinky pooch and lifted the dog up to eye level. She bared her teeth at him. "She bit the dogcatcher too," Paul added while the vet sized up the growling dog.

"Oh," Dr. Milt said to Scout. "So that's how it's going to be, is it, girl?" Then he turned to Jack. "When was her last rabies shot?"

Jack shrugged. "You'd know better than I would."

"I'll look it up in her file. If she isn't up to date, we might need to keep her for a while. You didn't happen to bring the skunk along too, did you?"

The men exchanged incredulous looks.

"If her shots aren't up-to-date, it could be quite a stay," he explained. "At least without the skunk to test." He waved a hand across his nose as the smell intensified. "Getting that smell out will take some work. Seems you'll have plenty to do just to get the smell off your own bodies. I'll take care of this one." He raised an eyebrow and looked at Jack.

"She's all yours," Jack said. "When should I pick her up?"

"I'll give you a call after I look in her file." Then he took Scout down the narrow hallway to one of the exam rooms, disappearing from view.

When they climbed back into the pickup, the odor of

skunk on their clothes was overpowering. Paul and Eli
rolled down their windows despite the cold and drove the
short distance to Eli's and then to Susan's house to drop
Jack off.

"Tomato juice is supposed to take the smell away,"
Paul said.

Jack nodded, his expression dour.

"What's wrong?" Paul asked.

"I sure didn't need a vet bill right now." He shook his
head.

"It'll be okay," Paul assured him. "Besides, the prize
money will more than cover that, right?"

Instead of easing the stress in his face, as Paul intended,
the statement twisted Jack's brow even more. It made
Paul wonder if he'd been taken for a ride, again.

THE TABLE WAS SET for a romantic dinner. The savory scent
of roast chicken and wild-rice stuffing filled the Hanlon
home. Kate had just finished transferring the mashed
potatoes to a serving dish and placing it on the table,
when the sound of Paul's pickup in the driveway reached
her ears.

"Perfect timing, Kate," she said. She pulled a match-
book from her apron pocket and lit the two white tapers
at the center of the table. They quickly caught, creating
the intoxicating atmosphere Kate wanted. Lately she and
Paul had been so busy with their various tasks—she with
the Harrises and her stained-glass project, he with church
work and those Wilson brothers—that they hadn't taken

time to be a couple. They liked to go on date nights often, either to a movie or dinner, or on some creative adventure that Kate enjoyed planning. But they hadn't been out in several weeks. Tonight that was going to change, even if it meant enjoying a simple chicken meal at home by candlelight.

She heard the pickup door slam, so she quickly took off her apron and hung it on its hook alongside the refrigerator. Then she went to the front door to greet her husband with a kiss.

But when he opened the screen door, the last thing she wanted to do was kiss him—the scent that accompanied him was overpowering.

"What did you do?" She covered her nose with her hand. "You smell like . . . like skunk!"

Paul touched the end of his nose. "Bingo," he said. "And my head is screaming. I think this smell is giving me a headache."

He lifted a foot to step into the house, but Kate pushed him back onto the stoop. "No, you don't!" she said. "I don't want my house contaminated with that smell."

"What am I supposed to do?"

Kate placed her hands on her hips and thought for a moment as the cold outdoor air chilled her. "Come through the garage," she said. "You can strip down there. I'll bring you your robe. And you can go get a bath." Then she paused. "Will a bath take that smell away?"

"I always heard it was tomato juice, but I didn't want to go into the store smelling like this."

"I'm sure the public is grateful. I'll have to go get some, I guess. Do they sell it by the barrel?" She lifted a teasing brow but quickly put a hand over her nose and mouth again as another gust of winter air brought the scent back to her. "How could you—?" Then, "At least go soak in the tub while I run out to the store. And don't touch anything!"

"I won't," he said sheepishly.

She shut the door on him and went to get his flannel robe from the back of the bathroom door. When she opened the door to the garage, Paul was ready for her. He slipped the robe on while Kate pinched her nose. "So much for my delicious-smelling meal," she moaned. "All I can smell is . . . you."

Paul shrugged. "It's not as if I planned this."

He went into the bathroom just off their bedroom and turned on the hot water, while Kate blew out the candles, turned the oven on *warm*, and set their meal inside. Then she reached for her car keys and went to get her coat.

As she was leaving the house, she called out, "Now don't move until I get back!"

"You don't want me rolling around the carpet?"

"Don't even joke!"

BY THE NEXT MORNING, most of the skunk scent was gone from Paul's person, though Kate decided to throw away the clothes he'd been wearing for fear that the scent would permeate her washer and dryer. He'd left early for the church, saying he needed to get caught up on his sermon preparations since he'd been scouring the countryside the day before in search of that dog.

Kate sat in her favorite rocking chair in the living room, enjoying the quiet of the morning as chickadees and blue jays fought over the seed in the birdfeeder outside in the backyard. She'd been praying and reading her Bible as she usually did before she took up whatever tasks the day held. She'd found over the years that when she didn't stop for those moments of peaceful contemplation and time alone with God, the worries of her day often overtook her and put her on a treadmill that went nowhere.

She'd been praying for Marissa and Patricia, that now that her chemotherapy treatments were coming to an end, Marissa would find energy to do the things she enjoyed, and that when the test results came back, she would be cancer-free.

Kate lifted her face toward the ceiling and closed her eyes. *Lord,* she went on, *give me wisdom to help, to show Patricia that she doesn't have to lean just on herself. That's been so exhausting for her. She needs your peace. She really does. Amen.*

When Kate lowered her head and opened her eyes, she saw that a male cardinal had landed on her feeder. He tilted his bright red head with its black mask, then dipped down for a taste of the black-oil sunflower seeds. A blue jay returned and chased him away. Kate didn't mind, however. Any birds were welcome to come, red or blue . . .

Blue. The word stuck in her brain. She rolled it

around, wondering at its significance. Blue was a color—so what of it? But the color of what?

Then it struck her. Why hadn't she thought of it before? Of course. She'd learned about genetics in high school.

She rose from her seat as excitement welled. Padding into the kitchen, she placed her cup and saucer in the sink, quickly rinsed them, and set them in the drainer. Then she dried her hands on a dishtowel. Grabbing her cell phone and purse, she went to the hall closet, put on her warmest winter coat, and made her way to her car.

She had to talk with Livvy. She *had* to. All her niggling thoughts hadn't been for nothing. She knew that now, but she had to make sure before she accused Patricia of lying.

Chapter Ten

It was a crystal clear day, the sky so blue it hurt her eyes to gaze at it too long. Even the snow seemed tinted in blue as it melted. It tugged at the branches of the ever-green trees along Smoky Mountain Road, dragging them down with the weight.

When Kate reached the outskirts of town, she could see that the inviting day had pulled many Copper Mill residents from their hibernation. Joggers moved at a steady pace along Hamilton Road. An elderly man with white hair and a hooded jacket pedaled the opposite direction on his Schwinn bicycle.

Kate made a right turn onto Main and a left onto Smith, then pulled into the library parking lot, which seemed unusually full for a Wednesday morning. Climbing out of her car, she tugged her purse onto her shoulder and made her way up the stairs of the historic two-story brick building.

Inside, the library was abuzz with activity. A group of children sat in a semicircle around a woman who was reading *Make Way for Ducklings* aloud to them in the children's area of the library. Even the periodicals section was filled with patrons perusing magazines and newspapers.

Kate glanced at her watch as she reached the checkout station where Livvy stood reading the computer screen.

"What's going on today?" Kate asked as her gaze moved around the large room.

Livvy lifted her head. "The preschool is on a field trip." She smiled and motioned to the four- and five-year-olds who were entranced with their story. "So, what are you up to?"

"I need you to do a little research for me."

"Okay . . . ?" Livvy said, raising her intonation slightly at the end of the word so it became a question. "What's this all about?"

"Do you remember our talk about Patricia Harris a couple weeks ago?"

"Of course."

"Well, I've thought of something new."

Livvy waited for her to go on.

"Do you have any way to look up old birth announcements from the paper? I mean, would they be on microfilm?"

"Sure they are. We could look at some online databases too."

Livvy clicked the keys of the computer. "Whose birth announcement are we looking up?"

"Marissa Harris'."

"Why in the—?" Livvy began.

"Just trust me. It's a hunch, but I think I'm onto something."

"Do you know her birth date?"

Kate searched her memory. It seemed she had seen something at the house . . . Then she remembered. "There was a cross-stitched picture in the hallway. I remember seeing it because I have one for each of my kids. It said 'Marissa Lauren Harris,' born . . . Oh, let me think." She chewed on her lower lip as she thought. "When did Elvis Presley die?"

"What does that have to do with it?"

"Just look it up."

Just then, three preschoolers came up with one of the teacher's aides to check out some picture books. Livvy attended to them, and once they left, she turned to her computer and googled "Elvis Aaron Presley" and "death." She clicked on the top link for Wikipedia, and within moments had the information she needed.

"Gotta love the Internet. August 16, 1977."

"That's it! Marissa was born August 16, 1985. I remember because it was two years after my Rebecca was born."

Livvy clicked around some more on her computer, but came up empty. "Let's see what microfilm can show us."

She waved Morty Robertson to the desk. He was a retiree who often volunteered at the library. "Could you watch the desk for a few minutes?" Livvy asked.

The white-haired man nodded. Livvy walked upstairs, with Kate right behind her, to a microfilm machine that was sitting at the far end of a long table amid computer stations, which were filled with patrons. Livvy pulled several microfilms from that time period from the file and set the first in place on the machine. She scanned the pages, quickly finding the birth-announcement section. Deciding the information wasn't on that one, she put in the next. Still nothing. She went through all the data from August through October of that year, but there was no birth announcement for Marissa Lauren Harris.

"Why wouldn't Patricia have had a birth announcement put in her hometown paper?" Kate asked as they made their way back downstairs. "Or wouldn't her parents have made sure their granddaughter's birth announcement was listed? Or someone?"

Livvy nodded in agreement. "This is a small town; folks here make sure every detail of their lives is journaled in that paper, including when their kids come home for a visit from college."

"Unless they weren't proud to be grandparents," Kate said under her breath.

Livvy thought about that. "You think Patricia and Ray were pregnant with Marissa before they got married?"

Kate shook her head. "No."

"I'm completely lost, then," Livvy said.

"What do you know about genetics?" Kate asked.

Livvy gave her another puzzled look. "Genetics?"

"I was always told that two blue-eyed people can't have a brown-eyed baby," Kate went on.

"I guess I heard that too."

"Sam Gorman said Ray had blue eyes."

Livvy squinted hers. "Yeah, I think that's right. Vivid blue as I recall."

"Patricia has blue eyes too. And Marissa's are dark, dark brown." She let the sentence hang for effect.

Livvy turned to her friend, her mouth agape. "Wow."

"I don't want to assume, though," Kate said. "I know what I was taught in high school—that the gene for blue eyes is recessive, so when two blue-eyed people get married, they've in essence eliminated any brown-eyed genes from the gene pool. But who knows what's happened in the last forty-five years of genetic research? I don't want to go talking to Patricia if I'm totally off base."

Livvy nodded. "Probably the wise course to take." By then, they'd reached the front desk and Livvy dismissed Morty to return to his cart of returned books.

"Would you mind looking into it for me?" Kate asked Livvy. "I have a hair appointment at Betty's in a few minutes, and besides, I know you'd find the information in a fraction of the time it would take me."

Just then, five more preschoolers and their teacher appeared at the front desk with books to check out.

"Mind if I do it once the crowd thins out?" she asked.

"When you get the chance," Kate said. "I'll swing by later."

"Don't worry. I won't forget!"

KATE PAGED THROUGH an old *Redbook* magazine as she waited on the padded bench in Betty's Beauty Parlor. All three chairs were filled with women, and a fourth woman was sitting under the noisy dryer in the corner.

The beauty shop was a time capsule in perfect early 1960s vintage. Even though Betty had taken over the establishment fifteen years before, it remained a testament to her predecessors. Posters of blonde Doris Day wannabes hung on the walls, the backgrounds faded to a pale puce color. The scent of perm solution was ever present, whether someone was getting a perm that day or not. The chairs looked as though they hadn't been changed since they'd been installed. They were a salmon-colored vinyl with white piping along their seams, and they complemented the white-and-aqua-checkerboard floor. There was a shampoo room in the back, with a couple of sinks and a desk across from them that served as Betty's office.

One of the women rose from her seat, gazing at herself in the mirror and touching her newly styled hair. It was a short, short pixie cut, carrot red in color. Kate hadn't seen many fifty-year-olds with such a style, yet she had to admit it did look good with the woman's green eyes.

"Wow," the patron said. "This is going to surprise Bob so much." She moved to the counter to pay her bill, then gave a quick wave and left.

"That means you're up, Mrs. Hanlon," Betty said. She was a cute woman, with short bleached-blonde hair and gray eyes. Kate didn't know her real well yet, but with her regular visits for manicures, cuts, and stylings, she knew they'd become very familiar soon, especially the way the woman liked to talk.

Kate and Betty made their way to the farthest chair, passing the other two stylists, who were chatting and cutting hair. Both girls looked to be in their twenties, fresh out of cosmetology school. Kate set her purse on the floor alongside the chair, then sat down. Betty draped a large vinyl bib around her, fastening it behind her neck. It covered her lap completely.

"So, what's it going to be today?" She fingered Kate's strawberry blonde locks. "I could give you some highlights, make that red more dramatic." She raised her eyebrows at Kate in the mirror and smiled.

"No," Kate said. "That's okay. Just wash it up and give me a trim, I think. And a manicure?" She held up her hands for Betty to see. "This polish is looking tired, and my cuticles could use some freshening."

"Good enough." Betty nodded.

She and Kate walked to the shampooing station, where Kate took a seat. Betty leaned Kate back so that her head rested in the crook of the hair-washing sink. The warm water felt good on Kate's scalp. Betty sudsed it up with gentle hands, rinsed, then added conditioner and rinsed that as well.

"You're squeaky clean," she said as she helped Kate sit upright and wrapped a towel around her hair turban-style. Then she removed the towel, still pressing it against Kate's hair to soak up as much excess water as possible. They returned to Betty's chair out front.

"So, what have you been up to this fine day?" Betty asked as she reached for a comb and started running it through Kate's hair.

"Nothing much," Kate said. "I spent a little time with the Lord, then came down to the library for some . . . research."

"Research, you say? Are you writing a paper or something?"

"Nothing like that. Just looking at some old birth records."

"*Hmm.*" Betty moved to the other side of Kate's head and combed that side as well. "I heard through the grapevine that you've been visiting the Harrises a lot lately."

Kate was stunned. "How . . . how did you hear that?"

"Their neighbor, Mrs. Healy, said she's seen you coming and going. Oh, she didn't say anything bad," Betty quickly added. "Just that she's seen your car there a lot and that Marissa is terribly sick."

"I've been . . . helping out here and there," Kate said. "Bringing a few meals." She gave a shrug.

"I wish more people would get out of their little boxes and look after the needs of others like that. What is this world if people don't care about their neighbors?"

Kate found herself feeling uncomfortable with the thread of conversation, yet the woman went on. "And those Harrises . . . if any family has been out there helping others, it's them. Ray used to volunteer with Habitat for Humanity. You know he was an electrician? 'Course you knew that. And Patricia . . . she was always there for all the school events, that one parent who went on every field trip."

Betty reached for the scissors and began to trim Kate's hair. How the woman could concentrate on her job and talk at the same time, Kate wasn't sure.

"And it wasn't easy for her, having Marissa at such a young age. Of course, Ray was quite a few years older than

her. And her parents . . . Well, they were a different breed
of people. She sure has changed since Ray's passing."

"Patricia?" Kate asked.

Betty nodded. "She used to come all the time before.
Now I never see her. I wonder who's doing her hair. Maybe
she's getting it done in Chattanooga . . . When I do see her,
she seems eager to get away. Have you noticed that?"

Kate looked up at Betty. She had to admit what the
woman was saying was true, at least of her early visits
with Patricia. Kate nodded.

"It's sad to see how some people just never get a
break. Well, I guess her marriage was a good one, but with
everything since . . . I mean it was bad enough that her
parents didn't even attend her wedding."

"They didn't?" Kate asked.

Betty shook her head. "Patricia told me once when
she was getting her hair cut. I mean, what girl doesn't
want her own mother at her wedding? You know her folks
never even met Ray before they got married? And there
was always this . . . sadness about her. Even when Ray was
alive. It was just under the surface, you know, like she'd
break into tears if you mentioned that one sensitive spot.
But I guess I could have been imagining it . . ."

That information wasn't new, yet something about it
resonated within her. She'd felt that way around Patricia
too, as if there was a switch inside of her that, once
tripped, would send forth a torrent of emotions. Hadn't
she seen it the last time she'd gone to visit, and when
she'd discovered Patricia with the photo album? Kate had
assumed it was because of Marissa's illness and Ray's

death. But was it more? If she'd acted that way even while
Ray was alive, surely there was another reason. But what?

WHEN KATE RETURNED to the library, all was quiet inside.
The preschoolers had cleared out. Livvy was at her desk
in her office, staring at her computer screen. She raised
her head when Kate came in. Piles of new books and
paperwork, puppets, and boxes of chocolates that would
be the rewards for the upcoming adult readers' challenge
covered the surface of one of the long tables.

"Hey, nice hair," Livvy said. "Betty didn't talk you into
a perm?"

"Not this time." Kate pulled up a chair alongside
Livvy's. "So, what have you found out?"

Livvy cleared her throat, then said, "I went to
Ask.com. Most people believe, as we do, that two blue-
eyed parents can't have a brown-eyed child. Yet, while it's
rare, it is possible. So, Ray and Patricia *could* have had
Marissa, biologically speaking. But the odds are against it.
It's not likely that Marissa is both Patricia and Ray's
daughter."

"Not exactly hard-and-fast evidence, is it?" Kate said.
"Maybe I'm just spinning my wheels. But I keep getting
this gut feeling, you know?"

"I know."

"I don't want to accuse Patricia of lying, and yet
there's just, well, more. I can't get past her saying that she
could stop Marissa's suffering. And the way she hid that
photo album . . . She's hiding something, and I don't know
if I can help her fully unless I know what it is."

Livvy nodded her understanding.

Kate paused in thought, then said more to herself than to Livvy, "Marissa told me that one time a friend of her mom's brought her a brochure on adoption, and Patricia got very upset . . ."

"And . . . ?"

"Why would she get so bent out of shape over adoption unless it was a sore spot in her own experience?"

"Perhaps Patricia herself was adopted. Maybe she found out her birth parents were in Chattanooga, and when she was in college, she contacted them."

Kate considered that possibility. "One of them could be a potential marrow donor, so they might be able to help Marissa . . . That would account for Patricia's statement. That's something we could look into."

"Or maybe Marissa isn't her biological daughter. Maybe she was Ray's daughter from a previous relationship, and Patricia adopted her?"

"Not likely," Kate pointed out, "since Sam said the reason they weren't able to have more kids was because of Ray's infertility."

They were silent for a few moments before Kate said, "Perhaps Ray adopted Marissa during a previous marriage. He was quite a bit older than Patricia was. That scenario would explain why Patricia herself isn't a match. Of course, biological parents aren't usually a match for such donations anyway. How long did you say Patricia lived in Chattanooga?"

Livvy thought for a moment before answering, "I remember she left town just after graduation my freshman year. Then when she came back, it was ..." She paused again. "Two summers later?"

"How old was Marissa at that time?"

"I don't remember," Livvy said. "But she wasn't a newborn."

"Not much time for a courtship and pregnancy."

SINCE IT WAS NEARING NOON, Livvy and Kate decided to head to the Country Diner for a bite to eat. Like every weekday at lunch, the place was jam-packed.

Kate and Livvy took a booth that looked out on the Town Green, though it was a patchwork of green and white at this time of year. All that remained of the snow cover were tall piles of white left from all the snowplows dumping their loads.

"So much for walking during my lunch break," Livvy said, drawing her attention back to her menu.

"I guess it is warm enough, isn't it?" Kate gazed at the menu. "But it doesn't hurt to take a break every now and then. Besides, you wouldn't want us to waste away." She smiled at her own comment.

"There's a high likelihood of that!" Livvy closed her menu.

"Decided what you're going to order?" Kate glanced up. She smiled when she saw J. B. Packer in the kitchen. J.B. had been suspected of setting the fire at Faith Briar Church, but once he was proven innocent, he took a job as a part-time fry cook at the diner, filling in for owner and head chef Loretta sometimes.

"Catfish, I think. With stack cakes."

"That sounds good. I'm leaning toward the chowder and a Reuben with Thousand Island dressing myself."

Just then LuAnne Matthews appeared, her horn-rimmed glasses dangling from the jeweled chain that hung around her neck. Her green eyes sparkled at them. "Hey, Livvy, Kate. Y'all interested in today's special? Meatball sandwiches with Cowboy Surprise?" the red-head said with a wink.

"What's Cowboy Surprise?" Livvy asked.

"It wouldn't be a surprise if I told you!" She laughed at her own joke, then said, "It's a soup, kind of. More of a stew with baked beans and bacon."

"I think I'll pass," Kate said with a smirk.

"Your loss," LuAnne said. "I had it this mornin', and it wasn't so bad."

They gave LuAnne their orders, then she hurried to greet new patrons at the front door.

Kate reached for her glass of ice water and took a sip.

"So, I think we've established that Ray wasn't Marissa's biological dad," Livvy said.

"I've never heard anyone say a thing about Patricia being an unwed mother though. Wouldn't word of that have gotten out? You went to youth group with her. Was that ever mentioned?"

"Maybe gossiped about, but I was a junior in high school, so I didn't exactly pay attention."

"Then the option that Marissa was adopted is still valid—either after Patricia and Ray were married or . . ." Kate said.

"No twenty-year-old would be allowed to adopt," Livvy

said. "There are minimum age requirements and length of marriage rules that come into play. I can't see that as a viable alternative. And most girls that age wouldn't choose adoption as their first option. That's usually taken up after failing to conceive biologically."

"Unless they had ideals about the social responsibility of adoption."

"Still, it wouldn't be allowed."

"Did I hear you two talking about Marissa Harris?" Renee Lambert suddenly appeared at their table, her dog Kisses markedly absent from her purse, where he liked to reside. Kate hadn't even heard her approach, so she was startled by her comment.

"Uh . . ." Kate said, then cleared her throat. "Would you like to have a seat, Renee?"

Livvy scooted over on her side of the booth, and Renee slid in.

"I overheard you both talking, and I just had to come over," Renee said, leaning across the table and talking in a whisper.

Kate and Livvy exchanged glances.

"Where's your dog?" Livvy asked, changing the subject.

"Oh, Kisses had a hair appointment. I'll pick him up in an hour or so, after his massage."

At seeing Livvy's raised eyebrow, it was all Kate could do to not burst out laughing.

"I know for a fact," Renee went on, "that Patricia Harris is the biological mother of Marissa." She leaned in and spoke in a low voice. "I saw a very pregnant Patricia once when I was in Chattanooga, though I wasn't totally sure it

was her at the time. I'd gone to town to do some sightsee-
ing and visit my Aunt Ruth. She has long since died, but
she was a dear woman. She liked to collect ironstone—
you'd appreciate her collection, Kate. Well, we were walking along, and I glanced across the street, and who do you
think I saw?"

"Patricia?" Kate and Livvy said in unison.

Renee nodded. "She was pregnant all right. I'd never
seen anyone so large. She'd gained a *lot* of weight. I mean,
she looked like she had a basketball under her dress, and
that was in early August. I was across the street that day
in Chattanooga, but I was fairly certain it was her."

She raised a hand for LuAnne to come to the table.
When the waitress arrived, Renee asked for a glass of lemon
water and placed an order for the blackened chicken salad.

As if to say, "Making yourself at home, are we?"
LuAnne lifted an eyebrow, which almost made Kate laugh
again. Then she shook her head at her friend, who went
back to waitressing.

"Well," Renee went on once LuAnne left, "I was going
to say hello to her, but before I could cross the street, a
bus passed between us. When it had passed, she'd disappeared. I thought she went into a large gray and white
Victorian house on Germantown Road, but it had a secu-
rity system, and I couldn't get in."

"*Hmm*," Kate said. "Let me ask you this, then. Could
Patricia have been adopted herself when she was a child?
Did you know her parents?"

"The Longs?" Renee scrunched up her face. "That's an
odd question."

"Do you think she could have been?" Kate pressed.

"No. I don't think so. Patricia looked a lot like her mother. They were too much alike for that." Renee touched the side of her perfectly styled hair as if checking to make sure it was still in place. "I didn't tell anyone anything about seeing her back then," she continued, returning to her earlier train of thought. "She wasn't married yet, at least not that I'd heard. But then she came back to Copper Mill even though she had no family here. That seemed odd to me, very odd. What's the point of living in a small town if you don't have family nearby?"

AFTER LIVVY RETURNED TO WORK and Renee excused herself to pick up Kisses from his spa treatment, Kate sat alone at the table. The story she'd come up with seemed simple enough. Patricia had gotten pregnant in high school. Who the father was, Kate had no idea. She wondered if Patricia's high-school boyfriend had brown eyes. What was his name? Mack...Mark? No, Matt. Matt Reilly. Upon learning of her illegitimate pregnancy, Patricia moved to Chattanooga under the guise of attending college when she was in fact entering a home for unwed mothers. There she met Ray. They fell in love, got married, and moved back to Copper Mill. It was simple, and none of Kate's business. Plenty of people had babies out of wedlock—it was hardly a big mystery.

Yet several thoughts still niggled at her. First, Marissa had never been told that Ray was anything other than the loving father she'd known him to be. Kate wondered if the bright girl had ever put two and two together on her own.

She was, after all, studying for the medical field. Surely she'd learned basic genetic theory. Then again, what child would want to believe such things about her mother? Kate knew plenty of people who chose to believe improbabilities because of the hurt the truth would no doubt bring.

While she didn't think keeping that secret from Marissa was necessarily the best course for Patricia to take, she could understand how such a thing could happen.

Second, there was still the question of what Patricia meant when she'd said she could end Marissa's suffering. Was she thinking she could find Marissa's biological father to see if he could be a bone-marrow donor? That was entirely possible. Yet why keep it all a secret now, when finding help for Marissa was so urgent?

And finally, what secret could that photo album hold —the album Patricia so obviously wanted to hide from her? If she discovered the answer to that question, Kate reasoned, she'd know the answer to all the others.

"YOU'RE DEEP IN THOUGHT." LuAnne interrupted Kate's musing as she refilled Kate's water glass.

"I'm sorry." Kate glanced up at the freckle-faced waitress, whose expression held concern. "I'm fine. Just thinking about the Harrises."

LuAnne set the water pitcher on the blue Formica tabletop and plopped down on the seat opposite Kate in the booth. She glanced around the now-quiet restaurant as if to make sure she wasn't leaving any patrons unattended, then she said, "You've been spendin' a lot of time with Patricia Harris lately, haven't you?"

Kate nodded, then took a sip of her ice water.

"There's something I need to tell you," LuAnne began.

"Oh?"

"I heard you talkin' to Renee and Livvy . . ." She dabbed her brow with the hem of her white polyester apron. "You see, Patricia dated my nephew Matt in high school."

Kate raised her head. "Matt was your nephew?"

"He was a great kid. Amazing baseball player, was MVP in the conference for three years running. I have his picture in my purse somewhere." She scooted out of the booth and waddled to the counter, then returned with a voluminous, flowered cloth bag, which she opened and began to dig through. Finally she pulled out an aged graduation picture of the boy. He wore a baseball jersey with the number fifty-four on it. He was good looking, with dark hair and deep brown eyes. It was like looking at a male version of Marissa.

"Wow," Kate mouthed.

"You see it too, don't you?" LuAnne's eyes were fixed on the picture. "When Patricia came home with that dark-eyed baby, I knew right away who she was. We all thought Patricia and Matt would get married after high school. It was such a surprise when they broke up. Then Patricia turned up married to someone else two years later, and with a baby no less. Matt was heartbroken. I think he was sure the two of them would get back together someday."

"Where is he living now?" Kate asked, her thoughts on the very real possibility that if this was indeed Marissa's biological father, he could be the key to her survival.

LuAnne's eyes clouded at the question, and she reached for a napkin from the stainless-steel napkin dispenser at the far end of the table. "Matt . . ." she began. "He died about four years after that picture was taken. He had so much hope, yet he . . ." She couldn't say another word. She held up a hand and took a deep breath. "His college roommate found him in his bed—he'd had a heart attack at twenty-two."

NOW KATE UNDERSTOOD why Patricia Harris had closed herself into her own safe cocoon. People did that when tragedy surrounded them. It felt safe there, as if nothing could touch them. But something had touched her, hadn't it?

Kate found Livvy at the library after her talk with LuAnne.

Livvy tucked a strand of her auburn hair behind her ear and said, "So Matt Reilly was Marissa's dad. I guess that makes sense. It was so sad when he died. *Shocking* would be the word." She took a deep breath. "So, there's nothing left for us to figure out. You should talk to Patricia—"

"That's not entirely true," Kate said. "There are some questions I still have, like why keep all of this a secret from Marissa?"

"A lot of adoptive parents do the same," Livvy said. "If Ray adopted Marissa, even if it wasn't a legal transaction, I could see the reason for not telling her."

"But in these dire circumstances, wouldn't you want the truth to be known?"

"I might not if I were Patricia, especially since she knows Matt died."

"Which leads me to the thing I can't get past," Kate went on. "If Matt's gone, then what did Patricia mean by saying she could save Marissa? And what was in that photo album?"

"There could have been pictures of Matt . . . Maybe he came to see Marissa when she was born."

"But you still haven't answered my first question," Kate probed.

Livvy threw up her hands. "I'm not coming up with a logical answer!"

Kate smiled at her friend and said, "We looked up birth records for Copper Mill, but we never tried the Chattanooga ones. Do you have those here at the library as well? It would make sense, since that was where she was living at the time."

"Of course!" They walked back to the microfilm files, and Livvy pulled up the pages from the Chattanooga paper and quickly scanned through, looking for any birth announcements that would match Marissa's birth date. Kate watched over her shoulder, scanning along with her. Then they looked at each other and gasped.

Chapter Eleven

Finally, there it was . . . the birth announcement they'd been seeking. It read: *Born to Patricia Long on August 16, 1985, twin girls Marissa Lauren, 5 lbs. 12 oz. 18 inches long, and Kara Raine, 5 lbs. 1 oz. 17.5 inches long, at Memorial Hospital.*

Kate sat back in shock. She placed a hand over her mouth. "That wasn't what I was expecting," she confessed.

"That's for certain," Livvy agreed. "But it explains a lot, doesn't it? At least why Patricia said what she did."

"Not everything, though."

"The only thing to do is to talk to Patricia. She knows the truth—and it's eating her up."

Kate nodded. "Even if it means she'll shut me out completely, I need to talk to her."

PATRICIA WAS ON A LADDER in the backyard filling her birdfeeders when Kate arrived. Kate had seen Patricia's Mercedes in the drive, so she knew she had to be home.

When no one answered the front door after she knocked, she walked around back.

"I thought I might find you here," she said.

Patricia turned toward her with a smile. "Kate. I didn't hear your car. Have you been knocking?"

"It's all right," Kate said.

Patricia lifted a bag of mixed birdseed and poured the remaining contents into a wood-and-glass birdfeeder with a copper roof. When it was full, she closed the lid and climbed back down the ladder.

"Marissa's gone for the afternoon," she informed Kate as she rolled up the paper seed bag and walked with Kate toward the house. She looked good. Refreshed. It was the first time Kate had seen her with makeup on, and she was struck by what a pretty woman she was, with those vivid blue eyes and short platinum hair.

"She's feeling better?" Kate asked.

"Much."

They entered the dark interior of the attached garage, and it took a moment for Kate's eyes to adjust. Patricia went to a metal trash can and tossed the bag in, then stepped up the two steps to the house.

"Her treatments about killed her, but now that she's done, she's coming around. She's spending the afternoon with some old friends from high school. Would you like some tea?"

"I never turn down a cup of tea."

They passed through the mudroom and into the bright

open kitchen. Kate took a barstool at the counter while Patricia filled the teakettle from the tap.

"I never thought something as simple as Marissa spending an afternoon with friends would seem so..." Patricia paused.

"Normal?" Kate filled in the word for her.

"Yeah. Normal is a good thing right now. I used to get so mad at her for being away from home constantly when she was a teenager."

"I had that problem with my daughters too," Kate said.

"You have daughters?"

Kate nodded. "Two. Melissa and Rebecca. And a son. Melissa is married with one child and lives in Atlanta, and Rebecca is single and lives in New York. She's trying her best to become a Broadway star."

"That's ambition."

"Scary is what it is. I worry about her all the time."

"That's part of motherhood, I think. Are your daughters close to each other?"

"Best friends. That's one of the things I like the most about having daughters; they enjoy each other's company so much. I'm glad they'll have each other even after I'm gone."

They sat silently for a moment. When the kettle finally whistled, Patricia turned off the burner and prepared their tea, then handed a cup to Kate across the counter. Then Patricia sat down and rested her head in her hands. Kate wondered if something she said had struck a nerve. She reached over and placed a hand on Patricia's. "I have to ask you something," Kate began, unsure of how to phrase the question. "There was something you said awhile ago that's been . . ." She paused and decided on another course. "I've been wondering about something."

Patricia withdrew her hand and sat up and took a sip of her tea.

Kate went on, "Do you recall saying that you could end Marissa's suffering if you chose?"

Patricia nodded, her gaze fixed on the counter.

"What did you mean by that?"

Patricia sighed. "I don't really want to talk about—"

"I know that Ray wasn't Marissa's biological father," Kate interrupted. She didn't want to divulge more for fear that it would cause Patricia to shrink further away, but she knew she had to push the issue if she was going to uncover the truth.

Patricia's eyes darted to Kate's.

"How could you possibly know that?"

"You and Ray both have blue eyes." Kate shrugged. "It's unlikely that you could have a brown-eyed child."

Patricia let out a pent-up breath and began to shake.

"I'm sorry," Kate said. She lightly touched a hand to Patricia's back. "I want to help you and Marissa. But I need to know the truth, and why you said what you did."

Patricia lifted her eyes to Kate's. "You're right. You've been a friend," she said. "I haven't told this to a soul. Not since Ray—" She took a shuddering breath.

Kate waited. She knew that whatever Patricia needed to say, it would come out now.

"You didn't give up on us. Even though I was so . . ." Patricia paused for the right word. "I wasn't very kind to you, and yet you kept coming. Thank you for that. For your persistence. I've felt so guilty about the way I treated you."

"You don't need to feel guilty about me—I understand."

"My guilt goes back a long way," Patricia confessed. "Twenty-three years to be exact." The tears came then— uncontrollable, gut-wrenching sobs. Patricia braced herself against the counter as she cried, her head down.

Finally her tears began to subside into a quiet stream. "I was eighteen," she said. "I thought I was in love. His name was Matt Reilly. He was a star baseball player. We dated all through high school." Her eyes met Kate's. "I found out I was pregnant . . ."

"You're what?" Matt said, his dark eyes flashing. He tugged his letter jacket tighter around himself against the cold late-November wind. They stood beneath the school's bleachers on a gray Thursday afternoon.

"I said, I'm pregnant. I took one of those home tests, and it came back positive." Patricia shrugged her shoulders. She tried to read his face, but all she saw there was surprise and then anger.

"How could you let this happen?" His voice rose to a near shout.

"How could I—?"

"I trusted you to take care of that. And now . . ."

His face was red, the veins in his neck bulging. "This will ruin my life. You did this on purpose! You're trying to trap me. Well, it's not going to work. How do I even know this is my baby?" He turned toward her and pointed a finger.

How could he think such a thing? Patricia felt herself shriveling inside. She'd thought he was the one she would spend the rest of her life with. Wasn't that what he'd told her when he'd been so persuasive? That they were meant to be together? He'd said he loved her, but he didn't love anyone but himself. That was all too clear now. As if his was the only life affected by this unexpected pregnancy.

How was she going to tell her parents? That thought, more than any other, terrified her. If Matt wasn't by her side, offering words of support, promises of marriage, how would she ever face her father? He was so strict as it was. This would probably kill him. Or he'd kill her.

She lifted her face to Matt's as tears coursed down her cheeks, and mustering as much courage as her weak heart could gather, she said, "You don't have to worry about it, Matt." How she got those words out, she couldn't even fathom. "My baby and I don't need you." She felt like crumbling with the words, lies that they were. "We'll find a way without you."

He softened then and touched her arm. "Patty," he said. He knew it melted her whenever he called her by that name.

She looked into his eyes, hope nudging its way back into her heart. She wanted to believe he was reconsidering.

"There is another way, you know," he said. "You don't have to go through with it. We could go on as we'd planned. Stay together."

"What are you talking about?" She prayed he didn't mean what she thought he meant.

"There are places you can go to take care of these kinds of problems."

Her hope deflated. "No. I can't."

He lifted his hands as if to say, "I wash my hands of you, then," and the hard glint in his eyes returned. "You're so stubborn."

Then he walked away. He didn't even turn to look back at her. He left her, shivering in the cold, to fend for herself and their baby.

In her mind, Kate could see the scene, and her heart broke for her friend as she thought about all the pain Patricia had suffered.

"When I told my parents, my father wouldn't even look at me. He was so disappointed. They told me I had to leave Copper Mill. They were afraid their precious reputations would be ruined if people at the church knew about my indiscretion." She shook her head at the memory.

"It must have been so hard for you," Kate said.

"There I was, all alone at a home for unwed mothers

in Chattanooga. My parents wouldn't have anything to do with me. Matt left for college without so much as a good-bye, and I found out I was having twins." She raised her head toward the ceiling. "It was a girl. I named her Kara Raine. Isn't that pretty?"

"She didn't . . . ?"

"Die? No. She was smaller and weaker than Marissa when she was little. The cord was wrapped around her neck, so she was blue for a few long moments. But she was okay. They put her in an incubator at first. Then she came home with Marissa and me."

"Home being where?" Kate asked.

"A tiny apartment above a drugstore. I was on welfare for a while, but even that didn't cover what I needed, and with day-care costs when I did find a job, there was just no way . . . Who wants to hire an eighteen-year-old with no college education, no experience, and two infants at home? I finally got a job at a grocery store in town, but that was barely above minimum wage." She took a long sip of her tea, then set the cup back in its saucer. "And I was exhausted. It was a miracle I'd been able to keep them both as long as I did, but I was barely with my girls those first few weeks. It just wasn't right. Then I got behind on my rent, and my landlord was talking about evicting me."

She wiped at her cheeks with a tissue from the counter. "What could I do? Live on the streets with my babies? The county would surely have taken them away from me, and I couldn't bear the thought of losing both of them. So I made the painful choice to give up Kara for

adoption, my tiny second-born. I figured an adoptive family would have better resources to care for her than I had.
She was so little, she'd never even remember that I was
her mother."

Another torrent of tears began, and Kate waited for
Patricia to regain her composure.

"I've missed her every day since," Patricia finally went
on. "I thought it would get easier with time, but it hasn't.
When Marissa would do something new—when she
learned to talk or walk, when she had her first solo in a
school concert—I wondered if Kara was doing the same
things. I'd see a little girl who looked like Marissa and
imagine it was Kara. And now that Marissa is so ill . . ."

"So that's what you meant when you said you could
end Marissa's suffering," Kate realized.

Patricia nodded. "I know it's wrong of me not to tell
her. I let her believe Ray was her father all her life
because I wanted to believe it. Then when I found out
Matt died"—she closed her eyes at the memory—"it was
easy to believe my lie. Matt would never come back to
prove me wrong. Ray loved Marissa as if she were his own
daughter . . . If only I'd met him before I'd given Kara
away. We could have all been together, and this horrible
mess . . ." She hung her head as tears filled her eyes again.
"But it was too late by then."

Kate held Patricia's hand and cried with her for a long
time. Finally Patricia rose and padded down the hall and
up the stairs to her bedroom. Kate could hear her footsteps on the risers. When she returned, she had the old

photo album in her hands, the one she had tried to hide from Kate.

As if she were extending a precious gem, she handed the album to Kate, who laid it carefully on the counter and opened its dusty cover. Inside were aged photos of Patricia with her two daughters. She looked so young, a baby herself. The twins were wrapped in pink blankets and snuggled beside each other in a white crib. Their cherubic faces smiled into the lens, revealing the deep dimples Kate recognized in the grown Marissa.

"Have you had any contact with her adoptive family since then?" Kate asked as she turned to the next page.

Patricia shook her head. "They wanted a closed adoption. It was the thing to do in those days. Not like today where adopted kids grow up knowing and spending time with their birth mothers. We believed ignorance was bliss. That was another lie, it seems."

"You need to tell Marissa the truth," Kate said when she'd paged through the whole album.

"I've been telling myself that for so long, but I don't know how to even begin. She'll hate me."

"She won't hate you," Kate assured. "She deserves to be told."

"She might be healthy now. Once we get the test results back, she might not even need a marrow donor . . ."

Kate gazed into Patricia's eyes. "You know this isn't just about the leukemia."

Patricia sighed. "I know. I've tried so many times to tell her . . . You have no idea. But I choke up. I'm terrified of it. I can talk to you about it so much more easily than I could with her. I've kept the truth from her all her life—how could she forgive that?"

"You did the best you could. You love Marissa, and she loves you."

"It was so perfect when Ray was alive," Patricia said wistfully. She ran a finger around the lip of her teacup, then lifted it for another long sip. "It was as if I had finally found forgiveness . . . And then the other shoe dropped. God is punishing me."

"God isn't punishing you," Kate countered. "He loves you, Patricia. Regardless of what you've done. He understands your reasons. He's not out to punish you. He wants to forgive you. Don't you see he's giving you another chance? That's what grace is all about . . . You need to forgive yourself too."

SEVERAL DAYS PASSED. Kate hadn't heard anything from Patricia, but she knew her friend needed time to work things out on her own. Patricia would tell Marissa the truth when the time was right. As for finding Kara Raine, Kate hadn't even brought the subject up. It was simply too soon. And if the doctor pronounced Marissa healthy, it was something they could do in their own time and their own way.

Kate knew if she were in Patricia's place, she'd want the same choice.

Kate had been working in her studio the past three days, on her surprise for the church. Twice Paul had come into the room from his study, taking a break from his Saturday-night sermon preparations, and had almost seen the piece, but she'd managed to cover it quickly with a bedsheet she kept handy for just such an occasion.

"What do you think I'm going to do? Go blabbing to everyone in the church about it?" Paul said.

"No," Kate said. "I just want it to be a surprise, that's all."

He'd shrugged his shoulders then. "If that's the way you want it, but you never know when I might sleepwalk into this room."

"You aren't a sleepwalker," Kate reminded him.

"I might take it up."

She laughed. Even after all their years together, Paul could still make her laugh.

The phone rang then, and Kate picked it up.

"Hanlons . . . This is Kate," she said.

A male voice that sounded slightly out of breath said, "Is Paul there?"

"Is this Eli?" Kate asked.

"Yes, it is. Hey, Kate."

Paul pointed to himself, asking if the call was for him, and Kate nodded.

"I'm calling about those Wilson brothers again," Eli explained, but Paul was already at her side, so she held the cordless phone out to him.

"Hello?" Paul said. "Yes, Eli."

He waited while Eli talked. "He didn't! What did Jack say?"

Kate couldn't make out Paul's words from where she sat, but she was fairly certain it had to do with that dog again.

"Can someone do that?" Paul listened. "Where are they now?" Again a pause. "I'll be right over."

He ended the call and came up behind Kate, resting his hands on her shoulders, giving them a squeeze. "Guess what?"

"Jack and Carl are fighting again. What about this time?"

"It seems Carl kidnapped the dog from the vet's, and Jack is suing for custody."

"You can sue for custody of a dog?" Kate asked.

"That's what I wanted to know." Paul left to go get his winter coat. When he returned, he said, "Don't wait up. Who knows how long I'll be arm-wrestling these two!"

AN EARLY FEBRUARY WIND bit Paul's cheeks as he walked up to the Wilson brothers' house. He could see Eli through the first-floor window. His back was turned slightly, and he was shaking his head.

Climbing the rickety stairs, Paul gave three knocks on the front door and waited for an answer. Eli opened it, a relieved expression on his face. He whispered as Paul came inside, "I'm so glad you're here."

Scout was barking and running in frantic circles around the two brothers. Jack stood, warming his hands by the potbellied stove that was central in the messy living room. Piles of old magazines and newspapers were

everywhere, as were clothes, blankets and books. It was a
kind of clutter stew, a little of everything all tossed
together.

Carl was sitting in a rickety-looking rocker, his arms
crossed in front of him. "Jack, this is ridiculous," he was
saying. "We aren't getting a divorce; you can't sue for custody of Scout."

"I can do whatever I want to do!" Jack shouted. "You
had no right to go get her from the vet!"

"She's *my* dog—I had every right. Besides, the vet
called me. What should I have done? Left her there?"

"I gave that flighty receptionist Aunt Susan's number.
The vet was supposed to call me."

"Maybe she never told the vet," Carl said. "Anyway,
does it matter? I picked up Scout. Big deal."

"But I'm the one they sent the bill to!" Jack protested.
Scout jumped up in front of him, but Jack ignored her.

Carl shrugged his shoulders. "That's not my fault."

Paul cleared his throat, and both brothers glanced his
way.

"Do you know what he did?" Carl said, glaring at his
brother. He handed a document to Paul, who scanned it
quickly. It was a summons for a court date, with the
details of Jack's custody suit.

"It doesn't have to be this way," Carl went on. "I'm tired
of fighting, Jack. We can find some middle ground." His
eyes entreated Paul's as if looking for some assistance.

The dog, no doubt tired from circling the room, hopped
into Carl's lap and licked at his face. Carl scratched Scout's

ears, and she leaned into the touch before settling down
to nap.

"This doesn't seem right," Paul began as he handed
the paper back to Carl. Both brothers looked at Paul. "Do
you really want to pay court fees and lawyer fees? It
seems so unnecessary."

"If he would stop interfering—" Jack began.

"You mean taking care of my own dog?" Carl started.

Paul held up a hand, and the two, thankfully, stopped
their tirades before they were fully off the ground. "I have
a solution."

"Go on," Jack said tentatively, crossing his arms in
front of him.

"What do you say to a little competition? You agree to
drop your custody suit, Jack, and I'll set up an obstacle
course of sorts for you two. You'll each run Scout through
a series of tests. Whoever Scout obeys the best and seems
more attached to will get sole custody of her."

"Who would judge the contest?" Jack asked. His gaze
turned accusingly toward his brother. "All it takes is for
Carl to bribe some judge, and—"

"Unbelievable!" Carl said. "Like I'd sink to your
depths. I'd have no problem winning the contest because
I know Scout is my dog." At hearing her name, the dog
lifted her head. Carl patted her head, and she lay back
down.

"We'd need someone impartial," Eli agreed.

"And neither of you qualify," Jack insisted. "Not after
that skunk fiasco."

"Okay . . ." Paul thought for a moment. "How about this? We ask someone from the dog-food company to come judge our contest. They don't know either of you. And they have a vested interest in seeing Scout in their ads."

Jack seemed to perk up at that suggestion, and Carl rubbed a finger across his stubbly chin as he considered. "They'd arrive the day of the contest?" Jack asked, eyeing his brother.

"They're only in Pine Ridge. I'm sure it won't be a problem," Paul said.

"And whoever wins, that'll settle the matter," Eli put in. "No backing out if the decision doesn't go your way. Once the decision is made, it's final."

"And the winner gets the five grand and gets to be in the ads," Carl added.

"Minus the vet bills," Jack reminded.

"It's a deal." Carl put out his hand to shake. His brother looked at it for a minute, then tentatively gave it a shake.

"It's a deal."

"And who gets Scout in the meantime?" Eli asked, more of Paul than anyone else.

"How about this?" Paul said. "We can see if your Aunt Susan will take the dog for the time being, until we can work out the details of the contest with the dog-food company. You two can keep living at home"—he looked from one brother to the other—"if you can get along."

They both gave the idea some thought. Paul hoped

the forced time together would work to heal their rift, but seeing their hesitance, he wondered if his suggestion was indeed the best one. Or would Eli be calling him to come out every day until the contest to settle the latest battle?

Finally Carl said, "I'm good with that."

To which Jack replied, "Fine. Me too."

THE HOUSE WAS QUIET the following Monday morning, except for the sound of the cuckoo clock in the hall. Kate pulled out a sheet of seafoam green glass and held it over the stained-glass window that was taking shape. Finally deciding where she wanted that particular color, she cut a one-inch strip of it, then began to cut out the smaller pieces. The cutter made a zipping sound as it moved across the glass, leaving a thin line on the surface. Kate moved the freshly cut piece to the side of the table, gave it a snap, and it broke along the line. She held it up to the template and decided it needed another cut to get the angle just right, so she scored it once more and used the pliers to snap it. It crunched off in tiny shards, so Kate moved to the grinder and pressed the glass against the rotating wheel until it was just right. This time it fit perfectly against its neighbor. She set it in its spot on the paper template.

She was almost finished cutting the glass for the good-sized window. It had been a lot of work, but having been home three days last week, she'd been able to accomplish quite a bit on the project. Next came cleaning any grinding dust and shards off the glass and wrapping the edges in copper foil. She reached for the roll of penny-colored tape and fitted it into its dispenser. Then she focused on centering the glass edge on the thin tape and wrapping the tape around each piece. The foil served as the metal to which the solder could attach. It had to be secure, or when it came time for soldering, the tape would pull off with the hot solder.

Kate was bent over her work when the phone rang. When she lifted the handset, she heard Patricia's frantic voice. She was crying.

"What's wrong?" Kate asked, her heart in her throat. "Is it Marissa?"

"We got the test results back," Patricia began. "The chemo didn't work. All that time, all that praying . . . and the cancer is still there."

"I'll be right over," Kate said and hung up the phone.

On the drive to the Harrises', Kate prayed for wisdom and comfort for Patricia. What could she possibly say that would be of any help?

She thought of Patricia's confession and realized there was still another way. If they found Kara, Marissa would have at least a chance of getting her marrow transplant. After all, siblings were much more likely to match on such tests, especially twins, though she didn't know if Marissa and Kara were identical.

She pulled into the Harrises' drive and cut the engine. When she climbed out of the car, Patricia was already standing at the front door. She let Kate in, and the two women embraced. Kate felt Patricia's thin frame shaking, and she patted her back.

"Where is she?" Kate asked.

"On the couch." She pointed toward the living room.

Kate moved past the wall of family photos and into the open living room at the back of the house. Sunlight streamed in through the east-facing bank of windows, filling the room with its warmth. Marissa lay sleeping on the plush, floral-print couch as the light played against her pale skin. She looked peaceful there, almost angelic. Kate sat in the wingback chair opposite her, careful to not awaken her, but Marissa's eyes opened in a flutter, and when she saw Kate, she lifted her head.

"I fell asleep," she said.

"You must've been tired."

Her gaze glued to her daughter, Patricia settled into the rocker opposite Kate. "How are you feeling, honey?"

"Good, actually." Marissa sat upright. "The doctor has to be wrong. I haven't felt this good in ages. Truly. I feel fine, Mom. Don't look so worried."

"What are we supposed to do?" Patricia took a deep breath.

"There's nothing *to* do," Marissa said. "We wait for a miracle. Do whatever the doctor tells us to do, and in the meantime, we live our lives." She reached for her mother's hand and gave it a squeeze. Then she glanced at Kate. "I hope you don't mind, but I'm in the mood for a long soak in the hot tub. Do you mind?"

"You go on ahead," Kate said.

The thin girl rose, kissed her mother on the cheek, and moved down the short hallway off the kitchen.

When she was out of earshot, Kate said, "I think maybe now's the time to tell her."

"I can't!" Patricia said. "She'll hate me. I couldn't live with that."

"Her sister might be her only hope. You can't *not* tell her. You're going to have to risk her not liking you." Kate knew her words were harsh, but she had to say them. "It could save her life."

Patricia nodded. "I know that, and that's part of the reason I called you. I can't look for Kara and take care of Marissa at the same time..." She sighed. "And I can't face seeing Kara. After all this time, after giving her away, who knows how she'd react..." Her words trailed away.

"I can look for her," Kate said. "You're not in this alone." She touched Patricia's arm. "I can talk to her about Marissa and ask if she'll agree to be tested."

The look of gratitude in Patricia's eyes melted Kate. "Even if she doesn't want to meet us...me," Patricia said quietly, "I want her to know that's okay. At least there would be a chance for Marissa."

Chapter Twelve

Livvy showed up at Kate's front door just after supper. Kate had seen her come up the walk through the bedroom window. The librarian was armed with a pile of books that looked as though it was about to topple out of her grasp.

"What's all this?" Kate heard Paul say as he opened the door.

"Books on adoption procedure." She said, handing the stack to Paul. "That about killed my back!" She stretched. "Where's Kate?" She glanced around the corner and caught sight of Kate, who was watching in amusement.

"I didn't know you and Danny were adopting," Paul teased.

"These are for your wife," Livvy said with a raised eyebrow.

Paul turned to look at Kate, his mouth slightly agape.

"Honey, how old are we?" Kate said.

Paul shook his head at her, then she kissed him on the cheek and reached for the top half of the stack.

Livvy and Kate retreated to the dining room, where they laid the books out and began their research while Paul watched the news on CNN in the living room.

All the books said essentially the same thing. Couples wishing to adopt prepared a home study, though some called it by other names. Essentially it was a document with photographs that gave the birth mother and the government an inside view of the background and home life of the couple who wished to adopt. When the birth mother decided to make an adoption plan for her child, she was given several of these packets to choose from. Thus, the birth mother chose the adoptive parents for her child.

Patricia had already given them what information she had about this. So Livvy and Kate knew that she had chosen the Family of Hope Adoption Agency out of Chattanooga and that the adoptive family was from a middle-class home. From what Patricia recalled, the mom was a stay-at-home mother, and the dad was a car salesman at one of the larger dealerships in town. But that had been more than twenty-two years before.

Kate flipped through the paperwork Patricia had given her and found the number for the agency that had placed Kara. "Here goes," she said to Livvy as she picked up the receiver and dialed the number. Livvy watched expectantly.

The phone rang several times, but then a recording picked up: "This number is no longer in service. Please check the num—" Kate hung up.

"Dead end number one," she said. Next she dialed Information in Chattanooga.

"May I help you?" a voice said on the other end.

"Yes, I'm looking for an adoption agency in Chattanooga. The Family of Hope Adoption Agency." She told the operator the address listed on the sheet and waited while the woman looked it up.

"I'm sorry but I don't have a listing for that business in Chattanooga."

Kate thanked the woman and hung up. "There's dead end number two," she said. She drummed a pencil against the tabletop as Livvy paged through another book. "I'm calling my son," Kate announced.

She dialed Andrew's home number in Philadelphia. It was a Monday, but he would be home from work by now. It rang three times before a male voice came on the line. "Hello, Hanlons."

"Oh, Andrew," Kate said.

"Mom? What's up?"

He sounded so much like his father, especially over the phone. Kate smiled to herself.

"Everything okay?" he asked.

She could hear her grandchildren's voices in the background. Andrew shushed them, and it became quiet.

"Fine, everything's fine," Kate said. "I have a legal question for you."

"Okay. Fire away."

"A friend of mine gave a child up for adoption twenty-two years ago, and she wants to find her daughter. Where do we begin?"

"You know I'm a real-estate lawyer, right?" She could hear the teasing in his tone.

"Of course I know you're a real-estate lawyer, but I figure you know everything."

He laughed, then his tone sobered. "I'd start with the adoption agency. Do you have that information?"

"They're out of business, or at least they've changed their number and address."

"Do they have a Web site?"

"I didn't check." Her gaze met Livvy's.

"If not, the Department of Health and Human Services will know what agency to contact to help with the search. The county can give you nonidentifying information— age, nationality, occupation, that kind of thing. But the placing agency would be the place to get the details. I don't know about Tennessee, but you might need a peti- tion of some kind to open those files. Was it an interna- tional adoption or domestic?"

"Domestic." Kate shifted the phone to her other ear.

"That makes it easier. You don't have some foreign government to work through, although ours can be plenty tricky too. If you can find out the name of the person who ran the agency, they might be able to help."

"I do have the name of the woman who ran it." Kate shuffled through the papers on the table until she found a sheet listing the name of the person in charge at the adoption agency. "Margaret Smee is her name."

"Talk to her first. She'll be able to steer you in the right direction at least."

When she hung up, she turned to Livvy. "Let's look up" —she read from the sheet again—"Margaret Smee, m'dear."

"It must be getting late," Livvy said with a chuckle. "You're getting punchy."

Kate looked at her watch. "It's only seven!"

Livvy lifted Kate's thick Chattanooga phone book. Only one Smee was listed—an M. Smee.

"It has to be her," Kate said. She reached for the phone again as Livvy read the number, writing it on a sheet of paper at the same time.

Kate was just about to hang up when a voice answered and said, "This is Margaret."

"Ms. Smee?" Kate began.

"Call me Miss, if you don't mind. Never much took to that women's lib hoo-ha. Who is this?"

"My name is Kate Hanlon—"

"You're not trying to sell me anything, are you? Because I don't buy junk off the phone. So if you are, you can just forget—"

"No, ma'am," Kate assured the woman. "I'm not selling a thing."

"So, what do you want?"

"I'm looking for the person who used to run the Family of Hope Adoption Agency."

"I'm the one. Still run it, actually," she said. Then she started coughing. When the bout passed, she asked, "What do you need to know?"

"I'm trying to find a girl who was given up for adoption in the mideighties through your agency. I don't know if you still have such information—"

"Of course, I still have it," Margaret interrupted, "but

I'm assuming since you're calling me that the adoption was closed?"

"Um . . . yes?" Kate said. "This is kind of an urgent case. You see, the girl that was adopted has a twin who is sick. We need to find her quickly . . . or her sister might not live." Kate knew she was begging, but it was the truth.

"Listen, it takes some time to track people down. I don't have forwarding addresses or that kind of thing."

"I understand that," Kate said.

"You'd be surprised how many people don't. They come thinking I've got their long-lost mother in my back room. Well, I don't. And I can't open sealed files for you unless you have a court order—that's how it works. I'm sorry, but I'll get in trouble if I let any old person look."

"Can we at least come talk to you?" Kate didn't know what else to say.

"Can't keep a person from talking," Margaret replied.

THE MOUNTAIN ROAD rose steadily in dips and swells. Conifers and deciduous trees towered over them as Kate and Livvy drove to the rural home of Miss Margaret Smee. She had said it was only a few miles southeast of Chattanooga. So far they'd driven twelve miles, and Kate's cell phone had gone out of range awhile ago. But as far as they could tell, they hadn't missed the turnoff. She'd told them to watch for a sign that said "Keith—48 miles," which seemed an odd name for a town. Then they were to turn left at the next dirt road.

"There it is." Livvy pointed up ahead.

Kate made the turn, and the road rose at a steeper grade. The little Honda complained but kept on. After a few miles, the road seemed to narrow, and the trees towered higher above them. They passed several shacks that looked as if they were about to collapse; their walls leaned in a gentle sway, and what paint had once covered them had now peeled off, revealing gray and weathered boards beneath.

Kate wasn't sure they'd find the information they needed from Miss Smee, but she was feeling frantic, and the thought of wading through government red tape only increased her sense of urgency. If she could at least find out a few details, some clues. Nothing illegal, but something to help them on their way.

Finally the road took a slight downturn, a sign that they were close to their destination, according to Margaret's directions, and they saw a dilapidated white house on the left. It peeked from behind a thick growth of pines. Kate turned into the drive as a large yellow Lab and a big black mutt came bounding out from a shed. The animals circled the car as Kate drove, and she slowed to a crawl for fear she would hit them. When she put the car into park, she noticed a dozen or more cats reclining on the covered porch of the house. They were an assortment of colors—some striped, others calico, others solid-colored. They seemed unconcerned with the dogs that panted in never-ending circles around the Honda. Black-and-white chickens pecked the snow-covered ground inside their coop just off the detached garage. The yellow Lab took off after one that had gotten out of its yard. The chicken flapped its wings and squawked in protest as it ran. Then the dog gave up and returned to Kate and Livvy.

"Do you think it's safe to get out?" Livvy asked.

"The dogs look harmless enough," Kate said. "At least they aren't growling."

It was then that Margaret Smee came out on the porch. She looked exactly as Kate had envisioned her on the phone. She was quite heavy, nearly as round as she was tall, and her feet pointed out slightly when she walked so she had a bit of a waddle. Her hair was a dirty gray, and short like a man's. She wore horn-rimmed glasses, and her clothes were so baggy that she had a bit of a potato-sack theme going on. Kate guessed her to be in her late seventies or early eighties.

"Mongrel, Mutt, get away from there," she shouted at the dogs.

Kate rolled the window down, and Margaret said, "Don't worry about them. They haven't bitten anyone lately."

Kate exchanged a look with Livvy before climbing out of the car and joining the elderly woman on the porch. The dogs followed alongside, panting and nudging Kate and Livvy's hands with wet noses.

"Thank you so much for allowing us to come," Kate began.

"Not a problem, not a problem," Margaret said. She motioned to the dogs to stay, and they did an about-face and returned to their home inside the shed. "I like to help folks reconnect whenever I can . . . Come on in."

"Do you still run your adoption agency?" Kate asked as she looked around.

"Yes I do, though there's a bigger agency in town that's taken over the lion's share of the placements. I still have my license, though, and find children for any who come looking. I used to have an office in Chattanooga, but I moved it out here several years ago."

Margaret led the way into the house that seemed a hodgepodge of additions. They moved past the kitchen and dining rooms, which were piled with dishes and empty food containers. An overweight orange tabby cat wove in and out through the obstacle course on the counters. "Scribble, get down!" Margaret said, though she did nothing to force the cat to comply. He simply gazed at her and turned to lick a bowl that had traces of cereal and milk in its bottom.

When they reached the living room, the woman stopped and motioned toward the overstuffed couch in a dark shade of green. "Please, have a seat."

Kate and Livvy complied, and the elderly woman returned to the kitchen. "I put a pot of tea on," she said loudly, from the adjoining room. "How do you take it?"

"Sweet and with cream," both women answered.

While Margaret prepared the tea, Kate glanced around the cramped living room. The walls were lined in shelves, some with closed bookcases and others open, but all of them held ceramic dolls in all shapes and sizes. There were Russian nesting dolls and homemade cloth dolls with dark-colored skin. Margaret had fancy-looking porcelain dolls with authenticating tags, and everything in between.

Every wall was covered with the inanimate creatures, except for where the television sat, and even that had a Raggedy Ann doll resting on top of it in a floppy pose.

Finally Margaret returned, bearing a tray with three steaming cups of tea.

"Thank you," Livvy said as she took her cup.

Kate said the same. Margaret placed the tray on a coffee table between them and sat in the heavy rust-colored La-Z-Boy chair that flanked the couch.

"You have quite a doll collection," Kate said. "It's very impressive."

"Thank you." Margaret looked around the room. "I started collecting them when I was a girl. Before long, everyone was giving me dolls for Christmas or my birthday. You should see my bedroom. I have a dresser in there with changes of clothes for all of them. I like to change them from time to time, so they don't get too bored sitting there staring at me." She laughed.

"How long have you run the agency?" Livvy asked.

"Oh"—she paused and scratched her double chin— "since 1970. Placed a lot of needy children during that time too. That's my calling in life. I never married, you see, so God put me in a place where I could help families find babies. And babies find their forever families." Her green eyes misted at the thought. "There's nothing as gratifying to me as being there when new families come together." She shook her head. "I don't know. Nowadays people go to such measures. All this medical hoo-ha, and for what? So you can have a baby who looks like you? I tell you, there are so many children out there who need a family to love them. Take China, for example . . . There aren't enough families to take in all the babies they're finding at train stations and orphanage gates. Yet folks let those beautiful children sit while they break their own hearts trying to conceive. It's insanity, I tell you."

Kate smiled at the woman, but Margaret seemed to be on a roll.

"Then there are the folks who complain that their child might grow up resenting that they're adopted. Well, they better get over that! Sure, there are some families with not-so-happy endings. Moses' adoptive mother didn't have such a happy ending, did she? Her son left her to return to his birth family and ended up ruining Egypt with all those nasty plagues. But still, she did the right thing, don't you think? Even though she took the risk that she could have been hurt, it was good that she pulled him out of that river."

Margaret lifted her cup and took a long sip, and Kate sent Livvy a look.

"You see," Margaret went on, "to me, helping families adopt is just a small thing I can do, my way of helping the childless and the orphans of the world find a better solution. It isn't ideal. Of course it isn't. But it takes a difficult situation and brings it . . ." Her words drifted into thought. "Grace," she finished.

The three women sat for a long moment, sipping on their tea. When Margaret returned to the present she said, "So, you're looking for a child you gave up?" She turned to Kate.

"Not *my* child," Kate said. "We're here on behalf of a

friend, Patricia Harris. Her name was Patricia Long when she made her adoption plan." She reached into her bag for the information she'd brought from Patricia. "She stayed at the Chattanooga Area Home for Unwed Mothers in 1985 . . ."

"You should have told me you weren't the birth mother." Margaret was shaking her head. "You wasted your time."

"What do you mean?" Livvy asked.

"I can't tell you anything about the case."

"But I—" Kate began.

"I'm sorry, ladies. But that's just the way it is. You'll have to bring this Patricia Harris back with you if you want any kind of information."

Chapter Thirteen

When Kate called Tuesday night to tell Patricia about the visit with Margaret Smee, she decided it might be best to tell her the news in person. Marissa was planning to spend the next day shopping with friends, so Kate invited the widow to her place for a change.

She didn't know how Patricia would respond to the news that she needed to visit Margaret in person and that she'd have to file a petition to see any court records. Patricia had been so fearful that Kate worried she'd give up on the search altogether. Yet she knew, for Marissa's sake, that this was out of the question. Patricia would simply have to work through her doubts and take that first step.

The coffeemaker beeped as the doorbell rang. Kate set two mugs on the counter and went to the front door.

It was an overcast day, though considerably warmer. The snow was melting and ran in tiny streams along the walk. The birds seemed to enjoy the lack of sunshine and had shown up at Kate's feeders in force. They flew off when Patricia walked by and then resettled in their places.

"What a nice place you have," Patricia said. She wore a pale blue jacket that brought out those vivid eyes, especially in contrast to her platinum hair.

"Thank you." Kate smiled and held the door as Patricia came inside. "The coffee's ready if you're in the mood."

"That sounds lovely."

Kate returned to the kitchen while Patricia made herself comfortable in the living room, but when she appeared with the tray of coffee and accoutrements, Patricia wasn't there. "Patricia?" she called.

"I'm in here."

Kate followed her voice into the studio.

"So, this is where you make your stained glass?" Patricia raised her head when Kate came in. She stood near the light table where several of Kate's sketches were laid out. The stained-glass window for the church was on the large table at the room's center, covered by a white sheet. Kate pulled it off to reveal the design that was laid out, with half of the leading yet to be completed.

"This is a surprise for the church," Kate confided. "Paul hasn't even seen it."

Patricia lightly touched the surface and said in a breathy voice, "It's beautiful. What a gift you have. You're really an artist." Her eyes met Kate's, and Kate felt herself blush.

"We all have gifts to offer," she said. "Not just me." She handed Patricia her coffee that steamed in rolling wisps.

Patricia took a sip, then said, "So, what did you find out in Chattanooga?"

Kate shook her head. "The woman wouldn't tell us anything. She says you have to come or our search is done."

Patricia blew out a held breath and sat in the chair next to the light table. Finally she said, "I was afraid of this. I don't know if I can—" Her gaze shifted to Kate.

"You have to," Kate said. "For Marissa."

Patricia nodded. "I know I do. But this is so hard. What if Marissa hates me? What if both of my daughters hate me?" A tear rolled down her cheek. "I tried to tell Marissa the truth while you were gone ... but I couldn't. She's feeling so much better now that the chemotherapy is over ... I just couldn't."

Kate reached for her hand. "The right time will come; you'll just have to seize it when it does."

"I'm terrified that whatever time I have left with her will be ruined, that she won't be able to forgive me. And Kara ..." She wiped a tear from her cheek. "What will she do when I come knocking on her door?" She lifted her eyes to Kate's. "I gave her to strangers."

"They aren't strangers to her," Kate assured. "They've loved her and made her their daughter."

"I still love her, you know? That doesn't go away when

you sign away your rights as a mother. But with us looking now when Marissa's so sick . . . will she think we just
want to use her to cure the daughter I *wanted*? After all,
we do have an ulterior motive, don't we? Kara owes us
nothing." She sighed and took another long drink of her
coffee. "I *did* want her. I did. But how will I be able to
convince her of that?"

"You tackle one problem at a time—that's how," Kate
said. "Besides, you could be selling her short."

Patricia looked questioningly into her eyes.

"Perhaps she is a loving, giving person who would be
honored to save her sister's life. You're offering her a
chance to be a hero. Not everyone would resent that. At
least come get the paperwork filed with the county," Kate
begged her, "and meet the adoption agent. If that's all you
want to do, that's okay. Livvy and I can finish the search
after that."

Patricia thought for a long moment, her gaze turned
toward the floor. When she finally raised her head, she
said, "I can do that."

Kate squeezed her hand. "I know you can. You can do
a lot of things you thought you couldn't."

THE NEXT WEEK, with the proper paperwork from the
county in hand, it was time to make the trip to see the
adoption agent. Patricia seemed ready to face her past,
though she hadn't told Marissa what the trip was really for.

LuAnne Matthews agreed to stay with Marissa while

Kate, Livvy, and Patricia went to see Margaret Smee. Marissa insisted she would be fine and was wasting LuAnne's time, but Patricia felt better having someone on call in case anything happened. When Kate asked if she'd be willing, LuAnne had gladly accepted, confiding that she'd always wanted to get to know Marissa better but that she'd never had a good reason to come calling. Kate sensed that she was sensitive about the issue of Matt's parentage and didn't want to intrude on the mother and daughter's privacy.

Patricia seemed uncertain about leaving Marissa in the waitress's care, but Marissa assured her she'd be fine. "It's just an afternoon, Mother. You never get to have fun with friends. Go! I spent all day yesterday with Suzanne; now it's your turn." The girl lay on the couch, a thick quilt pulled up to her chin.

"And when you came home, you were exhausted," Patricia scolded. She touched her daughter's forehead.

"I'll rest, and LuAnne will hang out. We'll get to know each other. It's not a big deal."

"She'll be fine," LuAnne assured. "And if anything happens, well, that's what I'm here for."

Patricia eyed her doubtfully, yet Kate saw that LuAnne's kindness had struck a deep place within the woman. "You don't even know us."

"Sure, I do," LuAnne reminded, her gaze firm yet sympathetic toward Patricia. "You're Ray's widow and a good mother."

MARGARET SMEE WAS FEEDING her chickens when they arrived at the ramshackle house later that Friday afternoon. It was a warm day, and though March was still a couple weeks away, the winds were blowing in lionlike form. Margaret's heavy form was bent over as she tossed cracked corn to the chickens, who darted for their feed with loud cackles.

She wore a shapeless navy-blue housedress, and her horn-rimmed glasses hung from a chain around her neck. She put them on when the threesome joined her near the chicken house alongside the garage.

"This must be the birth mother," she said, her gaze firmly on Patricia.

"Patricia Harris." Patricia held out a hand, which the elderly woman took. She held on and smiled into Patricia's eyes.

"It was *Long* before?"

Patricia nodded.

"I remember you. You always were a right pretty girl."

Patricia blushed.

"You had twins, right? Not many twins in my business, so when they come along, they're memorable. How's . . . What did you name the one you raised?"

"Marissa."

"That's the name." She patted Patricia's hand, still not letting her go. "Pretty name."

Patricia cleared her throat. "Marissa has leukemia."

The old woman's eyes clouded, and her brow furrowed.

"I'm so sorry. That's just wrong, isn't it? Someone so young. Just wrong. She's still with us, though?"

"Yes." Patricia choked on the word, and Kate could tell she had a hard time getting it out.

"You did the best you could," Margaret said. "You know that, right? You were in a hard spot, and you did the best you could. I guarantee you, the family who raised Marissa's twin was grateful for your choice every day of their lives."

Patricia didn't answer. She just stood there. Yet her expression filled with gratefulness for the healing words.

"Come," Margaret said as she turned and led the way into the house, her grip on Patricia's hand finally releasing.

This time instead of stopping at the doll-filled living room, Margaret led them to a small bedroom at the back of the maze of additions. There was no bed in the room, but stacks and stacks of papers. Along one wall was a collection of metal filing cabinets in varying heights and colors. Margaret went to one in the middle and said, "It was 1985, right?"

"Right," Patricia said.

Margaret pulled out a drawer and moved her thick fingers through the folders until she reached the Ls. "Long," she read. "Patricia Long, August 1985."

She took the folder and tucked it under her arm. "It's all in there, honey. But like I told these two the last time they came, don't expect it to lead us straight to your daughter. People move. Sometimes they don't want to be found. I'll help you with this process; that's what I do . . . I'll contact your daughter and see if she wants to meet you, or maybe exchange letters with you . . ."

Patricia turned and met Kate's gaze. Kate could see the fear that edged her features.

"Let's take it out to the dining room," Margaret suggested, her tone gentle, understanding. "I can give you some information—nonidentifying stuff. But I'll have to do the rest. I'll let you know when I've found your birth daughter—"

"You don't understand," Kate said to Margaret. "This isn't a typical case. Time isn't a luxury that we have. Marissa isn't in remission; her cancer is full-blown. We need to find her sister as quickly as we can, or Marissa will die."

Margaret's eyes held a deep compassion. "This isn't how things usually work . . ."

"All I'm asking," Kate asked, "is that you let me search. Right away. I can stay in touch with you if that's how you need to work this, but we don't expect you to do all this work so quickly."

Margaret paused in deep thought. Kate could see the struggle in her gaze. Finally she nodded and said, "I could get in trouble for this, but I'll give you the information I have. I have a fax machine that you can make copies on if you want, but the file has to stay here."

Kate sighed in relief, thankful for the woman's understanding. "We won't tell anyone," she assured her.

The dining room, like every other room in the house, was piled with junk. Margaret cleared off a round table, and Kate, Livvy, and Patricia began looking through the contents of the folder. Inside were documents about both Kara's medical background and the Olsens, the couple who made her their daughter. First was a birth certificate from the Chattanooga hospital where Patricia gave birth to Kara and Marissa, forms that Patricia had filled out regarding her health and family history, along with the home study that the adopting family had prepared. Patricia touched the birth certificate lightly, visibly overcome with the memory.

As Livvy looked through the papers, she came across several photos of the couple and handed them across the table to Kate and Patricia. Mary, Kara's mother, looked to be in her late twenties or early thirties at the time. She was a pretty woman with a dark, exotic look and broad smile. She gazed happily into the camera. Around her neck she wore a red scarf tied in a perfect bow, and her dark hair was fixed in a fluffy eighties style with big bangs and plenty of volume in the back. Robert, Kara's father, looked a bit older, perhaps in his late thirties. He had dark hair, slightly balding in the front, and equally dark eyes. He wore a white suit with a dark T-shirt that made Kate think of that TV show *Miami Vice*, also from the eighties.

"Here's the name," Livvy said, handing another sheet of paper across to Patricia. There in hand-printed letters was the new name of Patricia's daughter—Valerie Kara Olsen —and the address of her first residence across the bottom.

She clasped a hand to her chest as she stared at the words.

"What is it?" Kate asked.

Patricia lifted her face and said in a hushed tone, "They kept Kara as her middle name."

THEIR HEARTS WERE FULL as they made their way back to Copper Mill. The sun dangled low in the western sky, lighting the ridges of the mountains in glorious strands of tangerine and violet. Kate pulled off of the interstate at the exit for the winding road to Copper Mill. Patricia had barely spoken on the drive home, yet Kate sensed a new hope growing within her. Kate no longer sensed the fear that seemed to permeate every thought Patricia had of this child she'd given up.

They now had a name to go on—Valerie Kara Olsen. It was a starting place, at least, along with the address. Perhaps there could be a happy ending to this woeful story. Kate prayed that would be so.

And maybe if Patricia could see firsthand how God worked out those details, her heart would soften toward issues of faith. Or perhaps that was already happening, Kate thought. After all, Patricia had opened herself to Kate's persistence, and God was far more persistent than she could ever be.

Kate turned the Honda onto Main Street. The town was quiet in the early evening as families sat down to supper. The Town Green was empty, as were the sidewalks.

She dropped Livvy off at her home first, then turned onto Sweetwater and made a left onto Mountain Laurel Road a block before the Harrises' house. But when they pulled into the drive, everything was dark. Not a single light was on in the house.

"Something's wrong," Patricia choked out the words. Her hand touched her chest and her breathing quickened.

Kate gazed up at the house, studying it in the dim glow of the car's headlights. "There's a note on the front door," she said. "You stay here. I'll get it."

Patricia sat in the car as Kate walked quickly to the door and retrieved the note. She climbed back in the car and turned on the overhead light.

Patricia, the note read, *Marissa passed out. I couldn't wake her, so an ambulance came to take her to the Pine Ridge hospital. I'm with her there. LuAnne.*

Chapter Fourteen

Patricia sprinted through the front doors of the squat one-story brick hospital. Kate hurried to keep up with the younger woman. There was no one at the front desk, so Patricia started down the hall. Kate knew Patricia was frantic. To be honest, she felt pretty frantic herself.

They were halfway to the first room when a nurse appeared from its depths.

"Can I help you?" the short redhead asked.

"I'm looking for my daughter, Marissa Harris," Patricia said, urgency lining her words.

"She's in room 104." The nurse pointed down the hall, then paused. "But you should probably talk to Dr. McLaughlin first." She gestured toward the waiting room across from the front check-in desk. "Why don't you have a seat. I'll call him."

"Is she stable?" Patricia asked.

The nurse nodded. "Yes, she's stable. Just sleeping right now."

Kate saw Patricia's shoulders relax. She led her to the padded chairs in the waiting room, but Patricia was fidgeting, eager to get in to see her daughter. CNN played silently on the wall-mounted TV in the corner near the door.

"I knew I shouldn't have left her," Patricia finally said. "She was so tired after yesterday. I should have stayed here, where I belong."

Kate placed a comforting hand on her shoulder. "You heard the nurse. She's just sleeping; she's not in a coma."

"Why do I need to talk to the doctor first, then? And why are they keeping her here in the hospital?" Patricia looked at Kate with such sad eyes that Kate felt like crying. "It's all my fault. If I hadn't waited so long to look for Kara . . . I mean Valerie—" she went on.

"Mothers always blame themselves," Kate said. "The truth is, this could've happened whether you were here or not, whether you found Valerie or not. And you *are* trying to get help for Marissa. Remember? That's the reason you had to go."

Patricia's shoulders began to shake, then, in deep wracking sobs. Kate reached an arm across her back and let her cry. She didn't need to say anything else right then.

After what seemed an eternity, a lanky doctor with a shank of dark hair and a handsome face came down the hall. He wore a white lab coat, and when his gaze met Kate's, his eyes crinkled in a smile. The crow's-feet that marked them told Kate he was used to smiling often. He held out a hand to Patricia. "Mrs. Harris?"

Patricia nodded and rose to her feet as she reached for his outstretched hand. "How is she?" she asked.

"She was unconscious for a good hour, and she's very weak," the doctor began. He raked a hand through his hair. "Her red count is way down, so I gave her a transfusion and some platelets. That's why I want to keep her for a while—to make sure those numbers start going up again."

"She's on several prescriptions since finishing her last round of chemotherapy," Patricia said. "Do I need to bring those?"

The doctor nodded. "I saw that in her records. We'll keep administering whatever the doctor in Chattanooga prescribed."

"I can bring those the next time I come," Kate offered.

"Does she need to be in the Chattanooga hospital instead of here," Patricia asked, "since that's where she's gotten her other treatments?"

"That's up to you. They're part of our health-care system, so if she were to take a turn for the worse or need a different level of care, we'd transfer her."

"It *is* good to have her closer to home than Chattanooga," Patricia admitted. She lifted her eyes. "Can I see her now?"

Dr. McLaughlin nodded. "I'll take you to her room. I'd like to check her again before I head home."

He led the way along the quiet corridor to the room where Marissa lay sleeping. LuAnne Matthews was sitting in the La-Z-Boy chair alongside the bed. She stood when they came in.

"Oh, Patricia," she whispered. "I didn't know what to do. She had gotten up to go to the bathroom . . . and just collapsed." LuAnne's gaze turned toward the sleeping girl. "And your cell phone must've been out of range. I tried calling and left a message, but . . ."

Patricia stared at her daughter, who looked peaceful as she lay in the dimly lit room. The doctor walked over to her and pulled out his stethoscope to listen to her heart for a long moment. Then he took a look at her chart and wrote something down before saying farewell and disappearing back into the hall.

Marissa must have been exhausted, because even with their talk, she kept on sleeping. Patricia pulled a chair up alongside the bed and took a seat. She reached for her daughter's hand and held it tightly, bending to kiss it. Then she let out a heavy sigh. Kate touched her shoulder.

"Are you going to be okay?" Kate asked.

Patricia nodded. "Now that I'm here I will be. Why don't you head on home? I'm sure your husband is wondering where you are."

"I don't want you to be alone," Kate said.

"I can stay," LuAnne said. "Marissa and I were just getting acquainted, and I'd like some time to get to know her mother again." Her gaze met Patricia's. "If that's okay."

Patricia paused as if in thought, then she said to Kate, "I don't know what to do about"—she glanced at Marissa—"today. About what we discovered. I can't leave her again, but I know that's important too." Her eyes searched Kate's.

"We'll keep looking, Livvy and I. You don't need to worry. We'll do our best to get Marissa exactly the help she needs, even if we have to go to the ends of the earth."

PATRICIA HAD BEEN SITTING at Marissa's bedside for several hours, watching the rise and fall of her chest as she slept.

She thought of Kara . . . no, Valerie. She'd have to get used to that name. What was Valerie doing now? Was she well? Was she even alive? Had she gone to college and gotten married as so many of Marissa's friends had?

Marissa turned toward her in the bed. LuAnne lifted her head where she sat dozing in the chair on the opposite side of the room.

"I need a cup of joe," LuAnne said through the surgical mask she was wearing to protect Marissa from germs. "How about you?"

"That would be good," Patricia admitted and started to rise.

"You sit yourself down," LuAnne insisted. "I can make this run. You get the next."

After LuAnne left, Marissa opened bleary eyes as if she was unsure of her surroundings, and then her gaze settled on her mother.

"Good evening." Patricia stroked her daughter's arm. "You were sure sleepy."

"What time is it?"

Patricia turned to look at the large wall clock. "Ten o'clock."

"Did you have a good trip?"

Patricia laughed at the absurdity of the question, but then her laughter turned to crying as the stress of the day hit her full force. Tears streamed down her cheeks, and Marissa patted her hand.

"I'm sorry," Marissa said.

Patricia dabbed at her eyes. "You have nothing to be sorry for. But I"—her voice cracked—"I have so much to be sorry for."

This was the time—she knew it. And somehow a feeling of certainty and boldness came to her in a way she'd never felt before when she'd tried to tell Marissa the truth.

"I have a confession," she began. Marissa looked confused. "I should have told you a long time ago, but I was afraid you'd hate me if you knew."

"Hate you? Mom, I love you. I could never hate you." Marissa turned the rest of her body toward Patricia beside the bed, pulling up the covers and giving her mother her full attention.

Patricia took a ragged breath. "I hope not. Because I love you more than I thought it was possible to love a person. Your father did too. He loved you so much . . ." She stared at the floor.

"What is it?"

Patricia looked her daughter in the eyes as she began. "Ray wasn't your real . . . I mean, your *biological* dad."

"What are you saying?" Marissa tried to sit up, then fell back against her pillow.

"I was eighteen. I'd dated a boy all through high school. I thought he loved me, that we'd get married . . . Then I found out I was pregnant."

"You were pregnant?" Marissa said, her eyes reflecting her confusion.

Patricia nodded. "With you . . . Well, I couldn't stay in Copper Mill—your grandparents were too ashamed of me to let me have you here. So I stayed at a home for unwed mothers in Chattanooga."

"I thought you went to college there, that you and Dad . . . when I was born—"

Patricia shook her head. "No. I'm so sorry!" She lifted her face to the darkened window as she went on. "There are so many lies wrapped up in this. I should have been honest with you from the start, but once Ray came, everything seemed so perfect, and it was just easier to pretend that we were a normal, happy family."

"We *were* a normal, happy family," Marissa insisted.

"You deserved the truth. I met Ray in Chattanooga. He was an apprentice electrician who came to my apartment building to do some work after . . ." Her words trailed off again, and she began to sob.

"After what?" Marissa patted her mother's hand. "It's okay, Mom. You can tell me."

"There's more to this story. And it's the hardest part." She inhaled, and Marissa waited for her to go on. "You had a twin. I named her Kara. She was smaller than you, but she was pretty, with the same dark look you had, and the dimples . . ."

"I have a sister?" Marissa said. "And you never told me?" Her incredulous tone broke Patricia's heart.

"I know it was wrong. I can't apologize enough. That's what the trip to Chattanooga was about . . . We want to find her; we were trying to find your sister. Her name is Valerie now. We want to ask her if she'll be tested to see if she's a marrow match."

Marissa lay for a long moment in silence, her eyes staring at nothing. When she finally looked back at Patricia, she said, "How can you ask that of her?" Now Marissa was crying.

"I lost one daughter," Patricia said. "I'm not about to lose both."

IF THERE WAS ONE THING Livvy Jenner was good at, it was finding information on the Internet. She had a sort of sixth sense about such things that always amazed Kate. So when Livvy called on Saturday with news that she'd found the car dealership where Valerie's father worked, it didn't surprise Kate one bit.

"How about this?" Livvy said over the phone. "I have a Mountain View Ford on East Twentieth Street. According to the information on their Web site, the place has been in existence since 1979. You never know; the father might still work there. Or someone might know something about him . . ." She gave Kate the number, then excused herself to get back to work.

Kate dialed the dealership.

"MacKenzie Lincoln Ford Mercury," a scratchy voice

answered. It was a woman, and from the rasp in her voice, a heavy smoker.

"Hello, I'm looking for Robert Olsen," Kate said. "He's a salesman there, I believe?"

"Robert Olsen? We don't have anyone by that name here."

"Well, I guess he used to work there...maybe. Is there someone there who might know him? He would've been there in the mideighties, I'm guessing."

"Hey!" The woman shouted at someone on her end of the line. "You ever heard of a Robert Olsen? No, Jim, I'm talking to you. You ever heard of an Olsen who used to work here?" There was some muffled talk, then she came back on the line.

"Jim Parrish says he knew him. Said he quit a good ten years ago. And got a job at some big-shot dealership in Phoenix. That's all he knows."

"Can I talk to Mr. Parrish?"

"No, he's already back out in the lot talking to someone."

As Kate hung up the phone, her heart began to sink. Valerie couldn't be all the way in Arizona. There wasn't enough time for a nationwide search. She placed her hand on her forehead to think, offering up a prayer for help. Maybe this Jim Parrish was wrong.

They did have an address in Chattanooga. Or perhaps they'd moved to Arizona and returned to Tennessee. She wished she could simply call, but Livvy hadn't said anything about a phone number at the home address. She knew Livvy; she would've checked to see if there was any way they could find that information. No doubt their number was unlisted, or they'd switched to using a cell phone, as so many others had.

The only thing she and Livvy could do was head to Chattanooga themselves and try to track down Valerie on their own.

THE FEBRUARY MONDAY WAS WARM, almost sixty degrees. All the snow was gone except for the occasional dirty pile that the snowplow had left behind. The sun shone in radiance across the modest Chattanooga neighborhood, making it look more like the middle of summer.

The house where Valerie lived was small, with a stone facade and gingerbread details along the eaves, windows, and door. The backyard had a chain-link fence and an old-fashioned metal swing set. A large wolflike dog barked at them from the back as they approached the side of the house off the driveway and knocked on the screen door.

Livvy stood back a couple of steps while Kate waited in the front. "I hope our search is over," Livvy said.

"Let's hope," Kate agreed.

A bent, heavyset man answered the door. He had a thin layer of hair that was combed in a circular pattern over his mostly bald head. His thick brows furrowed together when his eyes landed on Kate and Livvy. "Who are you?"

"Good morning," Kate began. "I'm Kate Hanlon, and this is Livvy Jenner. We're looking for Robert and Mary Olsen, and Valerie Olsen . . ."

The man's expression was blank.

Kate cleared her throat and went on. "According to our information, they used to live here . . ."

"I thought I heard those names before," he said, holding up his index finger. "I bought this house from them in 1997."

"Did they leave any information about where they might have moved?" Kate pressed. "A forwarding address, perhaps?"

He scratched his stubbled chin. "They weren't exactly friends, so I don't know what happened to them after the paperwork was signed." He shrugged. "Could be anyone's guess where they are by now."

Chapter Fifteen

Kate and Livvy had never been more disheartened than they were at that moment. Climbing into Kate's Honda Accord, they sat side by side, neither of them speaking. Kate rested her hands on the steering wheel but didn't start the motor. A couple of cars passed on the quiet street.

"What does this mean?" Livvy asked, finally breaking the silence.

Kate sighed. "We don't have the time or the resources to go looking for her in Phoenix. It'd be like looking for a needle in a haystack."

"There has to be another way," Livvy said, pushing her hair back from her face.

Kate turned the key in the ignition and slid the gearshift into reverse. She glanced over her shoulder and backed into the street.

Livvy paused in thought, then continued, "We need something more concrete than the car salesman's word that they even went to Phoenix. Do you think the post office would keep forwarding records?"

Kate shook her head. "It's been too long." As they passed State Line Road, Kate glanced at her watch. It was eleven thirty. "Let's get some lunch." She pointed ahead at Andy's Restaurant on Dodds Avenue and pulled into the parking lot. "We need time to ponder and regroup."

Livvy reached for her purse from the floor of the car and got out. The two women walked up to the plain-looking restaurant.

The place was bustling, and the scent of fried chicken and barbecued pork hung in the air, making Kate's mouth water. A short young waitress with light-blonde hair and freckles dotted across her nose led them to a booth that looked out onto the street; she handed them their menus and placed two glasses of water on the table. She chewed gum as she spoke. "The specials today are pork riblets and chicken-fried steak. I'll be back in a few to take your order." As she bounced away, Kate and Livvy exchanged looks.

"I wish I felt like her," Kate said, making Livvy smile.

Livvy glanced at her menu, then said, "The question we need to ask ourselves is who would've known the Olsens well enough to keep track of them over the years?"

Kate meditated on that thought for a while as she perused the menu. Her stomach grumbled, and she pressed her hand against it.

"We're assuming, of course, that the Olsens are the kind of people who keep up with old friends," Kate said.

"It's all we have to go on right now." Livvy glanced back at her menu, then set it at the end of the table and took a sip of her ice water. "It's too bad we don't know what church they went to or if they belonged to any civic organizations."

The perky blonde returned to take their orders. "Heya," she said between chews on her bubble gum. "Do you know what you'd like?" She held the order pad aloft with a pencil at the ready.

"What do you recommend?" Kate asked.

"*Hmm*," the girl thought as she popped her gum. "I guess the barbecue? Otherwise, the hamburgers are really great. I like the chicken strips too."

Livvy raised an eyebrow, and Kate sent her a scolding look.

Kate pointed to a thin man with white hair who sat eating alone at the counter.

"What is he eating?"

"Oh, that's my neighbor, Mr. Leighton. He always orders the loose-pork barbecue. It's a hickory-smoked pork, off the bone. Has a very smoky taste. That's always popular."

"I suppose it's pretty fatty?" Kate asked.

The girl nodded and tapped her pencil against the order pad.

"I'll take the Cobb salad, then," Kate decided, "with blue-cheese dressing on the side. Does that come with a breadstick?"

"Yes, ma'am, it does. Is that okay?" the waitress asked.

Kate nodded.

"I'll have the loose pork," Livvy said. "And a fill-up on the water, please."

Kate watched the girl as she hopped to the next table, then she glanced at the man sitting at the counter—the waitress' neighbor. "*Hmm*," she said.

"*'Hmm'* what?" Livvy asked.

"I think the light is coming on. You know what we're missing?"

Livvy shrugged. "A clue?"

"That too. But no, that wasn't what I was thinking. We need eyewitnesses. And who are the best eyewitnesses?"

"You lost me at hello."

"The neighbors!" Kate said. "Of course the people who bought the house wouldn't have known the Olsens, but the neighbors might. There are always neighbors who stick around, especially in an old established neighborhood like theirs. Who knows, one or two might even still send Christmas cards to the Olsens."

WHEN THEY RETURNED to the neighborhood, it was almost one o'clock.

Kate and Livvy made their way up to the house next door to the Olsens' former home. Kate noticed the heavyset man they'd spoken to earlier peeking through the gauzy curtains at them. She waved, and he quickly shut the drapes.

The woman who answered at this residence was barely older than the waitress they'd just met. She had long brown hair that hung in braids down her back and dark circles around her blue eyes. Two preschool-age children tugged at her legs and screamed for attention when the door creaked open.

"Can I help you?" she asked, then shouted, "I said stay back!" She scowled at a little towheaded girl who had the same blue eyes as her mother. The mother's face flamed red as she turned back to the women. *Sorry*, she mouthed.

"Yes," Kate smiled. "We're looking for a Robert and Mary Olsen and their daughter Valerie. She would be twenty-two now. They used to live next door." She tilted her head in the direction of Valerie's former home. "Do you happen to know—?"

The mother was already shaking her head no. "I just moved here last year," she said. "I haven't even met the guy who lives there now."

The next two houses were no different. Neither of the residents knew the Olsens. And at the fourth and fifth houses, no one answered their knock. They were about to give up when they decided to try one more house. It was a white two-story with black shutters and a hedge of lilac bushes that ran the entire length of the property on three sides. Kate imagined it smelled heavenly when April and May rolled around.

Livvy rang the bell and stepped back beside Kate. They could hear the sound of someone shuffling around inside, so they waited even though it took several minutes for the door to open.

"Hello, ladies," an elderly man said. He had gray eyes

and salt-and-pepper hair. "To what do I owe the honor of your presence?" he asked, lifting his head and looking through glasses that had slipped down his nose. There was something about him that reminded Kate of Gregory Peck in his later years. Then Kate realized it was his rich-sounding voice. It carried that same warm honeyed quality she'd always enjoyed in the actor's performances.

"We're looking for someone, actually," Kate said. "Valerie Olsen? She's the daughter of Mary and Robert Olsen, who used to live at 313 on this street." She pointed to the house kitty-corner and across the street. "It would've been in the eighties when they lived there . . ."

"Well, sure I remember little Val. Cute button of a girl, that one. We were quite good friends with the Olsens. At least my wife was. I remember the day her parents brought her home. My Cora made them a cake, and we decorated the house with Welcome Home banners. What do you need with her?"

Kate felt a bubble of hope begin to rise within her.

"We're looking on behalf of her birth mother . . ." Kate explained, not sure if it was the right thing to say. But, she figured, if he recalled her homecoming, then he already knew that she was several months old on that joyous day. "She'd like to . . . meet her."

The man stroked his chin, then met Kate's eyes. "Why don't you come in? We can talk, and I'll tell you what I know of the Olsens." He stepped back and allowed Livvy and Kate to enter the lovely home.

Decorated in simple yet stylish furnishings, the place

felt comfortable and homey. The old man led them to a living room at the end of the hallway. Its windows looked out onto an expansive backyard with a rock garden and a fountain that was now dormant.

"I don't think I introduced myself," he held out a hand, "I'm Arnie Kerr."

Livvy, then Kate in turn, introduced themselves and shook hands with him, then they sat down on a high-backed formal couch.

"So, you're looking for little Val," he said, settling into a wingback chair. "My Cora had such affection for that child." He pointed to a small piano against the wall on which was a framed photograph of a woman. It was one of those photos that had been retouched as they used to do during the war, with paint applied to a black-and-white photo, giving it a painted portrait quality. The woman wore her hair in 1940s style, with perfectly sculpted curls that framed her face. She gazed prettily into the camera.

"We never had kids of our own," Arnie went on, "so Cora took in all the children in the neighborhood. She loved children. When Mary Olsen told her that they were going to adopt, well, that was real special to Cora. We probably should have adopted too, looking back. I wouldn't be alone now ..." his voice trailed away and his brow furrowed. "But it was too late by then." He shifted in his seat. "I'm sorry—I didn't offer you anything to drink. Would you like some lemonade?"

"No, thank you," Kate and Livvy said in unison, and Arnie scooted back in his chair to tell the story.

"Cora babysat little Val a lot in those early days," he said. "Mary worked as a secretary, so she needed day-care help, and Cora was happy to provide that. That child was a beauty—dark-haired and equally dark eyes. And she had these dimples ... I'm sure they made the boys weak-kneed when she was a teenager."

The description brought Marissa to mind, and because of it, Kate felt a connection to this child she'd never met.

"When she got a little older," he went on, "I guess about five or six, she always rode her bike up and down the street. I can still see it. And even after she was in school, she'd come in to talk to me and Cora and look at the jigsaw puzzles."

He pointed at several pictures throughout the room. Kate hadn't noticed before that they were puzzles that had been shellacked and framed as art around the house.

"We liked to put puzzles together in the evenings," Arnie said. "Cora and me. Helped pass the time."

"Do you know what happened to the Olsens?" Livvy asked.

He shook his head. "They moved in '97, I believe. They were doing well for a long time, but then we got word that they were getting a divorce. Mary told us in a Christmas letter a few years after they moved. I felt so bad for Val. She was probably a teenager by that time. I'm sure she was heartbroken. Her dad moved somewhere southwest—Arizona, I think. But Mary and Val stayed in the area for a while before they moved to Nashville. I got a Christmas card from them last year, even with Cora gone. That was nice of them to think of me. But I didn't get one this year."

He got up and hobbled over to a long oak cabinet and shuffled through a top drawer before returning to his chair. He handed Kate a card, still in its opened envelope. "This is from Christmas before last," he said. "You can keep it if you want."

Kate pulled out the card along with a photo of the mother and daughter. Kate stared at it. Valerie looked so much like her sister. If it wasn't for the hair, it would have been hard to believe it wasn't Marissa in the photograph. Her mother was dark-haired and dark-eyed too, with that exotic, almost-Mediterranean look she'd noted before. She no longer had the fluffy eighties hairdo of the photo Kate had seen in the agency file. If she hadn't known Valerie was adopted, it would have been easy to believe that the woman was her biological mother. She glanced at the envelope, noting the return address.

"So, this is where they live now?" she asked.

Arnie nodded. "As of a year and two months ago."

MARISSA HAD BEEN QUIET ALL DAY. Patricia tried to engage her in conversation, but the girl answered in curt, short answers. She wouldn't even look her mother in the eyes. Patricia thought her heart would break from the agony of it, but she also knew Marissa needed time to process the news. And time to forgive. She hoped she'd eventually be able to forgive her. She didn't know what she'd do if Marissa didn't.

She seemed weaker now too, and the doctor was more concerned about her low hemoglobin and red-cell counts. Her color, which had reappeared once her treatments were done, was now a faded gray hue. The dark rings under her eyes looked as if they'd sunk deeper into her skull, and her lips were cracked and parched-looking.

LuAnne had stayed with Patricia Friday night and part of Saturday, and then returned to Copper Mill for her evening shift at the diner. Before she left, she had promised she'd come back to visit.

Patricia had never known the woman well, other than knowing that she was Matt Reilly's aunt—Marissa's great-aunt. Another of the details she'd need to tell Marissa in due time.

They sat without talking as the television played mindlessly, Patricia in the chair alongside the bed. At least TV kept the awkwardness at bay.

"Did you want her?" Marissa suddenly asked through her mask, breaking the silence between them.

Patricia turned to look at her daughter. The hurt she saw in her daughter's face sent a barb into her own heart. "Valerie?" she clarified.

Marissa nodded.

"Of course I wanted her—" Patricia's voice broke on the admission, and tears rushed to her eyes. "I wanted both of you. But it was so hard. I was facing eviction because I couldn't pay my rent and pay for day care. I was all alone in a strange city . . . There was no way I could go to college to get a better paying job. I wanted better for my girls."

"So why her and not me?" Marissa asked.

"Oh, honey. You can't imagine how hard that decision was. Kara . . . I mean Valerie . . . was smaller than you were. She had a rougher start. I figured an adoptive family would have more resources to raise her and love her the way I loved her."

Marissa fingered the thin blanket that covered her legs. "Why didn't you give us both up?"

"I didn't give her up," Patricia said, her tone becoming defensive. "That sounds so callous. This was far from a heartless decision. I cried for a long time about it. For years I've regretted it, wondered how Kara was doing, missed her. Yet I knew I had no other choice. I kept you because . . . because I thought my heart would break if I lost both of you. At least with you here, I had a part of her too." She shook her head. "Maybe that doesn't make sense. Maybe it was selfish. In a perfect world, I *would* have had both of my children with me." She let out a humorless laugh. "I guess in a perfect world, I wouldn't have been an unwed mother, would I? But I'm so glad I had you—having you brought healing to my broken heart. Somehow that made everything better, even my parents' rejection."

Tears traced Marissa's cheeks, and Patricia reached out a hand to touch her face. Then she let it fall to the bed beside her daughter. "Ray loved you as if you were his own daughter."

"He didn't tell me the truth either." Hurt and betrayal lived in those words.

"He wanted to, but he felt it was my decision . . . And a poor one it was."

Marissa reached out and took her mother's hand. Patricia closed her eyes as a healing balm flooded her being.

"This makes so many things clear," Marissa admitted. "Why you acted the way you did about certain things . . ." Their gazes met.

Patricia mouthed *I'm sorry* again. Marissa leaned toward her, and mother and daughter touched foreheads.

"I want to meet her," Marissa said. "And not just to see if she's a match. I want to know my sister."

IT WAS DARK OUTSIDE. There was no moon, and clouds covered the stars. The interstate rolled beneath their tires with only headlights to illumine the way. Livvy slept in the passenger's seat.

Kate dialed Patricia's cell phone as they drove the rest of the way from Chattanooga to Copper Mill. She had to tell her the news right away. They'd found someone who knew Valerie. She even had a fairly recent photo of the girl who looked just like Marissa.

A tentative voice answered. "This is Patricia."

"It's Kate. How's she doing?"

"Weak, but she's okay. For now." Patricia spoke in a whisper.

Kate wondered if she was in Marissa's room and the girl was asleep. Then she could hear the sound of a door shutting.

"I told her the truth, Kate." Patricia's voice was louder now. "I told her about Valerie and . . . everything."

"How did it go?"

"You were right. She forgave me. All this time I wasted, and she forgave me."

"Of course she did. She's a great kid, and she loves you."

"I underestimated her," Patricia confessed.

"Do you think the doctors will let her go home soon?"

"No . . ." Patricia paused. "She's weak, Kate. I feel like time is running out, and that scares me. Through all her chemo treatments, I didn't feel the way I do now . . ."

Kate passed the twenty-mile sign for the exit to Copper Mill.

"I have some news that might help boost her morale," Kate offered.

"Oh?"

"We found someone who knows Valerie, or at least knew her. One of her old neighbors. His wife provided day care for her when she was little."

"Really?"

"Patricia, Livvy and I have a photo of her—she looks just like Marissa. She's so beautiful."

Kate could hear Patricia crying over the phone, so she waited before going on. Then she said, "We have an address . . . in Nashville. I'm going to drive there first thing in the morning. You just tell Marissa to hang in there," Kate said. "We're going to find Valerie for her."

AFTER HER TALK with Patricia, Kate felt an even deeper urgency. They had to find Valerie and find her soon.

Livvy couldn't make the long trip to Nashville with her. She had responsibilities at work, but Kate knew Paul could manage by himself for a while. She dialed him next. He answered on the second ring.

"Hey, honey. How's it going?" he said, no doubt having read caller ID before picking up.

"I'm going to have to make another trip," she said into her headset.

"Oh?"

"We think we've found Valerie, or at least her trail. But it's all the way in Nashville. I'm bringing Livvy home now, then I'll head to Nashville early tomorrow morning."

"Whatever you have to do, just be careful."

"I will be. And Paul?" she went on.

"Yes?"

"Remember I said I'd let you know when it was time for you to come to Patricia's aid?"

"Sure."

"It's time. She needs to know she's not alone, and I can't be the one to do that right now."

MARISSA SLEPT FITFULLY the rest of the night. Patricia watched as she twisted and turned under the covers. Thankfully the hospital had put La-Z-Boy chairs in the rooms for visitors rather than the hard vinyl and metal chairs Patricia was used to seeing in other hospital wards. She pushed back in the chair to recline and let her eyes droop shut.

Throughout the night the nurses came to check on Marissa, and the doctor even came in at one point to read her chart and bend over to listen to her heart. Though Patricia felt a huge emotional weight lifted from her shoulders from telling her daughter the truth, a new reality had dawned. Marissa was growing weaker.

When a knock sounded on the door, Patricia realized it was morning. She cleared her throat and glanced at her watch. It was eight o'clock. How had she slept so late? She stretched her back and pushed her hair into some semblance of order.

"Come in," she called, wiping the sleep from her eyes and straightening her clothes.

A clean-shaven man, who looked to be in his sixties, with salt-and-pepper hair and clear blue eyes tentatively entered, wearing a surgical mask.

"I hope I'm not disrupting anything," he said. "I'm Paul Hanlon. Kate's husband?"

Patricia put the recliner down and crossed the room to greet him. "I'm so happy to meet you," she said.

"I'm kind of early, aren't I?" he said after glancing at his watch.

"No, it's fine, really." Patricia waved the comment away with a hand. Her gaze turned to her daughter.

"Kate is going to Nashville today, so I thought I'd stop in and see how you two are holding up," Paul said.

Patricia crossed her arms over her chest. "That's a hard one to answer." She paused, still watching Marissa. "She's not doing well . . ."

"I'm sorry."

She met his gaze and felt the sincerity behind his words. "You and your wife have been so kind."

"We've only done what anyone would do."

She shook her head and looked away. "Believe me, that isn't true. I've been left alone more times than I care to remember, but you two have been such a . . ." She searched for the right word and finally said, "blessing." She was surprised by the word choice. But it was true.

When she turned back to the pastor, he was smiling. "We aren't the only ones who care about you, you know. We're trusting that God will find a way for your daughter."

Somehow those words didn't irk her as they would have a few short weeks ago. She'd seen loving compassion in the people of Copper Mill firsthand. And somehow, in that compassion she felt God's care for her. She supposed that as much as she had underestimated Marissa's ability to forgive her, she'd done the same with God.

A moment of silence passed between them. Patricia started to speak, then hesitated before she finally said, "Pastor?"

Paul's blue eyes were filled with kindness. "Yes?"

"Would you mind praying for us?"

LATER THAT MORNING a whole bunch of visitors started coming and going. Whether LuAnne Matthews had been the one to alert them or Pastor Hanlon or both, Patricia didn't know, but Marissa was enjoying the attention. And to Patricia's surprise, she was glad for the company too.

At ten thirty, LuAnne Matthews arrived, having scrubbed and gowned. "Hi-ho," she said as she came in. "How are you kids doin'?"

The redheaded waitress set a plastic bag on Marissa's bed and proceeded to lay out a full meal on Marissa's tray, including hot soup, canned peaches, a salad, and a dinner roll.

"I brought you some good food from the Country Diner," she whispered. "Hospital food is for the birds!"

In the first container was a steaming batch of chicken and dumplings; its scent of thyme and pepper filled the room. Marissa looked hungrily at the feast before her.

"She can have the hot food and peaches," Patricia instructed, "but the doctor said she can't have anything that might carry germs."

LuAnne pulled the salad and roll off the tray and winked at the girl.

When it was all ready, Marissa lifted her plastic fork

and tasted the dumplings. She closed her eyes in rapture. "This is wonderful!" she said. "You're right, LuAnne. Hospital food is for the birds." Then she dug in, a smile on her face. Patricia watched, grateful for the moment, and LuAnne said, "She'll gain her strength real quick if she keeps eatin' like this."

Several minutes later, Marissa sat back with an expression of satisfaction on her pale face. "That was very thoughtful of you, LuAnne. Thank you."

The plump waitress shrugged. "It would've just gone to waste sittin' around at the diner! You'll let me know if there's anything else you have a hankerin' for, won't you? I can sneak food out without a problem." She winked at Marissa again, and the girl giggled.

"I better get back to work," LuAnne said, looking at her watch. "The lunch crowd will be coming in soon. You know how crabby people can get if they have to wait for their meal!"

She waved good-bye and left.

At around noon Renee Lambert arrived. The older woman came bustling into the quiet of the hospital room. She was all made up as if she were on her way to a formal event—full makeup and false eyelashes, and an icy pink dress with matching nail polish and shoes.

"I heard on the prayer chain that you were here," Renee announced. Then she asked Patricia, "Do you remember me?"

Patricia knew the woman only slightly when she was a teenager. Renee had been an acquaintance of her mother's from the Rotary Club. Patricia smiled and walked over to the counter to retrieve a mask, which she handed to Renee.

Renee raised an eyebrow at it, then gingerly slipped it over her head, trying not to disturb her neatly coiffed hair. "I tried to sneak Kisses in," Renee admitted as she settled the mask into place. "He's my Chihuahua. But that mean nurse made me take him back to my car! They have rules about no animals. I think it's pathetic, if you ask me. What's more comforting than a snuggle with a little umpkins?"

"That was very nice of you," Marissa said. "What was your name?"

"Oh dear. I assumed that since your mom knew me, you would too. I'm Renee Lambert. I go to Faith Briar Church . . ." She paused, then said, "I heard about how poorly you were feeling. But I want you to know that we're all thinking of you and praying for you."

Renee stayed for over half an hour before excusing herself and offering to come back the next day. Patricia didn't know what to say to the woman. She thought of her initial reaction when Kate Hanlon had started visiting, yet that had turned into a good thing. Who knew? Maybe even visits with an elderly drama queen could bring joy into their lives. So she said, "That would be nice, Renee. Marissa usually gets sleepy a little before supper, so if you could come around the same time . . . ?"

"I'll plan on it," Renee said with a big smile.

A few minutes later, yet another visitor dropped by to

see Marissa—Betty Anderson from Betty's Beauty Parlor. She had been their regular hairdresser for several years, so when she poked her bleached-blonde surgical-capped head into the room, Patricia waved her right in. She too wore a gown, mask and gloves.

"Hey," Betty said. "I thought you two could use a visitor."

"You don't have a dog in your purse, do you?" Marissa asked with a laugh.

Betty wrinkled her brow, then winked at Marissa. "Now why would I have a dog in my purse?" She bent over to kiss Patricia on the cheek, then leaned back to look at her as she put back on the mandatory surgical mask. "You look awful!"

"Thanks!" Patricia said.

"I just mean that you look like you need to get some rest," Betty explained. She glanced down at her hands. "And a manicure wouldn't be a bad idea either!"

"She's right," Marissa said. "You do need to take better care of yourself, Mom."

"I'm just fine," Patricia said.

"Well . . ." Betty went on, this time to Marissa as she reached into the large tote that was tucked under her arm. "I came with an idea for you, young lady." She withdrew a makeup bag. "How about a little dolling up?"

Marissa touched her face, which hadn't seen makeup in ages, and then the flowered scarf that was tied around her bald head. "I doubt it would make a difference."

"At least let me try. I guarantee a little pampering will make you feel like a brand-new girl."

Marissa nodded and sat forward on the bed, tugging the IV stand, whose tube was attached to her arm, out of the way so Betty could sit next to her.

Betty pulled out a wig from another bag she'd set on the floor. "Want to try it on?" she asked.

Marissa smiled weakly and Betty nodded. "You're right. Now's your chance to go blonde," she said, pulling a long blonde wig out of the bag.

Marissa laughed and shook her head. "I'm not really a wig kind of person," she said.

Betty shook her head, pulling out a third wig, this one with short red hair. "You sure?"

Marissa nodded.

"I thought that might be the case," Betty said, "so I brought you a couple of new scarves." She pulled out two new head scarves, both in pretty, vibrant shades—one in blues and greens, the other in reds and oranges. "Can I?"

Marissa smiled and leaned forward as Betty removed the scarf she was wearing and wrapped one of the new scarves around her head, fastening it with a butterfly-shaped pin.

Then she handed Marissa a mirror. "What do you think?"

Marissa gazed at herself, turning her head one way and then another. She handed the mirror back to Betty and said, "I look like a new woman. Thank you, Mrs. Anderson."

Marissa smiled gratefully, but Patricia could see the weariness etched in the corners of her daughter's eyes It

had been a long day, and while she was grateful for the
kindness that everyone had shown, she also knew Marissa
needed to rest. She moved to Marissa's bedside and
helped the girl lie back as Betty gathered her makeup
supplies.

"This was so thoughtful of you," Patricia said to Betty.

Betty's eyes crinkled at the corners. "I didn't do anything. Really." She glanced at Marissa, whose eyes had
already closed in sleep. "Take care of her, okay? And take
care of yourself too." She met Patricia's gaze. "That's an
order."

When Betty finally left, Patricia sat back in the
recliner and closed her eyes. Marissa slept with a con-
tented expression on her face.

"You need to go home and sleep, Mom," she said later
that evening when she roused. "Betty was right about
that."

Patricia opened her mouth to protest, but Marissa
interrupted her. "You won't be any good to me exhausted
and sick. I mean it. I'll be fine. Go home and sleep."

Patricia finally agreed, and Marissa closed her eyes
and was soon breathing in a deep rhythm of sleep.

Patricia had thought the world had deserted them,
and yet today it had been made irrefutably clear to her
that she wasn't alone. Even though Ray was gone, life
didn't need to end for her. And as long as Marissa was
alive, she would fight for her and pray, because she was
beginning to see the power in that act. That sensation was
something she didn't want to let go of.

Her thoughts turned to Kate's trip to Nashville to find Valerie. Her stomach fluttered, both in nervousness and excitement with the possibilities that that discovery could bring. To have both of her daughters together, and to have Marissa healed of this horrible nightmare, would be beyond her wildest dreams.

Chapter Sixteen

K ate rang the apartment buzzer in the tall downtown Nashville building. After driving what seemed like an eternity, she'd finally located the address in the maze of streets. Her heart pounded in her chest with the hope that she'd finally meet Valerie.

"Yes?" A man with stringy blond hair, who looked to be in his late twenties, answered the door. He wore a green and gold knit cap with a bill. It looked like something she'd seen Bob Marley wear on TV. The young man's teeth were so crooked that Kate had to fight to keep from staring at them.

"I'm looking for a Valerie Olsen," Kate said. She held up the picture that the elderly man had given her in Chattanooga. "According to my information, she lived . . . or lives . . . here?"

"No Valerie Olsen here," he said. He started to close the door, then added, "You might want to check with the super. He lives downstairs in the first apartment."

Kate's frustration bubbled up. How many dead ends would she have to hit before the road went somewhere?

She made her way to the downstairs apartment. The elderly woman who answered hardly looked the part of an
apartment superintendent. She was a petite woman, no
more than four feet ten inches tall, with white hair in a
straight bob that gave her a youthful appearance.

"Now, who was it you were looking for?" she asked,
obviously confused by Kate's appearance at her door.

"The super?" Kate said.

"Oh, my husband's the super," she explained. "He's
out right now."

"I'm actually looking for someone who used to live
here. I'm not exactly sure when, although I'm fairly certain it was within the last two years . . ."

"We've lived in this building for fifteen years." The
woman leaned to get a better look at the photo Kate held
out.

Kate repeated the name as the woman gazed at the
picture.

"I remember Valerie," she finally said, nodding her
head. "Nice girl. Pretty. They moved not too long ago. I
think I have a forwarding address somewhere in here." She
motioned for Kate to come inside, then scurried to a file
cabinet that was tucked in a corner of the dining room.
Kate stood at the door and watched as the woman rustled
through the papers. When she returned, she had a sheet
of paper in her hand. "Here it is. They're in Memphis. I
recall the mother saying she'd gotten a job there, now that
I think about it. I think the daughter went with her. It was
just the two of them, you know."

Kate nodded her head. "I'm aware of that . . . May I?"

She reached for the sheet of paper and copied the address into a small notebook she kept in her purse. Then she thanked the woman and made her way back to her car.

Memphis was in the southeast corner of the state, a good three-hour drive away. Kate dreaded the long drive alone, especially if she got there only to come up empty again.

Deciding she needed to do a little more research before making the long drive, she stopped a young woman on the sidewalk and asked where the public library was. She quickly copied down the directions and wound her way to the regal-looking building on Church Street. Quickly moving to the checkout desk, she signed out a computer and found her way to an empty station. Kate gazed around the quiet sanctuary as other patrons perused periodicals and browsed the biographies section.

When the screen saver faded away and the desktop came to life, Kate connected to the Internet. Searching the online Yellow Pages for "Memphis" and "Valerie Olsen," she hit the Go button, but no matches came up. Next she tried "Mary Olsen." This time a phone number popped onto the screen. Kate keyed the number into her cell phone so she could call it once she was back out in the car. She clicked on a few more links to see whether any other Mary Olsens lived in the area. There weren't any, so she decided it must be the right number and closed the search window. If it was a dead end, she could always come back in and try again.

When she was back in the car, she hit the Talk button and waited for someone to pick up. She was just about to hang up when a female voice came on the line. "Hello?" the woman said.

Kate cleared her throat. "Yes. I'm looking for a Mary Olsen?"

"This is Mary Olsen."

"Are you the mother of Valerie Olsen?"

"Yes . . ."

Kate's heart pounded out a beat even as she ran out of words to say. She fumbled, then began, "My name is Kate Hanlon. I've been looking for Valerie . . . on behalf of her birth mother." She paused, bracing herself for the woman's reaction.

The phone was silent. "Mrs. Olsen?" Kate said.

"Wow," the woman finally said. "I guess I thought this day might come, but I'll be honest, I'm not entirely prepared for it."

"I'd like to meet you if that's okay," Kate said. "Rather than talk over the phone." A pickup and a car-hauling semi passed on the busy street.

"You're not her birth mother, then?"

"No," Kate said. "I'm just a friend." She watched through the windshield as a slew of pedestrians crossed at the next crosswalk.

"Okay . . . When would you like to meet?"

"Tomorrow?" Kate said. "I'm in Nashville right now, so it'll take me a few hours to get there."

"Tomorrow is good," Mary said. "Wednesday is my day off, actually, so I'll expect you around . . . ?"

"Let's make it one o'clock?"

"One o'clock at my house, it is."

TWO REPRESENTATIVES from the How Now Dog Chow Company from Pine Ridge arrived at the Hanlons' house the next morning. It was a warm day for the end of February. The judges wore stiff-looking dark suits. Paul half expected them to put on their Ray-Ban sunglasses and talk into hidden microphones in their neckties.

"Welcome to Copper Mill." Paul held out a hand to the men, who looked at it as if it were a cobra.

"Okay, then," Paul said under his breath. He stood aside so they could come inside, then led them to the dining room. "I'm glad you came."

"So, remind me, what is this all about, Mr. Hanlon?" the taller one asked. "I know we talked on the phone, but it seemed a bit peculiar." He had almost-black hair with a mustache and goatee, and when he said "Mr. Hanlon," Paul thought he could detect a bit of an accent in his tone.

"Both of the brothers say the dog is theirs. They aren't willing to share the prize, apparently. That's why we asked you to come. We needed someone impartial to decide. All we're asking is that you watch our contest and together decide who the rightful owner of the dog is—"

"And therefore who gets the prize and the ad spread," the shorter, blond one finished for him.

Paul nodded. "Basically."

"So, what does your contest entail?" the tall one asked as he folded his hands together.

Paul pointed through the dining-room window to the backyard, where he'd set up their course. "It's a good thing the snow melted," he said. "I thought we'd start with some basic commands—sit, roll over, stay—and have each of the brothers run the dog through that. There's also a tire swing to jump through, a balance beam, cones for her to zigzag through . . ."

"Impressive," the taller man said, nodding his head as he crossed his arms over his barrel chest.

The doorbell sounded, so Paul went to answer it. Aunt Susan was there, a broad smile on her round face as she held Scout in her arms. She'd dressed the cocker spaniel in a Tartan-plaid doggie coat with a matching hood.

"Hi there, Pastor Hanlon," she said. "Here's Scout for her little contest." She brought the dog inside and set her carefully on the doormat, wiping each of her paws with some diaper wipes from her purse. "Don't want her to track all over the place," Susan explained.

"I appreciate that, Miss Wilson," Paul said.

Susan started to take off her coat, but Paul motioned for her to keep it on. "The contest will be outside," he informed, "so you'll want to keep your coat on."

"Outside, you say?" She rubbed her hands together. "This ought to be fun."

The dog took off toward the back of the house, with Susan following behind, just as Jack and Carl arrived in separate cars. Paul could hear the dog howling, no doubt at the "secret agents" in the dining room.

Jack parked his restored '76 Ford Maverick while Carl climbed out of his Toyota Corolla and made his way toward Paul. Eli had called earlier, explaining that he was too busy at the antiques store to get away, so he wouldn't be there for the big event.

Paul wished his friend could have been here. He could use his perspective in figuring out how to navigate the waters with these brothers. He offered a prayer for wisdom to heaven, but it was still overcast.

"Good morning," Paul called to Carl, who waved back. Jack walked with his head down, offering a "Let's get this over with" expression when he reached Paul.

When they were all in the dining room and introductions had been made, Paul went over the ground rules, which were basically what he'd told the dog-food representatives earlier, including that both brothers had to abide by the judges' decision, whichever way it went. Scout wove through their feet in a hyper circle.

Both brothers agreed and signed documents to that effect. Then the group took the bouncing dog outside. Susan stood with the How Now Dog Chow men in a line near the house while Paul and the brothers moved to the obstacle course.

Paul flipped a coin, and Jack called heads. When the coin landed on heads, Paul asked the younger brother, "Are you going first or last?"

"I'll go first." He gave his brother a withering look, then took ahold of the dog's red leash and led her to the center of the course. Unhooking her, he gave the first command. "Scout," he said. Scout looked at him and tilted her head. "Sit, girl."

She tilted her head the other way, then turned in a circle and lay down. Jack squatted down beside her and pressed her bottom to the ground, forcing her to sit up. She licked his hand. "Argh," Jack said under his breath, though Paul could hear him plainly. "I said, sit!" This time she stayed in place.

Next he gave the command to roll over. Scout moved to standing and came alongside him. "I didn't say heel, you dumb mutt. I said roll over!" He plopped the dog onto her side and attempted to roll her over, but she struggled to get back onto her feet and growled at him, revealing her sharp white teeth. Paul was afraid she'd actually bite him, but she calmed down, and Jack went on.

Jack put his hands on his hips.

"Doing good there," Carl commented, chuckling to himself.

Jack turned on him and said, "Don't you even start!"

Seeing a break in the action, Scout bounded over to Aunt Susan for a head patting.

"Get back here!" Jack shouted. To his credit, the dog did obey that command, albeit with her tail between her legs.

"Let's do the course," Jack said, ignoring Paul's instruction to also demonstrate the "stay" command.

Leaving the dog at one end of the beam, Jack moved to the other end and called, "Come here, Scout."

The dog bypassed the beam and panted up to his side. So Jack grabbed her collar and dragged her back to the other end of the beam, attempting to get her to stand on the thin, long piece of wood. She put her front paws on the wood and barked at Jack.

"Get up!" he grimaced as he lifted her rear end. He

had her back paws on the beam for a moment before she plopped back down on the brown grass.

"Up!" He lifted her again, but at that moment a squirrel darted across the yard and into the woods. As soon as she spotted it, Scout was off and running. She barked at the furry creature and tore after it around the house, down the driveway and into the woods.

Everyone in the group exchanged disbelieving looks for a moment, and then they all took off after the dog, each calling her name, including the men in suits. Carl was in the lead.

Paul worried that they'd have another skunk incident. Yet within minutes, she was back, panting and slightly muddier.

Carl had her in his arms and handed her to Jack, who attempted to finish the course with her. But by that time, she was too distracted to pay any attention to him at all. She kept jumping up on him and barking. In turn, Jack muttered under his breath and at one point smacked the dog on the bottom. She made a tiny yelping sound, which caused Aunt Susan to gasp. Then he snapped the leash back onto her collar and brought her to Carl.

"Okay," Jack said. "Show me that you can do any better with this . . . this mongrel."

Carl took the leash, then bent down to look Scout in the eyes. She smiled her best doggie grin, and Carl patted her head. "Okay, girl," he said.

He walked with her to the center of the course, then took off the leash and gave the panting pooch a small

doggie treat. She smiled up at him as if ready to do his bid-
ding. "All right, girl," he said in a quiet voice. "Let's show
'em what you've got, okay?" She barked once, happily.

Then Carl straightened up and held out his hand.
Scout stood, all her attention on him, even though she
looked eager to head off for another run.

"Okay, Scout. Sit." He pointed a finger toward the
ground.

The dog looked at him for a few long moments, tilting
her head this way and that before finally obeying. Carl
leaned down, patted her head, and gave her another small
treat.

Next he gave the command to roll over, using a hand
signal that demonstrated the action. Scout laid down, and
Carl gave her a little help with the rest of the motion—
though to her credit, the dog did actually roll.

Finally Carl told her to sit again and then added,
"Stay, Scout, stay" as he walked to the far end of the
course. She squirmed a bit, her impatience obvious,
but she didn't move from her spot. When Carl turned
back to her, he paused and then said, "All right, girl! Good
dog!" She bounded to him for another treat and some
loving.

When he moved to the obstacle course, Scout
seemed to have figured out what it was Carl wanted from
her. Her gaze was locked on him, and the elder brother
managed to get her to obey, not perfectly, but she did do
the basics.

On the balance beam, he set her gently at the start,

then walked just ahead of her as she traversed its length.
She hopped through the tire swing when Carl poked his
head through and held out a doggie treat on the other
side. Finally came the cones. Carl simply walked ahead of
her, weaving in and out of the orange markers, and she
followed him. He snapped her leash back on and
returned to the observers at the side. Susan and Paul
applauded as the dog-food representatives whispered
between themselves. Jack stood at the back of the group
with his arms crossed over his chest.

After a few moments, the dark-haired suit stepped
forward and said, "It seems obvious to us that the dog
belongs to the last participant." He pointed to Carl. "She
obeys you better than your brother and seems to have a
great deal of affection for you. So it's our decision that you
should get the dog and therefore the prize from How Now
Dog Chow."

There was a sudden rustling noise from Jack's direction, and everyone turned to see what was going on. The
younger brother had swooped the dog into his arms.
She gave a yelp, but by then Jack was running down the
driveway toward his car at the front of the house.

When he was almost there, he turned and shouted,
"This isn't over! You'll be hearing from my lawyer!" Then
he shoved the dog inside, started the engine, and was
gone.

MARY WAS A PRETTY, slim woman in her late forties. She
had dark hair in a trendy cut and deep brown eyes that
gave her the Mediterranean look Kate had noticed in the

photograph Arnie Kerr had given her. She was preparing tea in the tiny Memphis apartment kitchen while Kate sat on the barstool at the counter. Mary set the cups carefully on a tray and blew out a breath, then stilled her shaking hands.

"I'm sorry," she said. "I guess I'm nervous."

"You don't need to be nervous with me." Kate smiled into her eyes as she imagined herself in the woman's place, surprised by a stranger with life-changing news. Kate's heart went out to her.

Mary set the teakettle on to boil. She was on the other side of the counter, standing with one hand resting on the surface and the other playing with a paper napkin. "Why didn't she come to find Valerie herself?" Mary asked.

"It's complicated," Kate began. "I want you to know that Patricia, Valerie's birth mother, completely respects your privacy. If you and Valerie don't want to meet her, that's okay. She doesn't want you to feel . . . pushed into anything you don't want to do."

Her brow furrowed. "I'm not following," Mary said. "I thought the whole reason you came was to find Valerie for her."

"It's not for her, exactly, though I feel certain that she would like to meet Valerie and you. She's told me how grateful she is for what you've done, and she completely respects you as Valerie's mother. But you see," Kate paused, "Valerie has a twin sister."

Mary's hand went to her mouth. "A twin? But why didn't the social worker mention that to me? We would have adopted her too if we'd known—"

"Marissa wasn't put up for adoption," Kate said. She leaned forward and met Mary's eyes. "It was too hard for Patricia to . . . give up both girls."

"I can understand that," she said, her eyes clouded. "So she wants the girls to meet?"

The teakettle sounded, and Mary went to turn off the burner. She set the tray of cups, sugar, cream, and an assortment of tea bags on the counter in front of Kate and then poured the water. The two women prepared their hot beverages in silence, the only sound that of their spoons clinking against the sides of the cups.

Then Kate looked up at Mary and answered. "You see, Marissa has leukemia."

"Oh . . ." Mary said, her stirring hand stilled. "That's horrible."

"We're hoping that Valerie would be willing to be tested to see if she's a bone-marrow match. The likelihood is higher among blood relatives, especially siblings . . ."

"I don't know how Valerie's going to handle all of this," Mary said honestly. "She's had her struggles with being adopted in the first place, and to learn that she has a sister . . ." She shook her head. "She always wanted a sister but . . ." she paused. "Well, her father and I didn't have the best marriage. By the time we would have adopted another child, things had started falling apart. We couldn't have biological kids." Mary looked away.

Kate wanted to comfort her, but she knew that would've made the situation even more awkward.

"I wish we'd had an open adoption," Mary confessed. "I think it might've made things easier for Valerie, instead

of always wondering about who she is and the circumstances that led her birth mother to give her up." She took
a sip of her tea.

"Any child would wonder the same," Kate said.

"I wish I could help you," Mary went on, "but my
daughter hasn't been real happy with me these last few
years, since the divorce. She's blamed me for her dad
moving away . . . I don't know if I'd even be able to get her
to talk to me, much less her birth mother. I could try, but
. . . she's been living with a girlfriend down near
Graceland—"

"Graceland?" Kate said. She remembered the many
Elvis trinkets she had seen around Marissa's room and
wondered if Valerie loved his music as much as her sister
did. Could such a common interest be biological? She
shook the thought off as crazy. Yet she'd heard far crazier
things about twins who first met in adulthood. Their lives
were often far more similar than any scientific research
could explain.

"Oh yes," Mary said, "she's always had a fascination
with that place. I don't know why. When I told her I'd gotten a job in Memphis, she was thrilled to move here just
to be closer to her hero."

Kate chose to take this news as a sign from God that
everything would work out just fine. But then the thought
crossed her mind that things hadn't worked out so well for
the King of Rock 'n' Roll.

PAUL FOUND JACK in the backyard at his Aunt Susan's
house that afternoon. Scout was tied to the dog run that

went out to the doghouse near the garage. Jack was split-
ting wood with long, angry whacks of the ax.

Paul made his way across the brown grass. Jack
looked up when he was halfway to him. Then he turned
his back to Paul, put another log on the stump, and lifted
the heavy ax overhead, bringing it down with a heavy
grunt. The dog barked, and Jack turned to scowl at her.
"Shut up, you dumb mutt!" he shouted.

"Jack," Paul said, closing the distance between them.
"This can't go on."

Jack shrugged and lifted one of the pieces of wood
that had fallen to the ground and set it on the stump for
another split. Scout let out another bark, then settled to
sleep in the doorway to her house.

"You know that the dog-food company is going to
make the check out to Carl regardless of whether you give
the dog back or not, don't you? You signed the release
before the competition."

"They can talk to my lawyer," Jack grunted.

"You don't want to do that, and you know it," Paul
said, hoping it was true.

Jack turned toward Paul, a hurt look in his eyes. "Why
does Carl get everything? Since we were little kids, it was
always Carl this and Carl that. Dad always put him
first . . ."

His words fell away, but Paul didn't miss their
significance.

"Did your dad give the dog to Carl?" he intuited.

Jack nodded. "He didn't give me a thing. I just wanted

him to think of me once. That was all. He had *two* sons, not just Carl. Yet he acted as if I didn't even exist." He set another small log on the stump and brought the ax down. The log split neatly in half, falling to the ground with a thumping sound. "I was the kid *Mom* wanted, the tack-on. He would've been happy if I'd never happened."

"I doubt that," Paul said.

Jack met his eyes with a look that said, *You never met my dad*.

"He's in a nursing home now," Jack went on. "With Alzheimer's. He doesn't even remember my name half the time. But he remembers Carl! Good old Carl." He bent to gather the pieces of wood from the ground, then placed them on the neat stack that filled the space between two tall pine trees behind him.

"So, you thought if you at least had Scout, you'd have a piece of your father's love?" Paul asked.

Jack shrugged. "At least Carl wouldn't rub my nose in it every day."

"Does he really do that?" Paul asked.

Jack turned his back again and set up another piece of wood. "I'll never have what I really want," Jack admitted. "You might as well take the dog."

SOMETHING HAD CHANGED. Patricia could feel it. There was something different about her daughter that Wednesday. Perhaps it was simply that she was tired after having so many visitors the day before. But there was more. Her skin, which was pale before, now was almost blue in appearance—it had the look of death. Patricia tried not to think that, but every time she gazed at her daughter's sleeping form, she saw it.

Marissa had been sleeping all day with a few stirrings here and there. Each time she would awaken, it was with an urgency, as if she were frantic about something. Her wide eyes would search the room until she found her mother, and then her tense body would relax and she'd drift away once again.

Patricia had asked the nurses to send their apologies to any visitors, except Pastor Hanlon. Marissa simply wasn't up to it today.

The curtains were drawn against the day. Patricia hadn't even looked outside to see if it was sunny or gloomy. She sat in the chair next to the bed and watched the rhythm of her daughter's breathing.

Another image flashed through her mind. It had only been a few short months ago, in this same hospital. Only then it had been Ray lying there, that blue tinge about him. His rugged, handsome form withered and struggling up until the very end, as Marissa struggled now.

Patricia touched her daughter's warm hand, which was turned palm-side up on the bed. Marissa closed her fingers around her mother's. Somehow that simple action gave Patricia hope. Marissa was still here. Patricia had to keep believing. *Lord*, she closed her eyes and sent up a silent prayer, *be here with us. Find a way to heal my daughter's body. I'm begging you. Because I love her so much.*

When she opened her eyes, Marissa was gazing at her. "How long have I been sleeping?" she asked.

"Most of the day," Patricia said.

"Has Kate called about Valerie?"

"No."

"She should have seen her by now, right?"

Patricia nodded. "I'm guessing so."

"Don't be scared, Mom." She squeezed her hand. "I'm not."

"About finding Valerie?" Patricia asked.

"No. About me dying." Her dark eyes penetrated her mother's blue gaze. "If I die, promise me you won't hide from the world. You have to go on with your life. For me. I want you to be happy and not shut yourself away like you did when Dad died. Take risks, even if it means hurting. At least you'll know you're alive. You have so much to offer."

"Don't talk about—" Patricia started, tears welling in her eyes.

"I have to, Mom," Marissa insisted. "Because I love you. And you have another daughter, who I'm sure would like to know you and love you too. If you'll just take the chance to get to know her. It's like you've been given a gift in my place, and that's okay. I'm going to be okay. Heaven will be a glorious place."

Chapter Seventeen

K ate parked her Honda on the street in front of the apartment building where Valerie's mother said she was living. It was a four-story brick building, modest but nice looking. The front was landscaped in cylindrical-shaped hedges and short, round evergreen bushes under the first-story windows. A cement sidewalk cut the brown lawn in half.

Kate stared through her windshield, gathering the courage to go in. She wondered how Valerie would receive her, especially without her mother there to ease the way. Kate had tried to talk Mary into coming with her, but the woman had insisted that her presence would only make it harder. Kate didn't know whether that was true, but it sure wasn't easy on her own.

Mary had warned Kate that Valerie's schedule was a bit unpredictable, since she was a student, but Kate was determined to wait for her. After a while a slight woman carrying a brown paper grocery bag made her way along the sidewalk toward the apartment building. She looked to be in her early twenties, and she had long dark hair that hung almost to her waist. When the young woman raised her head and Kate saw her face, she gasped. She had to be Valerie. Kate was sure of it. She had Marissa's face—those dark, penetrating eyes, and dimples—and the same hair Kate had seen in pictures of Marissa before the leukemia treatments caused it to fall out.

Kate climbed out of the car and walked toward the girl, smiling at her. "Valerie Olsen?" she called.

"Yes. Do I know you?" Valerie stopped walking and adjusted the grocery bag in her arms.

"I'm Kate Hanlon," she began. "I'm from Copper Mill, near Chattanooga. Your mother said I could find you here."

At the mention of her mother, the girl's eyes narrowed. "My mother sent you?"

"No," Kate said. "I was looking for you..." She glanced toward the apartment building. "It's kind of a long story. Would you mind taking a walk with me?"

Valerie studied her for a moment, as if trying to assess if she was trustworthy, then said, "I have to drop my groceries inside. Can you wait?"

Kate nodded. Valerie disappeared into the building for several long minutes before she came back outside. She pulled her jacket up around her thin shoulders and said, "So, where to?"

Valerie pointed down the street, and the two began their walk.

"So, you've been looking for me?" Valerie asked. "What's this all about?"

"Yes." Kate cleared her throat, trying to consider the best tact. Then realizing there was no easy route, she decided to dive right in. "I'm friends with your birth mother."

Valerie stopped walking, and her mouth dropped slightly open. "My birth mother?"

Kate nodded, searching her face for any sign of a reaction.

"Her name is Patricia Harris. She lives in Copper Mill, near where I live," Kate said.

Those dark eyes were unreadable, yet the pain in her voice was clear. "She sent you to find me? What would she want with me now? She's never cared enough to contact me before."

The gates of Graceland came into view ahead, with their musical staff and notes spreading wide across them, and the pillared mansion beyond. Kate walked that direction without answering her question. She needed to think. The last thing she wanted to do was further alienate Valerie from Patricia. Silence stretched as they walked, and Kate sensed that Valerie was dealing with a childhood of mixed emotions—hurts from so many unknowns, feelings of rejection, abandonment, betrayals.

"I know it isn't easy," Kate said, "to have some stranger show up unannounced ..."

Valerie glanced at her and tucked her hands into her coat pockets. They walked awhile in silence before she confessed, "I used to dream about finding my birth parents. When my parents made everything so hard, I'd think about my birth parents and imagine having a perfect life with them."

"Patricia is far from perfect," Kate said.

"I've come to realize that. Anyone who gives a child away like yesterday's trash—"

"Is that what you think she did?" Kate interrupted.

Valerie's hurt expression told her all she needed to know.

"Patricia loved you. If she could have found another way, she would've taken it. I know that for a fact."

"Right." Valerie turned away from her. A tear traced the contours of her cheeks. She swiped at it with the back of her hand.

They reached the sidewalk just across the street from Graceland and crossed to it. Valerie took a stuttering breath and touched the fence that surrounded the well-known estate with its manicured lawn.

"I knew this would be hard before I came," Kate said. "You weren't exactly expecting me . . . and I apologize for that."

Valerie met her eyes.

"There are so many things I wish I could help you see," Kate continued.

Valerie crossed her arms over her chest. Kate lifted her gaze to the white mansion behind the gates. Her thoughts went to Marissa and her bedroom decorated in Elvis's honor. What was it about this place that drew these twins, who were strangers?

Kate noticed Valerie gazing at Graceland and asked,

"Do you ever wonder why Elvis gave the place that name —Graceland?"

"No. I never heard that story." Valerie inhaled as if to compose herself. "But I always liked him," she said, sounding grateful for the change in topic. "Don't ask me why. He sure had his problems, but maybe that's *why* I liked him. He struggled like I did."

"We all struggle," Kate said.

"Some people don't."

"That's not true," Kate said. "I think some people suffer in silence and some more publicly. Like Elvis did. But it's part of the human condition. We all have losses in our lives as well as victories. The thing to keep in mind is that God loves us regardless of how good or bad we are."

"God!" Valerie mocked. "I'm sure he cares lots about me! That's why he's left me alone all these years, why my birth mother abandoned me—because he loves me. Right." Then under her breath, she added, "And after all the things I've done, I'm sure he's long since given up on me. Did my mother bother to mention that to you before she told you where to find me? That I'm not exactly the perfect daughter?"

Kate shook her head. "All your mother said was that she misses you and loves you."

Valerie's face fell a bit, and her eyes widened. Kate thought she would cry again.

"Maybe that's why Elvis called this place Graceland," Kate said kindly. "Because he found unconditional love here—grace. Grace doesn't depend on being good enough.

It's a gift, regardless of where we are or what we've done. It's a gift your mother . . . Mary . . . wants to give you too."

"And Patricia?" Valerie met her gaze. "What about her?"

Kate took a deep breath before she delved in. "Patricia tried to give you the best. She did all she could . . ."

"I find that hard to believe."

"Maybe if you heard the story from her, you'd understand." Her heart pleaded for Valerie to listen and not put up walls. But Valerie turned to walk away. Kate moved alongside her. "There's more," Kate said as a sense of urgency filled her again. "I need to tell you, at least so you'll know. Even if you don't want to do anything about it. You need to know."

"*Do* anything?" Valerie stopped. "What more could you possibly have to tell me?"

"You . . ." Kate began, "you have a sister. Her name is Marissa. She's . . . your twin."

"My twin?"

Kate nodded. "She has leukemia."

Valerie's eyes clouded.

"She's in the hospital now . . . and she's not doing well," Kate finished.

"So, in a few sentences, you gave me a sister and took her away. I really appreciate that." Valerie stepped off the curb and crossed the street back toward her apartment.

"You don't want to meet her?" Kate asked, struggling to keep up. "Or know anything about her?"

"Just so I can go through the pain of losing her like

everything else in my lame life? Why would I do that to myself?"

"Because you could save her life." Kate knew she was begging now, but she didn't see any other way. "You're the most likely person to be a bone-marrow match. If you could be tested . . ."

"Now I see how it is," Valerie said. "You're looking for my bone marrow, not for me! You want a cure for the daughter my birth mother kept. That's rich."

"I will admit we're hoping that you'll be tested and be a match," Kate said. "To save your sister's life. But she's as innocent in all of this as you are. She didn't know until recently about you either. You'd really like her, I think. I do. She loved to go sailing with her stepdad before he died, and she loves Elvis." Kate nodded back toward Graceland. "You should see her bedroom; it's filled with Elvis memorabilia. She's an open, honest person. She'd make a great friend."

Valerie stopped walking and crossed her arms against the warm breeze.

Kate repeated, "Don't blame Marissa. She had no idea you existed until a few days ago."

Valerie's shield seemed to drop a fraction.

"Marissa wouldn't care one way or the other if you matched her marrow," Kate said. "She'd be happy just to meet you before she dies."

Valerie wrinkled her brow, then glanced away as tears began to fall.

"You wouldn't have to meet them unless you wanted

to," Kate went on. "Or if you just wanted to meet Marissa, that would be okay too. But if you could consider being tested . . . People do this all the time for strangers."

"She is a stranger," Valerie said, though the anger had diminished from her tone. "Listen, I feel bad for this . . . Marissa. But you've sprung this on me awfully fast. I need to think. I mean . . . I've been so angry at my birth mother for so long. And now to find out I have a sister, a twin . . . Well, it's an awful lot to take in."

"I understand that." Kate dug in her purse for a card with her name and number. "Here." She handed the card to Valerie, who gazed down at it. "At least consider helping, even if you don't meet. Just think about it and give me a call. Marissa doesn't have much time left."

Valerie nodded. "I'll think about it."

As KATE DROVE the long distance from Memphis to Copper Mill that evening, she couldn't help but feel that she'd blown it. She'd finally found and met Marissa's twin only to be turned away.

She just prayed her failure wouldn't be Marissa's undoing.

She'd called Paul and told him the disappointing news. When Kate finally dragged herself into Pine Ridge, it was seven o'clock. She was exhausted, but she needed to stop at the hospital to check in on Marissa and Patricia and give them the news.

Her cell phone hadn't rung with a call from Valerie the whole way home, though Mary had said she'd try to talk to her daughter. Considering Valerie's reaction to any mention of her adoptive mother, Kate didn't have much hope that that interaction would yield any results.

Parking in the hospital's small lot, Kate made her way into the one-story brick building. The hospital was quiet, with only the occasional nurse wandering between rooms. Kate scrubbed in and donned a gown and mask, then quickly made her way down the hall to Marissa's room.

She knocked quietly on the door and pushed it slightly open. A light was on, and she could see part of Patricia's shoulder and the back of her head, where she sat facing Marissa's bed. Patricia turned toward her and rose when she realized it was Kate. "You're back!" she whispered.

Kate crept inside and saw that Marissa was asleep. The girl looked so frail, her thin cheeks sunken into her face and her skin ashen. It broke Kate's heart to see her that way, especially with the news she had.

Patricia glanced at her daughter, then motioned for Kate to join her in the hall. When they'd closed the door to Marissa's room, Patricia said, "So? What happened?"

Kate's shoulders drooped, and she looked Patricia in the eye. "I met her." Kate reached into her purse and pulled out the photo that Arnie had given her. "This is the photo I told you about."

When Patricia's eyes landed on her daughter's face, they immediately became misty. "She's beautiful," she breathed. "She looks so much like Marissa, you'd think they were identical."

"They aren't?" Kate asked.

Patricia shook her head. "No." She lifted her gaze to Kate. "Is she going to come?"

Kate shook her head. "I don't know. I don't think so." She glanced away as a nurse passed them in the white hallway, then looked back at her as she said, "She said she'd think about it, but she didn't sound real encouraging . . . I'm so sorry. I wanted to bring you good news."

Patricia closed her eyes. Kate could see that she was struggling with the news. No doubt she'd hoped beyond hope for the fairy-tale ending that Kate had tried to find.

"It's okay." Patricia touched Kate's sleeve, the shimmer of tears in her gaze unmistakable. "I can't tell you how grateful I am that you tried, how grateful I am to have a friend like you right now. You've encouraged me in so many ways. I've been praying . . . asking God to help us." She laughed. "Who would have thought that? But it's been good. Thank you, for everything."

Kate met her eyes, and the person she saw was no longer the protective, anger-filled woman she'd first met. Instead, she saw a person of courage . . . and faith.

"I've had the best talks of my life with Marissa these last two days," Patricia said. "Finally we're able to be honest. I've lied for so long, I started to believe my own lies. But now that she knows the truth . . . it's so healing. Even if it's too late, I know we'll be okay. *I'll* be okay."

Chapter Eighteen

On Sunday, after church and an afternoon nap, Kate wandered into her studio, a cup of steaming coffee in her hands. The stained-glass piece for the church was as she'd left it, still covered by a sheet on the worktable. Setting down her cup, she lifted the cover and neatly folded it, placing it on its designated shelf in the closet. Then she turned to gaze at her masterpiece. It seemed forever since she'd last worked on it, yet it was mostly finished. There were a few more small pieces to recut and solder, and the frame to attach, and the black patina to rub on. But that wouldn't take any time at all. She'd have to talk to Eli Weston about readying a place for the window in the sanctuary once she had the final dimensions. It would be tricky to get that done without everyone in the church knowing about it before the final unveiling, but she'd find a way.

She thought about heading back to the hospital, but Patricia had assured her that she'd call if she needed her and that Marissa was sleeping most of the time anyway.

So she set herself to work. There was something about creating that never ceased to calm her, even as the tumult that was life seemed ready to push her under.

Pulling the supplies she'd need from the drawers, she was soon engrossed in her work. When the phone rang, she almost jumped out of her skin.

"Hanlons," she answered after the third ring.

"Is this Kate?" the voice on the other end sounded so much like Marissa, Kate knew instantly that it was Valerie. Her heart skipped a beat.

"Yes, this is Kate. Valerie?"

"I've decided to be tested." The words resounded in Kate's ears, and with them utter joy.

"I can't tell you how happy that makes me. Marissa will be so grateful."

"I realized," Valerie said, "after talking with my mom, that I'd be shortchanging myself and my sister if I didn't at least try. Life is short as it is. I can't waste it now only to live with regrets later."

"That's very wise of you," Kate said.

"Those were my mom's words—I can't take credit for them." She paused as if to consider something, then said, "I'm going to be tested here in Memphis, tomorrow. I don't know how long it takes for the results to come back...I want to meet her—my sister. I don't know about Patricia. I'm still struggling with that one. But I do want to meet Marissa. I know time is of the essence, so I was thinking tomorrow after I get tested...?"

"That's easy enough to arrange," Kate said. Her mind

filled with a myriad of details—getting Valerie to the hospital, calling Marissa and Patricia with the good news . . . "She's still in the hospital, but you're more than welcome to stay with me and my husband here in Copper Mill. There's a hotel in town—the Hamilton Springs Hotel. It's kind of pricey, though. And, of course, there's a hotel in Pine Ridge."

"We don't have much money," Valerie admitted. "And my mom would like to come too."

"Of course," Kate said. "There's a foldout couch in our guest room. Tell her she's welcome to stay here too."

"That's very kind of you."

"We're just glad you're coming."

KATE COULD BARELY contain herself as she dialed Marissa's room phone. When the call finally connected, and Patricia said, "Hello," she blurted, "She's going to be tested!"

She heard Patricia suck in a breath. "Valerie?"

"Tomorrow, in Memphis. She just called."

"Oh my. I need to sit down." Then a few moments later, "What did she say?"

"She wants to meet Marissa."

"But not me?" The disappointment in her voice was unmistakable. There was a long pause. "That's okay," Patricia said. Kate could sense she was trying to reassure herself.

"She might change her mind," Kate said.

"It's okay," she repeated. "She doesn't owe me anything.

I'm just grateful she's going to be tested and she wants to meet her sister."

"Now all we have to do is pray that she'll be a match."

LATER THAT AFTERNOON Kate readied the guest room that doubled as Paul's study. She vacuumed, dusted, and changed the sheets on the foldout couch, though the ones that were on it were perfectly clean. Then she cleaned the windows that were mostly hidden behind blue curtains and set out a bouquet of fresh flowers.

When she stood back to inspect the room, Paul came up from behind and slipped his arms around her waist.

"I didn't know you were there," she said, leaning into his strong chest.

"The room looks ready to me," he said, grinning. "Of course it looked ready before you even started."

Kate nudged him with her elbow, though she didn't pull away from his embrace.

"This is a good thing you're doing," he said. "Having Valerie and her mother here. You've been a good friend."

She turned to face him. "It isn't anything you wouldn't do yourself." She smiled up into his eyes, and he bent to kiss her.

"I love you," he said.

"I know." She pulled from his grasp.

"Did you also know that you left the door to your studio open?" He lifted a flirtatious brow.

"You didn't see my surprise, did you?" She punched his arm.

Paul feigned injury, clutching the spot where she'd hit him. "I didn't see a thing," he said. "Just mentioned that the door was open. You don't have to be so distrustful!"

"Paul Hanlon!" She was grinning at him. "Your teasing is going to get you into big trouble someday!"

Kate marched down the hall to the open studio and shut the door, this time making sure it was locked. She held the key out of his reach. "Now you can't snoop."

"So you think . . . Ow," he said as he rubbed his arm, "you really hurt me."

AFTER HIS CONVERSATION with Jack the previous Wednesday, Paul hadn't had a chance to talk to Carl. He'd hoped the brothers would finally talk their differences through themselves, yet Jack continued to live with his Aunt Susan. So when Paul had a free hour in his schedule late that Sunday afternoon, he made the short drive to the Wilson brothers' home behind Weston's Antiques.

Scout was in the yard, sniffing the brown, wet ground. She lifted her golden head when Paul approached and trotted over to his car. "Hey, girl." He scratched her between the ears, and she jumped up for more. "Get down," Paul said, and the dog surprisingly obeyed.

"She's learning," Carl said from the screened front porch.

"Who brought her over?" Paul nodded toward the dog.

"Aunt Susan did, last night," Carl said. "Come on up. I was wanting to talk to you."

He opened the door for the pastor to make his way

inside. Scout ran ahead, jumping to greet her owner as she passed Paul. They walked into the house, the smell of woodsmoke filling Paul's nostrils. Carl cleared a stack of *Outdoor Life* magazines from a padded chair so Paul could sit down. Scout nudged Paul's knee for another pat.

"Can I get you anything?" Carl asked.

"I'm fine." Paul scratched Scout's head again, and she grinned at him before circling back to her owner for attention. "I wanted to talk about Jack."

"He hasn't been talking to me," Carl confessed as he took the seat opposite Paul. The wood stove next to him radiated warmth throughout the room.

"I figured as much. Did he tell you why he did all this?" Paul asked.

"I'm as clueless as ever. Did he say something to you?"

"He gave me some good clues." Paul leaned forward in his chair and rested his forearms on his knees.

Scout took that as a signal and came to nestle beside him. He stroked her shiny coat as he talked. "The whole dog thing was about your dad . . . Jack seems to think your dad doesn't love him. I gathered he's mourning that loss."

"That makes sense."

"Jack said the dog was a gift?"

"From my dad," Carl confirmed. "Actually, she was Dad's dog until he got too sick to care for her. He's in the memory unit at the nursing home in Pine Ridge. He has Alzheimer's pretty bad. Only seems to remember what happened in 1940 or 1950, but if you ask him what he had for breakfast, he's usually a blank."

"Was Jack ever close to your father?"

Carl shook his head. "Maybe when he was little, but not for a long time. Those two were so much alike, they drove each other nuts. They'd try to have father-son time, but most of the time they'd both come home angry about a fight they had. After Mom died, things got really bad. She was their go-between. I tried to bridge the gap, but Jack would just get mad at me . . . I think because he was jealous that I understood where Dad was coming from and he didn't."

"That explains why he thinks you're the one your dad loves. He said he feels like you two have been in a competition for your father's love. And he's the loser."

"That's ridiculous," Carl said. "Dad loves him. In his own way. Problem was, Jack wanted him to show it on his terms—couldn't accept it for what it was. Sometimes he's just . . . stubborn." Carl shrugged.

"I can see that," Paul said with a grin. "So what would it take for Jack to see the truth?"

"You've got me. I've tried everything I could think of."

"Would you be willing to give it another try with me?"

"Why not? If you can get him to listen."

"Can you make up some excuse for him to come over?"

"Sure."

Reaching for the phone, Carl dialed his aunt's number. Susan must've answered because Carl said, "Yes, ma'am, I'm doin' well . . . Oh, Scout's just fine too. She misses you, though. She sure loves your homemade doggie chow."

Carl was quiet for a moment before finally saying, "I'm actually wondering if Jack is there . . . Yes, ma'am. I want to make things right too."

He exchanged a look with Paul as he waited for his brother to come on the line.

"Jack, it's Carl. Hey, I've got some of your stuff packed. You might as well come get it if you're going to stay with Aunt Susan . . . Yes, *now*." Then he hung up and said, "He'll be right over."

A few minutes later, Jack's Ford Maverick pulled up in front of the rundown old house, and Jack climbed out. Paul and Carl watched him through the front window. He must've recognized Paul's pickup because he stopped and looked at it, and then at the house, before coming up the walk. The screen-door spring stretched and creaked as Jack came inside, then he let the door slam shut behind him. Scout padded to his side, looking up at him expectantly, but he ignored her.

"What's Pastor Hanlon doing here?" Jack asked.

Paul waved hello to him from his seat. Carl was standing near his chair at the stove. He'd gotten up to add a few more logs to the blazing fire.

"Paul wants to talk to us, and I think we should listen," Carl said as he took his seat again.

"So the call about the boxes . . . ?" Jack raised his hands.

Carl pointed to a pile of boxes near the front door, and Jack turned to look.

"Fine," Jack said. "I'll take them to Aunt Susan's when we're done here."

Jack picked up some scattered jackets and sweatshirts from the love seat and set them on an adjacent rocker that already had a similar mound on its cushion. Then he took his seat on the overstuffed yet comfortable-looking piece of furniture. His gaze shifted from Carl to Paul.

Paul began, "Jack, you need to tell your brother how you feel about your dad."

"What is this—some kind of intervention?" He started to stand, but Carl motioned for him to stay seated.

"I care about you, Jack," Carl said. "You're my brother. I'm tired of this rift between us. I want to be friends again, and I want you to move back home."

Jack's face fell, and Paul could see that Carl's words had struck a chord.

"I don't want to compete for anything—most of all Dad's love," Carl went on. "That's what Pastor Hanlon told me you said, that you think we've been in a competition for Dad's love all these years. It's just not true. This is a hard time for the two of us. First, losing Mom, and now with Dad going downhill so fast . . . We need each other, Jack. We don't have time to waste on silly dog competitions. I want my brother back."

Jack crossed his arms and considered Carl's words. They sat in silence for what seemed a long time before Jack finally admitted, "I've been jealous of you my whole life, Carl. You're smarter, gifted in sports, you had lots of friends . . . and what was I? The smart-mouthed little brother who tagged along and got in the way."

"You're good at a lot of things," Carl said. "I could

never take a junker and make it into a beautiful car the way you do. That takes talent—"

"Dad always loved you," Jack interrupted. "There was never any question ... Now he barely remembers my name, and it's too late."

"He remembers you," Carl said. "If you'd ever visit him ..."

"It's never too late to make things right," Paul added. "Even if your dad doesn't remember or can't understand, you can make it right with yourself."

Jack rubbed his forehead, then said, "I don't know." He lifted his head to look his brother in the eyes. "I'm sorry I put you through all this." He nodded toward Scout. "With the dog and all."

Scout, recognizing that she was once again the topic of conversation, hopped to her feet and stood facing Jack, barking loudly at him. "That dog is annoying!" the younger brother said.

"So are little brothers," Carl said with a smile.

THAT EVENING Paul drove the Wilsons to see their dad at the nursing home in Pine Ridge. He figured he could pop in and visit some of his regulars—longtime Faith Briar members who'd had to give up independent living for round-the-clock care—while the brothers talked to their father.

After he'd said good-bye to Violet Hicks, his last parishioner—a petite woman with white hair and a straight smile, who'd suffered a stroke the previous year—

he made his way back to the memory unit, secured behind a locked door. A heavyset nurse with too-short hair let him in and pointed him down the hall to Zeb Wilson's room. The door was wide open, and the gray-haired father was sitting between his two sons on the narrow bed. He didn't look that old, when Paul studied him, probably in his early sixties.

Father and sons were paging through an aged photo album, their heads close together.

Paul didn't want to disrupt them, but he couldn't take his eyes off the scene. It reminded him of the last time he'd seen his own father.

"That's you, Jack," Carl said, his finger resting on a photo.

The old man had a blank look, as if he couldn't place where he'd seen the boy. "Wasn't he the cutest little kid, Dad?" Carl added.

Jack sat back, the look of disappointment distinct in his features.

"See, he's feeding a stray kitten with a baby bottle. I found that mewing thing under the front porch. Remember? Mom had a fit when she saw it. Didn't want me bringing a mangy animal into the house! Do you remember that?" he said to Jack.

Jack nodded, exchanging a glance with his elder brother. "Yeah, I remember."

"He named the cat Taxi so that when we called it, we had to say, 'Here, Taxi.'" Carl laughed. He was trying so hard to bring the two men together that Paul felt a lump rise in his throat.

Finally a spark of recognition came into the older man's eyes. The father lifted a finger to point at the picture. "I remember that cat."

Jack's shoulders fell, and Paul heard him take a heavy breath. But the elder Wilson went on, "It was Jack's cat." He lifted his eyes to his youngest son. "Your cat, right, Jack?"

"Yes, Dad," Jack said. "He was my Taxi."

Zeb smiled at the name.

"That was a funny name. Did you think of that?"

Jack nodded. Then Zeb reached over to pat his son's knee. It wasn't anything monumental. Just a touch from father to son. But Paul could see how it affected Jack. His eyes darkened as he searched his father's face for something. But that was all the man had to offer. The cloud that had crowded his mind returned, dimming the sunlight once again.

Carl and Jack both stood when they realized Paul was there. "Well, we should get going, Dad. Pastor Hanlon is our ride home."

"So soon?" Zeb's eyes moistened, and Paul felt bad for the old man and the loneliness he must have faced when his sons were gone.

"Would you mind if I came back to visit you?" Paul asked. "I come every week, and I'd love to get to know you better."

Mr. Wilson's face brightened. "That'd be nice, young man."

Paul smiled at the term *young man*, especially since they were probably close to the same age. He hadn't been called that in more than forty years.

Carl and Jack turned back to Zeb to say their farewells. First Carl, who bent over his father in a hug, and then Jack.

Mr. Wilson said nothing, merely patted his son's back with that absent look. Then he gave Jack a kiss on the cheek and patted his hand. All he said was "Jack." But it was enough.

WHEN THEY REACHED COPPER MILL, Jack asked to be let off at home with his brother. Paul pulled up in front of their house and put the gearshift into park.

"No sense in staying at Aunt Susan's anymore," he said, glancing at his brother. "I'm ready to come home, if you'll have me."

Carl smiled and slugged his brother in the arm. "Thanks, Pastor. You should go home now too," Jack said, smiling at Paul.

Paul looked down at his watch and realized that Kate's guests from Memphis were arriving the next day. "I'll get home, but I probably won't be hitting the hay anytime soon. I've got company coming tomorrow."

"Family?" Carl asked.

"No." Paul shook his head. "Do you know Marissa Harris?"

"I went to high school with her," Jack said. "Pretty girl with dark hair and eyes. I asked her to homecoming one year."

"Really?" Paul said.

"She turned me down, but man, I had a crush on her." He cleared his throat.

"She has leukemia," Paul said.

"I hadn't heard that," Jack said, a look of concern in his eyes. "Is she doing okay?"

"Not too well. She's in the hospital, hoping to find a bone-marrow donor. A bunch of us from church have been tested, but so far no match. The people coming are her . . . family. We're hoping one of them will be the right one."

"And if she doesn't find someone?" Jack asked.

"She doesn't have any other options."

"That's harsh," Carl said.

"Indeed," Paul agreed. "Sometimes life is harsh."

Chapter Nineteen

Valerie and Mary arrived the next day a little after one. Kate pointed them to the guest room to drop off their bags and showed them where their bathroom was. As she pulled a batch of cookies from the oven for lunch, Valerie padded into the small kitchen. She was dressed in stylish jeans with embroidery down the front and a layering of T-shirts with a green wool jacket to top it all off.

"We can't thank you enough for letting us stay here," she said and ran her hands through her long hair as if to comb it.

"You must've started early," Kate said. She set the cookies on the counter and transferred them to a cooling rack. "I have a snack if you're hungry."

"It smells heavenly. The visit to the hospital was quick—just a swab of my cheek. So we were on the road by seven-thirty."

"So, you and your mom mended fences?" Kate asked.

Valerie fingered a paper napkin on the kitchen counter. "I was being childish, and it was just time that I grew up."

"I'm glad to hear things are working out between you two," she said. Kate lifted a steaming cookie onto a square plate and handed it and a glass of cold milk across the counter to Valerie.

Valerie took a bite and closed her eyes as she tasted it. "That's delicious," she said.

Kate grinned. "A cook always likes to hear that."

She led Valerie to the kitchen table, bringing a plate of cookies that had cooled earlier. "So, it's a big day," Kate said. "Are you ready for it?"

"Who is ever ready to meet their sister for the first time?" Valerie paused as if to say more, then added, "I've decided that I want to meet Patricia too."

"Really?" Kate smiled. "She'll be so pleased."

"When I was talking to Mom, she convinced me that it wouldn't kill me to meet my birth mother. I don't know what I thought would happen. But I can't be afraid to live anymore. I want to meet my birth mom and have her meet the woman who raised me and still loves me."

Just then Mary Olsen came into the room. Her dark hair was combed back, and her face looked freshly scrubbed and shining. "Your forever mom?" She bent to kiss her daughter on the top of the head.

"Yes," Valerie said, touching her mother's hand that rested on her shoulder. "My forever mom."

KATE WONDERED how Patricia would react to meeting Valerie. They might carry the same blood in their veins, but they were still strangers, after all. Kate had called to tell her that Valerie was asking to meet them both. She could hear the joy in Patricia's voice when she'd told her —and the fear.

Finally they were there, standing outside Marissa's hospital room. Kate knocked on the door tentatively and heard a faint "Come in." She turned to Valerie. The girl held her mother's hand and drew in a deep breath as she nodded.

The door slowly opened, and Kate entered, followed by Mary, with Valerie behind her. They'd already scrubbed and gowned.

Marissa had a pretty orange and red head scarf tied neatly on her head and makeup on her wan face. The eye shadow, blush, and pale pink lip gloss made her look almost healthy.

Valerie's dark eyes locked on Patricia's. Kate could tell that Patricia was holding her breath.

"Hello," Valerie said in a small voice.

Patricia moved forward, and they shook gloved hands. "I'm Patricia Harris," she said. "Your—" she stumbled on the word.

"Your birth mother," Mary filled in for her, her voice gentle.

Patricia turned to this woman who had raised her precious daughter. A track of wetness lined Mary's cheeks.

"I'm Mary Olsen," the woman said.

"I'm so pleased to meet you," Patricia said as tears welled in her eyes. She grasped Mary's hand. "I can't tell you how grateful I am . . . for everything."

Mary's eyes smiled into hers. "It's so good for Valerie to finally meet you. She's wondered about you for a long time."

Patricia's gaze shifted back to Valerie, who was watching from the other side of the bed. Kate silently observed the scene, feeling humbled to be part of this moment, to see the coming together of this broken family.

Finally, they turned to Marissa.

"Valerie," Patricia said. "This is your sister, Marissa."

Valerie moved to her bed and extended a gloved hand. "Hello."

Marissa took it and said, "Thank you for coming." She was grinning from ear to ear. The two sisters held hands, and Valerie sat down on the bed alongside Marissa.

"How long have you been sick?" Valerie asked.

"A few months," Marissa said. "But I feel better now." She lifted a smile to her mother.

"Let's hope you get healthy real soon." Valerie lifted her gaze to her mother. "When will we know if the marrow matches?"

"Soon, I think," Mary answered. "They have my cell number."

"They'll let our doctor know too," Marissa said, still holding hands with her sister. "Tell me about you," Marissa said. "I want to know all about you."

Valerie looked back down at her, her eyes clouding. Kate sensed the well of emotions Marissa's simple question brought out in her sibling—the desire to know and be known. It was a powerful thing.

When Valerie lifted her gaze, Marissa added, "What do you like to do? Did you go to college?"

Valerie nodded. "I'm still in college, actually. Studying to be a nurse."

"No kidding!" Marissa said. "I was studying to be a physical therapist."

Valerie's eyes crinkled in a smile. "We could work in the same hospital."

"Absolutely," Marissa agreed, then asked, "Do you like to sail?"

"I haven't been much, but I do like the water. I go whitewater kayaking with my friends whenever I get the chance. I don't own one or anything, but my boyfriend has a few, so we do that once in a while. There are some great rivers for kayaking in Tennessee."

"That sounds awesome," Marissa said, her gaze far away. "I'd love to get back out on the water again . . ."

Valerie touched her shoulder, drawing Marissa back.

Seeing the gesture, Kate choked up. These girls had missed so much by not being together, by not having shared their childhoods. Kate glanced at Patricia, who had tears streaming down her cheeks.

Just then a nurse came in with a tray of food for Marissa—a boiled dinner of potatoes, carrots, some sort of bland meat, and a cup of milk.

"I should have brought you a fried peanut-butter-and-banana sandwich," Valerie said as she squinted at the boring-looking meal.

"Peanut butter and banana was one of Elvis's favorites." Valerie nodded knowingly.

"Oh my goodness! You're an Elvis fan?" Marissa practically shouted.

Valerie nodded again. "Kate told me you are too." Then she added, "I'll have to take you to the Sun Studio Café in Memphis. They have them on the menu there."

"That's near where Elvis made his first recording as a birthday present for his mother, right?"

"Next door."

Filled with amazement, Marissa's eyes flew to her mother, then back to Valerie. "You'll have to come see my room," Marissa went on. "It's wall-to-wall Elvis. I've been collecting since . . . I can't even remember when."

Valerie was intent on Marissa, and in many ways, Kate was grateful for that. She knew Marissa was safe for Valerie. After all, her sister hadn't caused any of the pain in Valerie's life.

After the girls had had a while to talk and Marissa began to grow sleepy, Kate suggested they head out for a bite to eat. "No!" Marissa protested, "I want to hear everything!" But the exhausted look on her face said she needed rest.

Patricia leaned over and touched a gloved hand to her daughter's forehead, even as Marissa's eyes drooped shut. "I'll take notes and tell you everything that we say later, okay? You get your sleep."

"We'll come back to talk some more," Valerie promised. Mary nodded in agreement.

Finally Marissa acquiesced. Her eyes closed, and the soft breath of sleep overtook her.

The four of them crept from her room and agreed to

meet at the Bristol, the new restaurant at the Hamilton Springs Hotel just east of downtown Copper Mill.

Valerie and Mary rode with Kate, and the trip was painfully quiet. Kate knew this would be the most diffi-cult part of this day, when birth mother and daughter finally had the chance to talk. She'd sensed it in Patricia, the way her body stiffened and her glance kept shifting to Valerie when Kate had mentioned going out to eat. She sent up a prayer for both of them and pulled into the pine-tree-lined lot next to the Hamilton Springs Hotel. Formerly the Copper Creek Hotel, the historic building had recently been renovated after years of disrepair. Patricia's car pulled in behind them alongside the two-story building. They climbed out and made their way to the hotel.

Wide double doors opened onto a stunning, massive foyer with double staircases that wound their way up to the floor above. The room was a warm honey tone, with a blazing fireplace in its center and mounted deer and elk trophies on the polished wood walls. The floors shone from years of visitors coming and going, and thick beams lifted toward the ceiling. Woven Indian rugs gave the room definition, with seating groups placed around them throughout the space.

Kate led them to the Bristol, which was to the left of the foyer, a sunny room with banks of divided windows on three sides. The waitstaff bustled between tables, and a gentleman wearing an expensive-looking suit showed them to a table overlooking a pond. Sensing her friend would need a boost of encouragement, Kate moved alongside Patricia and took the chair to her right.

"My house is on this road," Patricia told Valerie and Mary as she pointed toward the woods to the west. "On the other side of town. I'll have to show you Marissa's Elvis collection."

"Maybe . . ." Valerie said tentatively.

Kate could see the doubt her response caused in Patricia, who fingered the tablecloth awkwardly.

"I mean," Valerie went on, "I'd hate to take away from Marissa the joy of showing it to me herself."

"Oh . . . of course," Patricia said. She breathed, catching Kate's eye, and attempted to smile.

The waitress appeared to tell them about the daily specials and to hand out menus. They stared quietly at the tall laminated sheets for several long minutes before the waitress returned to take their orders. When she scooted off to the next table, Mary took a deep breath and said, "I know this can't be easy for you, Patricia." Her gaze shifted to her daughter. "It's not for us, either. In so many ways, I wish we'd always known you."

Patricia's eyes widened. "But it was a closed adoption . . ."

"That was our mistake," Mary said. She touched Valerie's hand that rested on the table between them. "I think it would've been healthier for Valerie if she'd grown up knowing you and Marissa, instead of always wondering, having that mystery hanging over her head."

Valerie raised her head, a tremulous smile on her lips.

"Because I didn't know who my birth parents were or

the circumstances around my adoption," Valerie began, "I made up a fantasy about you." Her face turned a deep shade of red.

"That's normal," Kate said.

"I always wondered *why*—that was my biggest question. Why?" Valerie looked at Patricia.

The anger and hurt in her face made Kate cringe. She sent up a prayer for Patricia, that she would be able to speak truthfully without breaking down.

Kate touched her arm, and Patricia gave her a quick smile of acknowledgment.

"I can't make things right for you, Valerie," she began. "I wish I could. I'd redo everything, but I made the best choice I could at the time. My options weren't great." She inhaled a ragged breath. "When my parents found out I was pregnant with you and Marissa, they disowned me. Till the day they died, they washed their hands of me, even after everything seemed okay."

Valerie crossed her arms over her chest, but Patricia went on, "That left me with few options. I was eighteen, just out of high school. I had no way of getting a good-paying job, though I tried to keep you and Marissa together."

Tears streamed down Valerie's face.

"I wanted you and Marissa to be together. You need to know that." She lifted her head to the ceiling. "I couldn't come back to Copper Mill; small towns are hard places to be a single mom anyway—at least in the eighties they were. Still are, I'm sure. I wasn't keeping up on my rent, not with the cost of day care for two babies. And there weren't any subsidized apartments available in Chattanooga at the time . . . I was afraid the county would end up taking both of you. I couldn't bear that."

"So, why me and not Marissa?" Valerie swiped at her eyes, and Mary reached for her hand on the table.

"Marissa asked the same thing," Patricia said. She inhaled, then looked Valerie in the eyes. "You were smaller, frail. I knew an adoptive family had more resources than I had to make sure you were healthy, and loved—" Her voice broke, and she lowered her head to cry.

Kate patted her back, and Mary offered a look of empathy. They sat in awkward silence while Patricia cried and dabbed at her cheeks with a tissue from her purse.

"You gave me the greatest gift of my life," Mary finally said, her gaze firmly on Patricia. "The ability to be a mother." She squeezed Valerie's hand. "My husband and I had tried so long to have kids, but we just couldn't. Then we finally chose adoption . . ." She too dabbed at her face with a tissue. "You can't imagine what a miracle that was for us, to finally be parents and to have this beautiful child to raise. I've counted it a privilege every day for the past twenty-two years, and I'm so grateful. I know it was hard for you to let her go, and I appreciate that." Then she turned to her daughter. "And I know you've struggled too, Val, but I love you, and I'm glad you're my daughter."

By the time the food came, they were one big sobbing mess. Mascara streaked their cheeks, and used tissues dotted the table. The waitress looked at them curiously, but no one offered an explanation. Patricia gave Kate's arm a squeeze, and the women exchanged glances. But Kate knew what she meant by the gesture—she'd found the forgiveness she'd been seeking. It had been there all along, but she'd finally taken hold of it.

Chapter Twenty

The next day, as Marissa and Valerie worked on a Sudoku puzzle together, and Kate, Patricia, and Mary looked at old photos of the girls, the news they'd been waiting for finally came. Dr. McLaughlin pushed open the door and entered the room. His blue eyes were somber, which gave Kate an uneasy feeling.

"I...uh..." He cleared his throat. "I have some news." He turned toward Marissa, whose expression was hopeful. "The test results from the marrow match are in." He shifted his gaze to Valerie. "You're not a match."

Valerie gasped.

"I thought since they were twins—" Kate began.

"The odds were good," Dr. McLaughlin reassured, "especially since they're twins."

"But we're not identical," Marissa guessed.

The doctor nodded. "That would've been a sure match. As siblings, you had about a thirty percent likelihood of matching."

Kate looked at the shocked expressions around her.

"We'd put so much hope in Valerie being a match," Patricia said slowly. "I . . . I don't even know what to do now."

Marissa began to shake. Valerie reached her arms around her and held her. The doctor offered his sympathies and reminded them that there were still other options before quietly turning to leave. Everyone sat in stunned silence as they absorbed the news. Finally Marissa leaned back against her pillow. Her eyes were ringed in red, and her skin was blotchy. Kate handed her a tissue, and she dabbed at her face.

"I'd been hoping," Marissa said.

"We all were," Valerie said, her eyes welling with fresh tears.

BY THE NEXT DAY, Marissa seemed to have already slipped another notch. Her eyes were dull, a blank, empty look. When Kate, Valerie, and Mary came to say good-bye, she barely lifted her head from the pillow. Patricia sat next to her bed, poised, as if at any moment she would be gone.

"It's not right," Valerie whispered to Kate and her mother at the far end of the hospital room. "I can't leave her like this. I told you this would happen," she said to her mother. "My heart is breaking in two."

Mary cupped Valerie's face in her hands. "But you're not alone, honey." She sighed and glanced over at Marissa, whose gaze was fixed on the windows. "You have school, and I have work," Mary whispered. "What else can we do?"

"I'm coming back," Valerie insisted as she glanced at Marissa. "I'll drive back this weekend."

"It's already Wednesday," Kate reminded her gently. "You'd just be turning around once you got home."

"Then I'll move here," Valerie said. "I can transfer to Chattanooga, get my nursing degree there."

Mary patted her daughter's hand, her expression serious. "We can talk about that," she said. "I don't want you to move across the state from me, but I do understand. Let's talk on the drive back."

Valerie finally nodded. Then she turned with a sigh and moved to Marissa's bedside. "We've ... got to get going," she said. "I don't want to go, but I have to. Mom has to. I promise I'll be back, okay?"

Marissa nodded.

The sisters held each other for a few moments, both with closed eyes. "I'll be okay," Marissa said, though they all knew that wasn't so.

They wrote down their e-mail addresses and promised to write daily until Valerie's return, with Patricia promising to courier the messages between home and the hospital.

Then Kate and Patricia walked Valerie and Mary out to the parking lot. The sound of their shoes clicking on the tile corridor filled the silence between them.

When they reached the car, Valerie hesitated, then turned to Kate. "You've done so much," she said, taking a deep breath. "I don't know how to thank you." Her dark eyes reflected her gratitude.

"That's thanks enough." Kate reached out to give the girl a hug.

Then Mary reached for Patricia. "We'll keep in touch," she said, patting her back.

"Absolutely," Patricia said. She looked so fragile, Kate thought she would break apart at any moment.

Patricia's gaze turned to Valerie. They paused in awkwardness, then Patricia said, "Valerie, I'm so honored . . ." Her words trailed off. "I wish we'd met under different circumstances . . ."

Kate knew the two still had much to work out in their relationship, yet they'd taken a huge step. That was more than they'd done in the past twenty-two years.

Valerie moved to her birth mother's side and reached for her hands. "I'm glad I met you too . . . I am."

Then Mary and Valerie climbed into the small celery green economy car. Mary turned the key, bringing the vehicle to life, and with a wave, they pulled out of the parking lot and disappeared down the street.

Patricia took a heavy breath, then looked at Kate.

"Are you okay?" Kate asked.

"I'm stronger than I thought I was," Patricia admitted.

"She's a nice girl." Kate's gaze turned toward the street. She watched the cars pass by and tried to think of something better to say.

"That was her mother and father's doing," Patricia said.

Kate simply patted her shoulder, and they turned to walk back into the hospital.

WHEN KATE AND PATRICIA made their way back inside, something seemed different. There was a hubbub at the nurses' station. Immediately both women looked at each other, then hurried toward Marissa's room.

Marissa was where they'd left her, but a tall spidery-thin nurse was checking her vitals.

"Is something wrong?" Patricia asked.

The nurse finished whatever it was she'd been doing, then turned to face Patricia. "Nothing's wrong," she said. "They've found a marrow donor for your daughter."

Perhaps it was the unadorned way she communicated the news or that it was simply too good to be true, but whatever the case, Kate couldn't believe her ears. "What?" She closed her mouth, then opened it again, trying to form coherent words. "Who?"

"I know him," Marissa said from the other side of the tall woman. "It's a guy I went to high school with—Jack Wilson." She smiled. "He asked me out once."

"Jack Wilson?" Kate frowned. "Why is that name familiar to me?" Then it dawned on her. Jack was the man who'd been suing for custody of his dog. She immediately picked up her cell phone and dialed Paul at the church.

On the second ring, Paul's secretary, Millie, answered. "Faith Briar."

"Hello, Millie, is Paul there?"

"Who is this?" the aged secretary asked in her raspy voice.

"It's me. Kate. His wife?"

"Oh." She cleared her throat. Then there was a clicking sound, and the phone rang again.

This time Paul answered. "Faith Briar Church. This is
Paul Hanlon."

"It's me, Paul. You know, you really need to help that
woman with her people skills," Kate said.

"Millie? I know. I think that's my main job here.
What's up?"

"Did you know that Jack Wilson was tested?"

"You mean for Marissa?"

"Yes, for Marissa." Kate's tone rose with her excitement.

"No . . . but I guess I did tell him and Carl about her
the last time we were together, after visiting their dad.
Why?"

"He's a match!" She was practically shouting, but she
didn't care. "He's the one we've been looking for."

"Wow," Paul said softly. "I didn't see that one coming."
He laughed. "When will the transplant take place?"

"I don't know yet, but tell him thank you if you see
him. And honey, thank you too. I have no doubt that your
wise counsel helped all of this come about."

"It wasn't me," Paul said matter-of-factly. "God gets
the credit."

"THIS IS THE ANSWER to our prayers," Marissa said weakly.

Kate nodded and smiled at the frail young woman laying on the gurney. Just two days ago, on Wednesday, they
had thought all hope was lost. Then God had sent them a
donor. Since then, life had shifted into hyperdrive. The

previous day they had transferred Marissa to the larger hospital in Chattanooga to begin preparing her for the transplant, and now Marissa was about to be wheeled down the hallway to the ICU. There she'd be kept under complete sedation while she underwent two intensive days of chemotherapy and radiation. Nurses had constantly been at her side to check for infection and monitor her status.

These latest treatments were much more intensive than any treatment she'd had before. In her prior chemo, they'd only been killing cancer cells. In this treatment, they would be killing not only those pernicious cells but Marissa's very bone marrow as well. Her ability to produce blood at all would be gone, if not for the donor. If something happened to him in the meantime, she would be dead. Kate realized that death was a very real possibility for Marissa no matter what. Many leukemia patients died before they ever received their transplant.

When the procedure was done, she would not only assume Jack's blood type, if it was different than hers, but she'd also take on any of his allergies and antibodies and lose any she'd had prior to the procedure. In effect, the procedure was much more than a simple transfusion. This was no coming together; this was a complete blood transformation. The old would be completely dead. And if it went as planned, a new Marissa would rise.

Marissa held Patricia's hand as Kate and a heavyset black nurse waited for mother and daughter to finish their conversation.

"I'll just be glad to have you home and in one piece," Patricia said. She leaned over to kiss her daughter's forehead, despite the green mask that covered her mouth.

"I love you, Mom," Marissa said. She put her arms around Patricia.

"I love you too, honey." They stayed like that for a few minutes until the nurse cleared her throat. Patricia sighed and pulled back. The nurse lifted a dark brow and said to Marissa, "All ready, missy?"

"Yes, ma'am," Marissa answered as the nurse grabbed hold of the gurney and wheeled her through the swinging doors marked ICU.

Patricia stared after her for a long moment, then turned to Kate.

"She's going to be fine," Kate said, hoping her words sounded more reassuring than she felt. The very real possibility that the intense chemotherapy and radiation could kill Marissa loomed as a shadow over them.

They walked toward the ICU waiting room down the hall. Inside, several Faith Briar members were already holding vigil, among them Eli Weston and Paul.

LuAnne Matthews came over with a steaming cup of coffee in her hands. She smiled and held the cup out to Patricia, who took it and sipped gingerly at the hot liquid.

Paul was seated in one of the orange vinyl chairs next to a blond-haired man whom Kate had never seen before. Paul stood when Kate and Patricia entered and made his way to them. "How is she?" he asked.

"Braver than I am," Patricia said with a laugh. "But that doesn't take much!"

The tall blond man who'd come up with Paul reached a hand toward Patricia. "I'm happy to meet you," he began.

"Oh, I'm sorry," Paul said. "Kate, Patricia . . . this is Jack Wilson's brother, Carl."

Patricia's eyes focused on him, and she shook his hand. "I can't tell you how much we appreciate your brother's sacrifice," she said.

Carl's face glowed at her words, and he shrugged. "Jack wanted to be here too, but he had work to finish up before . . ." His voice trailed off. "When he found out it was Marissa . . . Well, to be honest, he had the biggest crush on her in high school."

"Well, nonetheless," Patricia went on, "we're grateful."

They took their seats for what felt like an eternity, taking turns to get up and pace the hall or bring more coffees from the vending machine.

Kate glanced at Patricia, who was fidgeting with her hands. She watched her pick up a magazine and page through it, though given the quick rate at which she flipped the pages, Kate was sure she wasn't reading.

"You okay?" Kate finally asked.

Patricia sighed. "I'm a wreck." She smiled despite her statement. Paul looked up and smiled back. "I wish Ray were here," Patricia said, looking at Kate. "That's what I keep thinking. He would have wanted to be here for this . . .

for his daughter. Because, you know, he really was Marissa's father in so many ways."

Kate squeezed her hand. "Of course he was."

Patricia turned slightly to face Kate. "You've been . . . the best friend I've ever had, other than him. You've shown me so much. I was wrong before . . ." She gazed at the large clock on the wall near the door, then back at Kate. "I'm glad you didn't give up on me."

"That's what friends do," Kate said. "We nag each other."

Chapter Twenty-One

An hour later, a doctor appeared at the waiting room door. He was a small man with straight white teeth and a spark in his green eyes. He wore scrubs and a surgical mask, which he pulled from his face as he started to talk. Everyone in the room quieted to hear what he had to say. Patricia stood, as did Kate.

"She's sedated now, and we've started the chemotherapy," he said. "She's doing well, but we'll need to keep an eye on her counts." His gaze turned to Patricia. "She can't have visitors, as she's at major risk for infection, and she has no ability to fight it right now."

Patricia nodded her understanding.

"There won't be much you can do around here," the doctor went on, looking around the room. "I suggest you all go home and get some rest. It's going to be a long haul."

TWO DAYS PASSED, and Marissa was pronounced ready for the transplant. Kate drove to Chattanooga as soon as church was over, and made it in time to see Marissa before the transplant. After scrubbing and gowning, she walked into the gray room where Patricia had kept vigil.

Kate had never seen a living person look more death-like. Marissa had no color in her face, and her eyes were dull and filmy.

Patricia moved to her bedside, and the girl did her best to smile. "I don't feel so good, Mom." By her tone, she'd said it as a joke, but Patricia merely sat, stroking her cheek. Kate took a seat in the padded chair by the window.

"The hard part is over," Patricia assured her. "At least that's what the doctor says."

"I don't think I could handle much harder," Marissa said. Then she breathed as if the effort of speaking had taxed her energy.

"Is Jack in surgery?" she finally asked.

Patricia nodded. "He went in about half an hour ago. The doctor says it'll only be an hour so . . ." Her words fell away.

There wasn't anything else for them to say, so Kate began to pray. She asked for God's protection over Jack and Marissa, and she asked that Marissa's body would accept the marrow and begin to heal. She prayed for patience and trust for those who could only sit and wait, and she asked that God's grace and peace would cover them all. When she finished, Marissa smiled. Then they sat in silence. The March day was warm. The sun shone through the miniblinds, warming the room with its cheer.

Forty-five minutes later, the chaplain came in with the doctor and a nurse carrying the life-giving marrow in a plastic bag. The chaplain said a prayer over Marissa, then the nurse attached the bag to the Hickman catheter in Marissa's chest. The marrow would be infused into her body over the next four to six hours.

The doctor placed a hand on Marissa's shoulder and said, "You'll be feeling good in no time." Then he winked at her, and she smiled.

Kate felt like crying at the relief that flooded her. "Is Jack doing okay?" she asked the doctor.

"It'll take him awhile to come out of anesthesia, but he did great." He smiled. "He'll be here a couple days, so you'll get to see him, I'm sure."

Relieved, Kate let out a deep breath. She hadn't realized she'd been holding it.

THE LIGHTS IN THE ROOM were dim, with only side lights creating ambience. Marissa had fallen asleep, as had Patricia, no doubt from the tension of the day. Kate was resting in a side chair near the window as the sun set. Marissa was still attached to a heart-and-blood-pressure monitor, though the IV had finished doing its job.

Her skin had already begun to take on a pinkish tone. Kate found herself staring at the girl. She really was a miracle.

"Hey," Marissa said groggily as she opened her eyes.

Kate moved alongside her. "How are you feeling?"

"I'm ok," Marissa said, smiling weakly.

Patricia made a small noise, then lifted her head and stretched. When she saw that Marissa was awake, she quickly got up and moved to the other side of the bed to hold her daughter's hand. She gazed at Marissa with a deep tenderness. "Look at you," she said. "You're going to be okay."

Kate had a sudden urge to talk to her own children and tell them how very much she loved them.

THE NEXT DAY when Kate came to visit, Marissa was talking to Patricia about her future, when to pick up her schooling again and if she should stay in physical therapy or switch to something a little less demanding. Yet, she reasoned, once she was fully recovered, that wouldn't be an issue.

Her mother was clearly grinning at her through her mask, judging by the way her eyes were crinkling.

"What are you smiling at?" Marissa complained.

"You're certainly feeling better!" Patricia said. "It's only been a day."

"Why, yes I am, ma'am!" She gave her mother such a cheesy grin that they both broke out in laughter. The sound was music to Kate's ears.

"Maybe I could start back to school when Valerie transfers to Chattanooga." Marissa said. "We could go together."

"*If* Valerie comes," Patricia reminded her.

A knock sounded, and Kate recognized the blond man they'd met in the ICU waiting room. He wheeled in a younger man with dark hair and striking dark eyes. Both men wore surgical gowns and masks.

"Hello . . ." Marissa said.

The younger man's head was hanging down, so Marissa lowered her own as if that would help her make eye contact with him. He awkwardly flicked his hair back out of his eyes and cleared his throat.

Sensing his discomfort, Patricia was instantly on her feet, crossing the room to meet the younger brother. "You must be Jack," she said.

"Yes, I am," he said.

"Jack Wilson? I haven't seen you in a long time," Marissa said. He lifted the mask from his face for her to get a better look at him. She blushed and touched a hand to her head scarf. "Wow . . . You've . . . grown up!"

"So have you," Jack said. His smile was shy. He was an attractive man, his dark features a distinct contrast to his towheaded brother. But he was definitely the kind of man a young woman would look twice at. "Are you feeling okay?" he asked, his gaze firmly on Marissa.

"Thanks to you, I feel like a new woman." She shifted toward the edge of the bed as if to get down, then when her mother shook her head at her, sat back against her pillows.

"Jack, I'm so glad you came to see me. I wanted to say thank you and tell you how much all of this means to me and my family."

Jack grinned sheepishly and said, "When I heard that you were sick, I couldn't stay home . . ." His tentative gaze met hers. "They're discharging me tomorrow," he continued. "Though they're telling me I can't do much for a week or so."

"They want to make sure he doesn't start bleeding," Carl interjected.

"Where did they...?" Marissa began to ask, then dropped the question, obviously embarrassed.

"From my hip." Jack leaned forward a bit and pointed to the ice pack that was wedged between him and the wheelchair.

"Is it uncomfortable?"

Jack shrugged. "Naw."

"I'm sorry you're leaving so soon..." Marissa said. "I hoped we could... catch up."

"Well, would you mind if I came to visit? Once you're feeling better, I mean?" He laughed uncomfortably. "Gotta make sure my marrow is doing okay."

"Definitely," she said with a grin.

HOME HAD NEVER LOOKED more beautiful than it did the day Marissa came home from the hospital. For three weeks she'd been in reverse isolation in the ICU. And when the marrow began to produce blood cells on its own, she'd moved to a "transplant house" near the hospital where she'd been close enough for regular checkups and frequent monitoring for four more weeks. The danger now lay in the possibility of rejection, though the doctors seemed pleased with her progress.

With each day she became more and more her old self, regaining her strength as well as some of her hair. Kate and Patricia had driven to Chattanooga together to bring Marissa home. The leaves were greenish silver on the aspens in the Harrises' front yard, and the grass was a lush coat. The late April winds blew gently across Kate's cheeks as she came around the passenger's side of Patricia's Mercedes to open the door for Marissa.

"I don't need help, you know," Marissa scolded with a teasing glint in her eye, though the rest of her face was hidden by a surgical mask.

"I can help if I want to," Kate defended.

Marissa gasped in joy and pointed to a banner over the front door that read "Welcome Home, Marissa."

"Did you put that up?" She smiled at Kate.

"I didn't have a thing to do with that." Kate smirked.

"Are you two going to stop that banter and get in the house?" Patricia scolded.

"Oh, all right." Marissa grinned.

They moved toward the house, and Kate could hear the sound of voices inside. "Something's going on," Marissa said. Her eyes were alight with expectation. Then the door mysteriously opened, and a chorus of voices shouted, "Welcome home!"

The girl squealed in delight. "You guys!"

Just inside the door were Valerie, Mary, Paul Hanlon, and Eli Weston, though Kate could tell there were more people in the back. The open kitchen was filled with flowers and helium balloons in a multitude of colors and shapes.

"This looks amazing," Marissa said. She leaned over to

sniff a bouquet of red roses with delicate white baby's breath tucked between the stems. The card read "Get well soon.—Jack."

"I love roses," she whispered. Her gaze traveled to all those gathered around. Even Renee Lambert and Livvy Jenner were there. "You all . . . Thank you. I feel like I'm on one of those celebrity cruises!"

"The ladies even cleaned the house for us," Patricia said. Then she gestured to the lineup of foodstuffs that covered the counter. "And we have enough food for several parties."

"We're going to get spoiled really fast," Marissa said.

The girl's face was bright with joy. Kate glanced at Patricia, who was grinning at her daughter, and sent up a prayer of gratitude for all that God had accomplished in this woman's life. Sure, Kate had had some part in that, but it was God who had done the work. On her own, Kate would still be looking at a slammed door.

Paul stepped forward, and everyone hushed. "Marissa," he began, "we want you to know that we're all thrilled that you're doing so well. And we're still here for you, no matter what. We believe that this home-coming is simply the first step toward a long and healthy life."

The group applauded in agreement.

"I feel good enough to run a marathon," Marissa said.

Valerie was the next to speak. She stepped forward and gazed at her newfound sister. "I'm glad to have found you." Her eyes were locked with Marissa's. "You're a great person.

Someone told me I'd think that." She glanced at Kate and winked. "I'm grateful for the opportunity to find out for myself just how amazing you are."

"Okay, now," LuAnne Matthews piped up. "This girl needs her rest, and we're keeping her from it." Her green eyes sparkled, and Marissa smiled at the woman she had recently learned was her great-aunt.

"You're all going to leave me?" Marissa whined.

LuAnne bent to kiss her on the forehead. "We'll be back, missy. Don't worry, and don't overdo it." Then she grabbed Renee Lambert's hand. "Come on, Renee."

"LuAnne Matthews, get your paws off me!" Renee pulled her hand back and batted at LuAnne with the other. Then she straightened and moved with a dignified air to Marissa. "I'm pleased that you're home and well, dear," she said. Kisses whined from her designer bag, and she petted his head. "Would you like to hold Kisses?"

Marissa shook her head. "Thanks, but I guess I am feeling a bit tired."

Others began to file out, offering their good wishes and promising to return in the coming weeks.

When Paul and Kate finally made it home, a wave of relief swept over her. She closed her eyes and reveled in the sensation.

"Are you okay?" Paul asked.

"I'm fine."

He reached an arm around her waist and held her close. She leaned into him, feeling his strength seep into her being.

"I didn't realize how much this was taking out of me," she confessed.

"I did," Paul said. "But that's who you are, Kate Hanlon. It's the reason I married you."

Kate lifted her face and kissed her husband.

KATE HAD FINISHED the surprise for the church during Marissa's recovery, but she'd put off unveiling it until Patricia and Marissa could be there for the event.

Kate spent the week leading up to the unveiling working on various projects she'd started. Getting back into glasswork had made her realize that this hobby she so enjoyed was something she might like to spend more of her time doing. It gave her flexibility to do whatever she needed to do—like help a widow find her long-lost daughter—yet it was something she could always come back to without a boss's expectations of a certain number of hours per week. She toyed with the idea. Perhaps she could start with a Web site. Her son-in-law, John, was a genius at all things connected to the Internet. She was sure he'd be willing to make a site for her. She could post photos of pieces she'd created in the past, and if an order came in, she could simply duplicate that art until she had time to come up with some new designs. She also decided to talk to a few of the businesses in town to see if they'd consider selling her pieces as well. As she put the finishing touches on a sun catcher, Kate realized that maybe the move to Copper Mill was a chance to start over in many ways.

Chapter Twenty-Two

The next Sunday, the church was filled to capacity. Spring's warmth filled the sanctuary as did bouquets of lilacs, their scent permeating the warm air of the buzzing sanctuary.

Patricia was there with Marissa, Valerie, and Mary, sitting near the front. Even the Wilson brothers came.

In the front pew, Kate felt a flutter of nerves as she sang the first hymn of the service. Paul's rich tenor voice led the congregation in "Crown Him with Many Crowns." It was one of Kate's favorite hymns. When she sang it, she envisioned that final day when all the people of the world would be gathered, and Christ would receive the worship he so deserved. She concentrated on the words, trying not to think about what she was about to do.

When the song ended, Paul waited for everyone to settle into their seats. He glanced at Kate and sent her a smile of encouragement.

"It seems my wife has a little surprise for all of us," he began, pointing to the white fabric that clung to the wall behind him.

They had arranged that when the service first started, Eli, who had installed the window, would remove the covering on the outside of the church so that the morning light could penetrate the window full strength at the unveiling.

"I'll have you know," Paul went on, "she's been very . . . *deceitful* about this project these past few months." The congregation laughed. "She kept it hidden under lock and key in her studio at the house. Wouldn't even let me in there! And if she did, she had a sheet over the thing. So I'm as curious as all of you are to see what she has in store for us." He extended a hand to Kate, and she stepped up to the podium.

"I have *not* been deceitful!" Kate said as she leaned into the microphone. "Just private. You should see your pastor, by the way. He's the nosiest man on the planet!"

Another laugh went up.

Then Kate took a breath and gazed across the faces gathered before her. "Seriously," she began anew. "When we had our first real service here after rebuilding the church, I noted several things. First, how totally bare this place looked." She smiled, as did many faces before her. "You know how I am about decorating! But more importantly, I noticed how resilient you all are."

She looked at Livvy Jenner and her clan up front, then at Eli Weston and LuAnne Matthews, and finally at Joe

Tucker and Renee Lambert near the back. "You took this church that looked for all purposes . . . *dead* and lifeless, and you breathed new life into it, giving us this beautiful place in which to worship." Her gaze traveled to Patricia and Marissa. Mother and daughter were holding hands and smiling up at her. "And over the past few weeks, I've seen how, as a people, you've done the same in the lives of others in Copper Mill—caring for them and loving them. Praying when hope seemed lost." She paused before going on.

"These are such wonderful examples of redemption, the little resurrections that God brings us in our everyday lives, bringing something beautiful from dismal situations. So I had the idea of creating this piece as a symbol of that redemption." She tugged on the cloth, and it pulled free, fluttering to the floor.

The congregation gasped in awe when they saw it, and a murmur of conversation filtered through the sanctuary.

An oak was at the center of the large circular window. Its branches spread across the surface like tendrils seeking light. They twisted upward, and at their tips, tiny green buds were visible. The interplay of browns and greens and blues was simply breathtaking in the morning light.

Kate turned back to the congregation. "A tree is like that," she explained. "In the autumn it dies. Only faith keeps us from cutting it down, because we know that come spring, it will be filled with new life, a new resurrection of sorts. So I created this in honor of all of you, and of the hope we have for new life." As she turned to step down, the congregation broke out in thunderous applause. Then they stood to their feet, Paul grinning and clapping at the front.

Kate lifted her face to the light, as the vibrant colors filled the sanctuary with a kaleidoscope of shifting hues and grace covered them all.

About the Author

BEFORE LAUNCHING her writing career, Traci DePree worked as a fiction editor for many of the best Christian authors in the country. While still maintaining her editing career, Traci loves creating new worlds in her novels. Her hope is that, just as in Copper Mill, Tennessee, her readers will see God's creation and inspiration within the people in their own lives. Traci is the author of the best-selling Lake Emily series, including *A Can of Peas*, *Dandelions in a Jelly Jar* and *Aprons on a Clothesline*. She makes her home in a small Minnesota town with her husband and their five children, the youngest via adoption.

Mystery and the Minister's Wife®

Through the Fire
by Diane Noble

A State of Grace
by Traci DePree